MI
NE

MINE

MARLENE
HAUSER

The Book Guild Ltd

First published in Great Britain in 2023 by
The Book Guild Ltd
Unit E2 Airfield Business Park,
Harrison Road, Market Harborough,
Leicestershire. LE16 7UL
Tel: 0116 2792299
www.bookguild.co.uk
Email: info@bookguild.co.uk
Twitter: @bookguild

Typeset in 11pt Minion Pro

Printed and bound by CPI Group (UK) Ltd, Croydon, CR0 4YY

ISBN 978 1915603 531

British Library Cataloguing in Publication Data.
A catalogue record for this book is available from the British Library.

To my family, for everything.

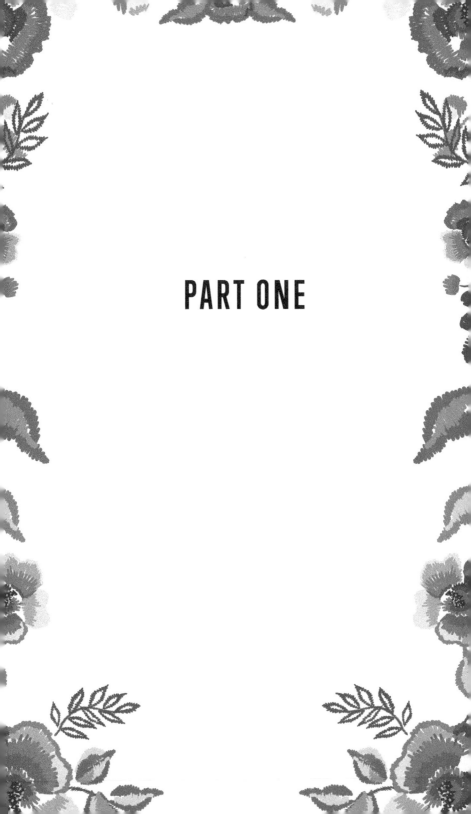

PART ONE

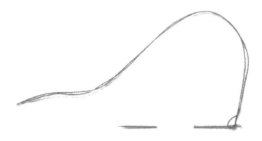

ONE

Sophie Taylor loved the North, the Far North, the frozen silence, the sleds pulled by reindeer, the intricate red embroidery sewn into the hem of a blue wool skirt. The love affair, made strong by a childhood adventure in Finland, started even earlier with an illustrated, oversized, leather-bound book of fairy tales that her mother Anne had brought home from Norway, where she had gone to study ice, snow and the receding Engabreen glacier.

Fairy Tales by Hans Christian Andersen, especially the story of the Snow Queen, stole Sophie's attention. She considered the Queen in all her spidery finery, snug in a high-backed sleigh, protected from the whirling snow, commanding her malamutes, the Arctic fox and two snapping tundra swans. Her fur-trimmed cloak had billowed up, out and over them all.

With the treasured volume wrapped in her thin arms and a willow branch rapping against her bedroom window, Sophie never imagined then that one day she might meet, marry and move within miles of her favourite Far North.

"Estonia," Tucker Mägi had said, spreading jam on a toasted bagel during breakfast at a local deli in Rye, New York.

"Really?" Sophie answered, picturing the country on the map, below Finland and across the Baltic Sea. "Is Mägi an Estonian name?"

"Yes, and so is Tõnis, my real first name."

"Tõnis?" she repeated, wrapping her tongue around the strange sound.

"Tõnis. Bitch of a language, Soph. I don't speak it, never tried. Too many umlauts. My mom tried to teach me once, that and folk dancing."

"No interest?"

"Zero."

Tucker's grandparents originated in Estonia, which for Sophie equalled the Far North, or close to it. This alone made Tucker stand out, and while she never bought into 'the one and only' theory, this single fact appeared to be a bit of sorcery. She didn't want her age to be the reason why she hoped so, but it was true that at thirty-nine, time was running out for her, especially if she wanted a child, which she did and which she felt was one of the best reasons for getting married.

While Tucker read the *New York Times* and helped himself to a second bagel, Sophie imagined Estonia, the country now shaded a pale blue in the atlas, like the other two Baltic states, lumped together, tucked away at the top of the world, riding the shoulder of Russia, the Great Bear. She remembered when this part of the world, the Old Soviet Union, was a no-go zone, always and forever shaded a bright red, stamped with a monolithic USSR.

Who would ever go there?

On a lazy Sunday morning, when they both wanted nothing more than to escape to the beach, anywhere along the Sound, Tucker hustled into the kitchen of his small, rented house on a relatively quiet, historic street in Rye.

"Take a look at this." He placed a stained document on the table.

4

"What is it?" Sophie asked, pulling the wicker picnic hamper from the top of the refrigerator, and in the same instant tossing her beloved spaniel Daisy a crust from her morning toast.

"Dusty paperwork from Pops."

"Let's see."

Tucker spread the paperwork out and Sophie leaned in to get a closer look.

"These look like old property deeds. Are they in Russian? Estonian?" Sophie questioned.

"I think he thought I might be interested."

"He's not?"

"Never. You couldn't get him or his father back there ever."

No one in Tucker's family had any interest in Estonia. The Mägi family, now well established in Louisville, Kentucky, for the past two generations bred Derby-winning thoroughbreds.

"It is Russian," Sophie said, studying the document closely, "and I'm guessing the flipside is Estonian? You should get them translated. Whatever they're referring to may be worthless, but on the other hand..."

"Fortune made?"

"Fortune made." Sophie laughed as they headed to the door and Tucker unlocked his rusted Audi. "And then maybe you can trade in this wreck."

Tucker had the papers translated, and discovered he might own a long-disused sawmill and extensive timberland. In addition, it appeared he held rights to a manor house, or maybe just four crumbling walls and a few outbuildings.

"I should marry you or hire you," he said. "Left on my own, I'd have thrown the paperwork out, or at least shoved it in the back of beyond for another day."

"Marry me or hire me?"

"Yes."

"No, thanks. I have a job."

"Well, keep the offer in mind."

"Thank you." She smiled. "Noted."

Tucker's father Gaabriel realised early on that his son had no talent for horseracing. His only appetite was for building. He left his imprint wherever, whenever he could. Whether with coloured blocks or snap-together Lego, the young Tucker developed, designed and built sturdy, practical enclosures, seafront towns or seductive cities with efficient traffic flow. Later, whatever Gaabriel asked the adolescent Tucker to do – tackle a milk shed, a hay barn or a viewing stand – his son fulfilled the task, quickly, efficiently and with money to spare. Second only to building was Tucker's nose for money.

While he flew to Tallinn, the Estonian capital, to explore his newly acquired deeds, Sophie found her way to New York's Estonian House. Just a short taxi ride from her office at Ascent Magazines' headquarters, the quiet, almost sleepy, Beaux-Arts building stood sentinel on East 34th. Buzzing herself in, Sophie paid attention to the odd, tight security in what seemed like a private members' club, then ascended a wood-panelled staircase, taking in the scent of baked bread, strong coffee and cooked cabbage. The sharp odours reminded her of dark earth, upturned on an early spring day, when frost might still cling to the underside of a metal spade.

On the walls along the flight of stairs hung a gallery of images: an onion-domed church with Orthodox crosses, an endless field of wheat and a timber house that spoke of distant places.

"May I help you?" an accented voice called out as she reached the top step, leading into a gift shop and what appeared to be a library.

"I'm interested in Estonia," Sophie began. "I mean… I have a friend who is Estonian. Or… actually his grandparents, his parents, were Estonian. Came to the USA in—"

"And he is called?"

"Tucker Mägi," she answered. "Well, Tõnis is his birth name."

"Mägi?"

"Tõnis Mägi," she emphasised.

From the dark recesses of the library, beyond the concession, a newspaper rustled and a chair scraped against the floor. A tall, elderly man with thinning hair stood up. Towering over the glass partition that appeared as much for protection as privacy, a fixture more appropriate for Moscow than midtown Manhattan, he looked down his long nose at Sophie.

"I knew a Tõnis Mägi," he said. "I went to school with him. We were engineers together. He was a friend. From Pärnu. Where is he now?"

"Really?" Sophie asked, at first spellbound, then, realising the improbability, she suggested, "Maybe you mean his grandfather?"

"Maybe his grandfather," the man echoed, his shoulders sagging. "Tell me about your Tõnis."

"He lives in Rye, in Westchester County," Sophie replied, "but his family is in Louisville, Kentucky. He runs his own property company, sort of, took an MBA at Columbia. No siblings and his mother – Eeva Meri Mägi – recently passed away, but his father and grandparents run the Louisville stud farm. Maybe you two should meet?"

The man nodded, still standing, while Sophie carried on. "His father sent him some old paperwork, deeds, and he's gone off to Tallinn. He's not particularly interested in things Estonian, but I am."

"Smart boy, and one with a nose for money, by the sounds of it," the old man laughed, tapping the side of his nose, "like all the Mägis. They once owned most, if not all, of the Pärnu city centre, as well as the seafront. I think some buildings in Tallinn, too. Things will be different now, after Independence. He'll have a passport. He'd be Estonian if it weren't for the war. People are going back now."

7

Sophie nodded.

"On the other hand," the man said, "there might be nothing left for a young Mägi. I'm not going back. Never will."

He excused himself with Old World charm but before he reached his chair turned back, remembering something. "There was a manor house that belonged to the Mägi family. Twelfth-century, outside Tallinn."

He rustled and snapped his newspaper, as if strong-arming disappointment, then looked away, but not before giving her a small salute, while the simply dressed, elegant woman who had originally asked if she might help bustled forward. In her arms, she carried books: *The Czar's Madman*, *The Forest Brothers* and *A Brief History of Estonia*.

"These might interest you," she offered.

Sophie bought all three titles, along with an Estonian flag in blue, black and white.

"The colours of Estonia," the woman said, as she wrapped the package smartly, in a way that Sophie thought quaintly antiquated, in natural twine and brown paper. "Deep blue for the sky," the woman went on, "black for the forest on the horizon and white for endless snow."

"Thank you."

"Eat in the cafeteria, if you wish," she offered.

"I will," Sophie said, as she checked her watch, realising she might shortly be missed at the office.

The warm bread served in the café was cut from a dark loaf, oval-shaped, homemade and tasting of another century. The soup, fresh and made of cabbage, carrots and caraway seeds, reminded Sophie of someplace cold and remote. The square napkins, thin and red, along with the coffee, thick and black, served in a heavy porcelain demitasse, spoke of the Soviet Union, the North and frugality. Cinnamon flavoured her coffee, and Sophie sat just for a moment savouring Estonia in the canteen's semi-darkness.

8

"You should have seen the place," she told Tucker later when he picked up the phone. "Dimly lit in a homey sort of way, spiced coffee, toasty warm… hard to describe. I felt that if I looked outside, there'd be six feet of snow, with more coming down. Strange… one part Soviet, one part ancient, medieval, Scandinavian."

"Sophie," Tucker responded, "you've described it. If you saw where I am sleeping now, it's definitely ancient, medieval, Soviet, but buzzing with the new. Bring the books when you come."

"When I come?"

"I'm not coming back. The sawmill and timberland turned out to be nothing. It may have been at one time, but it's been cut up and parcelled out so many times that ownership is untraceable. It's a farm collective, or something, now. The manor house is interesting, though, but not commercially. So basically the deeds are worthless, but the place is humming. Estonia itself is totally viable. These people are just wrapping their heads around the idea of private property or that a contract is binding – that your word is your bond or that a signature actually means something. I can start from nothing here, Sophie," he paused, "and can make something of myself."

"Yes," she answered, "you can."

In October, four months after Tucker had left, Sophie found herself on her way to Estonia, with Daisy safely staying with a neighbour. The stopover at Helsinki Airport felt familiar. Reindeer-fur boots and rugs hung on display, Nordic glass vases lined the shelves, catching daylight as if frozen in ice, and embroidery as rich and sprawling as red lichen spread itself across naturally dyed linen and woven blue wool. Sophie bought a clear vase and a box of foil-wrapped mints if only to distract herself from the sharp-edged needlework that piqued her imagination.

As she looked out of the window on the short flight to Tallinn, she imagined sleds sliding over the endless, frozen expanse of the blue-black Baltic Sea barely visible below.

A fluke, early snowfall dusted the red-tiled roofs and mostly square fields, as towering firs gave way to ancient city walls, where through intricately carved windows lights flickered. Stewardesses now served Kalev mints, speaking to Sophie in Estonian, then alternating to Russian and Finnish, as the plane prepared for landing.

"I'm sorry," Sophie said, "I only speak English."

They tittered in disbelief. Obviously, they thought, she could speak Estonian; she just chose not to. She looked Estonian, with her blonde hair, height and blue-grey eyes. They stared incredulously as Sophie made her way down the portable stairs, over the slippery asphalt and into the terminal, where Tucker met her with a single, foil-wrapped rose.

"They think I am Estonian," she said.

"Well, that's good. Because I am."

Tucker ground cinnamon and coffee beans in the morning in his freezing apartment, served toasted black bread with butter and promised Sophie he'd pick up some lingonberry jam in the afternoon. They negotiated with Soviet maître d's in order to eat in restaurants that were virtually empty but resolutely 'Reservation only'. They met a group of Estonians who were working on something called 'video chat', who claimed Tallinn would one day be the digital capital of the world. "Like Japan," they enthused. "After the war, we'll leapfrog today's technologies. We are a family, a small one, so we can do anything."

Arm in arm, Sophie and Tucker snuck into the Soviet sculpture garden, and sat on a statue, the back of Lenin's head pushed squarely down into the snow. In a restaurant called The Donkey's Stall, they ate delicate blinis, black caviar and rich sour cream. Over wild mushroom soup, roasted pork, and a redcurrant *kissel*, they both agreed Estonia might actually be 'home'.

"I don't want to go back to Rye." Sophie studied her spoon.

"I'm not going back." Tucker smiled, motioning for what Sophie thought was coffee.

Instead, a man dressed for the outdoors in a darkly stained wool muffler and a shiny puffer jacket approached the table. One waitress murmured to the other, as Tucker paid the bill and then extended a hand to Sophie.

"So last century," she said, as he buttoned her coat. Outside in a light drizzle, Tucker helped her into a polished red troika with three horses abreast, one hundred brass bells and a regatta of multicoloured streamers.

They made their way across Raekoja Plats, over slick cobblestones, the bells sounding a counterpoint to the reciprocal drumming of the horses' hoofs, only slowing down on turns and momentarily as they made their way out of Suur Rannavärav, the great coastal gates to the outskirts of town. Bundled in blankets, Sophie and Tucker leaned one into the other, silent, thoughtful, watching the countryside open and close behind them, with the drizzle now having turned to snow.

When the horses came to a halt, and the bells across the bridle, saddle and harness stopped ringing, Sophie dismounted from the sleigh.

"The manor house?" she asked.

"Yes, here it is." Tucker grinned.

The looming stone facade of a once grand twelfth-century mansion stood unevenly on unkempt ground, quietly invincible. Barely visible, a trace of rose paint shone under a lone bulb on an unscathed portico, which seemed to anchor the ancient building into place.

"What do you think?" he asked.

"Extraordinary."

Tucker motioned Sophie into the house, as the driver walked away. "It's ours."

"Ours?" Sophie smiled.

"Yes. Happy fortieth birthday, Soph." He tilted his head. "The manor and marriage…" He opened a small box. "Is it a deal?" he asked.

"It's a deal," she answered, slipping on the gold ring hammered round for a song in a shop just off the Plats known for its prehistoric amber and its stolen icons.

The troika took the long way back to Tucker's through the dark and slush. At home they made hot cocoa, tried to fall asleep, as if that would hold off morning and Sophie's return to Rye, but finally, wrapped in blankets in front of the porcelain-tiled stove, they could only discuss how their future together was going to work.

"Give up my job?" Sophie hesitated.

"Digital is happening here."

"I know."

"It's not fantasy. It's fact."

"Tuck, okay, I only have one condition."

"Go ahead?"

Tucker poked the fire, adding another log, despite the early-morning hour, the sound of birds filtering through the dawn light and their need to get to the airport.

"I want us to have a baby."

"A baby?" He paused. "No problem with that, Soph."

Too soon, Sophie found herself back on Estonia Air, then Finnair into New York. Rye appeared stripped down now, bare compared to Tallinn. She felt as if she had stepped straight from the depths of a feudal tapestry into a sharped-edged work of modern life. Could she find even one tree in Rye as old as any in Kadriorg or a building as ancient as Peter the Great's hunting lodge? No braided pastries and bejewelled cherry tortes sold from darkened baskets adorned the shelves of her local Shoprite. She ached for the cafés in Old Town, the thick city walls and the ever-present nip of cold.

Tallinn would never blow away in a gale-force wind, but back in Westchester County she felt that everything could be gone in an instant, with one decent sweep of a hand. Even the walls of her condominium felt like cardboard.

Over the next few days Sophie floated between her old life and one she imagined with Tucker.

Give up work? Live in the Old Soviet Union?

America was distinctly, unflinchingly free. She couldn't point to one quiet corner in Rye where people huddled, whispered, spied, as it appeared they still did in Tallinn. Not so long ago in Estonia, the wrong thing said or indicated – even an eyebrow arched – at the wrong time and in the wrong place might have resulted in disappearance or even death. Did the Soviet secret police still exist? Would Russia always keep a toehold?

Sophie couldn't imagine living in that sort of unease, never mind giving up work. Westchester County did not have a KGB building allegedly with a meat grinder in the basement used for, well, murder, or metres-deep holes dug outside the city limits that could be primed with TNT to bring about the appearance of an earthquake, collapsing walls, never mind the oldest remaining medieval castle town in the world.

Back at Ascent Magazines, with hardly time to say hello, never mind resign, Sophie found herself in front of George Nygaard, the CEO. After putting a series of gruelling questions, he asked her to take over the analysis of the company's intent to digitise its portfolio of magazines. Apparently, Simon Garth, their star analyst and marketer, had left for higher ground, and time was short. A meeting was coming up. Ascent Magazines intended to plant both feet firmly into the Internet boom, and they needed a couple of star bankers to get them there.

"Money to be made. You know the drill. You're Simon's clone, I am told."

"Yes." Sophie nodded, wondering when to say 'yes, but I'm leaving, too', yet not wanting to. Being the prime analyst and marketer on a major digitisation deal was a dream come true for her.

"So?" George asked.

"Yes – I'm not exactly his clone, but, yes, I know the drill."

"You'll have everything you need, but you personally will be responsible for the meeting with Morgan Stanley and Credit Suisse. Virtual shopping, online magazines – all of it."

"Video chat?" Sophie interrupted him.

"Video chat?"

"It's a software interface between—"

"Is there money in it?"

"Yes."

"Good. Add it. Where'd you hear about it?"

"In Estonia."

"Estonia? Who the Sam Hill lives in f'ing Estonia?" He paused, looking carefully at Sophie. "Look, these guys took Netscape public. This is the real deal."

Who the Sam Hill lives in Estonia?

I do, Sophie said to herself, as she picked up where Simon left off, analysed the new digital future, took it a step higher, worked late into the night, prepared the data for Morgan Stanley and Credit Suisse, while all the while fighting against the image that felt like a dangerous undertow: the spring, herself, Tucker and a small child wrapped in soft wool, rocked in the Baltic sunshine.

TWO

With Ascent Magazines' Internet scheme signed, sealed and delivered, and both Morgan Stanley and Credit Suisse on board, Sophie resigned. Less difficult than she'd imagined, she said goodbye to NYC, *adios* to Rye, and hello to the rest of her life. Most surprisingly, George Nygaard gave her a parting bonus and a promise of a rehire into senior management when she got her MBA.

"Hell," he said, "you could be my right-hand man. Send us postcards. Or I guess, if it's Estonia, it'll be video chat?" He smiled.

Back on Finnair with her now-familiar strong coffee, served with her favourite Fazer mints, Sophie visualised Tallinn, its turrets, red tiles, cobblestones and all, while the woman beside her flipped through a copy of *American Baby*. On the cover a blue-eyed toddler with a full head of hair peeped from behind a green, loosely knit blanket. Articles, sequentially ordered, one title after the next – *Baby on the Way*, *Nighttime Kisses* and *True Stories of Childbirth* – spun about the baby's head, promising insight or dread.

Sophie pulled out her own magazine, *Vogue Bridal*. At forty, she wondered if she should feel embarrassed; as a more mature bride, perhaps she should be marrying in a raw silk, A-line skirt and edge-to-edge jacket – an age-appropriate Chanel suit instead of the luminous gown she had chosen, with its snug, full-length sleeves, tiny, close-fitting waist, full skirt and thirty-two satin-covered buttons down the back.

"Am I too old to have bridesmaids? A veil?" Sophie had asked the sales assistant.

"First, you look no more than thirty," the woman said. "And second, who cares? Bridesmaids? So what? A veil? Yes. Simple. You do know you are beautiful, don't you? Do what you want."

In Estonia Tucker tackled the wedding celebrations like any other project he put his mind to. He pulled a team together and put all the pieces in place, from flower girls to menus.

Sophie's mother Anne couldn't have been more overjoyed when they told her. She said it was the moment she'd most looked forward to and most dreaded since the day Sophie was born – giving her away. Anne Taylor paid for as much of the wedding as Sophie and Tucker would allow her. They were both financially independent and preferred to keep it that way.

Anne Taylor was not just Sophie's mother but also her best friend in the way that only a single parent of a sole child could be. Doctors believed that Sophie's father's unexpected death, shockingly young, from an undiagnosed heart problem, had caused Anne to give birth prematurely, a storm both mother and daughter had weathered successfully.

As Sophie grew up, Anne taught her to step out and into life, to be unafraid, to travel, everywhere, anywhere, to investigate, to respect people, places and cultures, to be of service. Above all she had said, "Be yourself, and remember every problem represents an opportunity."

Sophie's fellow traveller slipped her magazine into the back pocket of the seat in front and turned to Sophie.

"Nice ring," she said. "When's the wedding?"

"Shortly," Sophie said, closing her magazine, both wanting and not wanting to talk.

"In Helsinki?"

"No. Tallinn."

"Lovely," the woman said. "How'd you decide? To marry, I mean. I was never 'in love' in the way I think you're supposed to be."

"I want a family and the right guy came along."

"I'm starting a family. IVF."

The blue-eyed toddler peered at Sophie from the pocket of the seat in front. Momentarily lost for words, Sophie recalled a woman she used to see at Oakland Beach in Rye every summer. The woman and her entire family – sisters, brothers, parents, and a large number of nieces and nephews – staked out the same place, at the same time, every Sunday in every summer in every year. This woman, although she'd had a partner, always sat apart, with no babies crawling on or off her lap. But then one summer, with the same kids swarming around, a bit older now, she sat with the most beautiful young child perched on her knee.

At the outdoor shower, while waiting in line, Sophie couldn't help herself.

"Beautiful… your baby is genuinely lovely."

"IVF," the woman had said, gently rinsing her child.

Sophie's fellow passenger continued, "Second try. I might be pregnant now. I'm based in Helsinki… involved in a telecom startup there… but I'm originally from New York. If you need anything while you're over, call me. My name's Helen. Helen Turnbull." She handed Sophie her card.

"Helen." Sophie nodded. "Thank you. I will."

When she disembarked Sophie took Helen's copy of *American Baby* with her. The odds of finding a baby magazine in English in Tallinn, while not impossible, were slim.

Having moved house again, Tucker showed Sophie the new apartment, even closer to Old Town this time and literally abutting the city walls. Sophie loved the thick, solid rock ramparts that kept the Baltic winter at bay, and pressing her hand, sometimes even her cheek, against the time-worn, neatly cut rock as she walked the circular stone stairwell to the tower, to her new apartment, she sensed herself more deeply at home than ever.

With her wedding looming, she felt part of the energy, the buzz, the heartbeat of Tallinn, with its nonstop building and renovation. Gone almost overnight were the blood-red, Soviet brown walls; even the airport looked more European now than Soviet. As Tucker luxuriated in his newly installed hot tub, reeling off ideas, the rector of the newly reopened *Püha Vaimu kirik*, Church of the Holy Spirit, an Australian, telephoned.

"Whenever you want," he said, "the diary is empty. I can do a marriage whenever. Now, for instance." He laughed.

Later, under the church's medieval clock, rooted to the spot, Sophie marvelled at the fact that she was actually getting married, in Tallinn, and Tucker had agreed to a baby.

Down the street over the sound of drills, hammers and workmen, Tucker barked orders at his builders who were transforming an ancient abbey into a boutique hotel. In Yankee Odd Lots, Sophie found cookbooks, one in French and one in Italian. Just able to make out a mushroom, onion and chicken recipe, she had a go at the shops in search of ingredients. Traders in leather vests with quick fingers flew over worn abacuses. Charmed, Sophie watched those same deft fingers wrap Estonian cheese, chicken and mushrooms with paper and string. The bread, deliciously black, reminded her of an afternoon spent in Estonian House, in midtown Manhattan, in the semi-dark.

Back at the top of the turret, in her new apartment, Sophie pulled a decades-old cast-iron pot from her Soviet-era oven.

"Look," she said, "a feast from an Odd Lots Italian cookbook. I had to mime-shop my way around Tallinn to find everything."

"Victory." Tucker smiled.

"Bliss," she said.

Sophie took the hydrofoil to Helsinki. Not only did she need something to wear for the civil ceremony, before her wedding at the Church of the Holy Spirit, but also she wanted to call Helen Turnbull.

How's the IVF going?

Helen sprang for lunch, reported the IVF was going well and tagged along for the shopping. At Stockmann, they found everything Sophie wanted: an ivory shift, a simple hat with a small brim, gloves and shoes; and at the harbour, where Sophie once again boarded the hydrofoil, they promised to stay in touch.

"Send photos."

"You, too. Come back when you need a breath of fresh air, some civilisation."

On deck, with the ferry underway, Sophie did take a breath of fresh air. She was happy for Helen, who was definitely pregnant, after her second attempt at IVF, and showing, and who was equally thrilled with her telecom startup. Apparently, a sale was in play for seventy-five million dollars with Telefónica Móviles being the first bidder.

Sophie knew Helen was at the top of her game: baby on the way, her business for sale and a clear understanding of how she intended to ride the Internet wave. Sophie pictured her now happily strolling back up the esplanade from the harbour as it buzzed with jazz musicians, cyclists, summer smells and clanking trams. Contentedly, Sophie knew she didn't need Helsinki for a 'breath of civilisation'. Tallinn was her society, one that had survived one occupation after the next. Tallinn was her warm place, her longed-for slower and genuine pace, and Kadriorg, 'her park', offered what she liked to think of as the freshest air in the world. Maybe it was the trees, the ancient firs, but the Great Kadriorg Park, built by Peter the Great for his Estonian bride Catherine, might just as well have been built by Tucker Mägi for Sophie Taylor.

"You can't smile before the surprise," Tucker teased Sophie at the ferry landing.

"Why not?" she asked as he whisked her and her bags off to a harbour restaurant in a stationary Soviet submarine, complete with outdoor fairy lights wrapped around its towering radio antenna. Over a bottle of wine from Crimea, Tucker presented her with a single strand of pearls.

"Thank you," he said.

"For what?"

"For taking the job."

Sophie and Tucker awoke on the first of their two wedding days to the sound of traffic, specifically a derailed truck full of fish, now spilt on the sidewalk, with gulls reeling and squawking. Anne called her daughter from the airport to say she was getting herself to the hotel and would see her at the town hall. Tucker warmed milk for coffee and volunteered to collect Sophie's bouquet. They too would meet later at the town hall; Sophie should take a taxi.

Clad in natural wood with stained-glass windows of orange and yellow, the hall resounded with the commotion of marriage, and congratulations all around. Anne beamed, shook hands and agreed, "Yes, very lucky." As Tucker's family never left the United States, and definitely wouldn't travel with foals arriving on the stud farm, they sent greetings and apologies, along with love and two monogrammed passport holders. Sophie and Tucker both knew that with good reason both his Estonian father and grandfather would never set foot in Tallinn again. They had lost family and friends to the Soviets, and both feared that the Russians still operated covertly in Estonia; it was their fixed belief that a return ticket was no guarantee that once they arrived in Estonia that they'd ever be allowed to leave.

The pink-robed Justice of the Peace pronounced her words slowly in both Estonian and English. Did they understand? "In Estonian law, you are now wife and husband." Sophie and Tucker nodded, and outside in front of a large group of Tucker's employees,

Sophie tossed her bouquet while someone served champagne. The sun shone unusually warm.

Quickly escaping, the newlyweds made their way this time by car to the Mägi manor house, where Tucker had proposed that snowy night. By daylight the manor remained ramshackle. The collapsed walls of the chapel only remained semi-standing thanks to the saplings and rampaging ivy that sprouted from them, tracing the outlines of crumbled windows and the beam that marked the apex of a long-vanished timber roof. Wind disturbed the surface of a fast-flowing river nearby that spooled back upon itself, breaking into cascades. Tucker embraced his wife, kissing the top of her head, as they stood on the banks of that river outside the thousand-year-old chantry.

"Long way from Rye."

"Yes. Long way from Rye," Sophie said, pausing to take the day in. "What's that?" She pointed to a low, narrow, thatched cottage.

They walked over and found the door open.

"Too strange," Tucker said as he flicked the side of a red donation box and ran his hand over thick glass display cases full of small Viking artifacts: coins, beads and crosses, black-and-white photos of ghosts, some in aprons, others mottled with time, ships in a harbour, peasants with infants and thick socks, and then, on a card starkly stamped 'Tõnis Mägi', an announcement of their own wedding inside a simple black frame.

"Stranger and stranger," he whispered. "Too weird. Too *Twilight Zone.*"

"It's an honour, Tuck. It's family. You're part of it now, Independence, you're home."

At the reception Sophie and Tucker replicated their favourite Estonian meal: blinis, wild mushrooms, roast pork and creamy, sweet *kohupiimakreem.* Anne toasted her children and the Wild, Wild East. Most of the wedding party departed early as they had to be up and ready for the blessing of the marriage in the morning at the Church of the Holy Spirit.

21

"Okay," Tucker said, as they tumbled into bed, "let's make that baby."

The next morning, in the 1906 chauffeured Rolls Tucker had ordered from St Petersburg, driving from Kadriorg Park to the *Püha Vaimu kirik*, Anne and her daughter got lost in the maze-like streets of Tallinn's Old Town, with the driver finally going to the wrong church, explaining as he went, "This is *Toompea*, built in 1227 by the German Knights of the Sword—"

"Thank you," Sophie said, "but it's the Church of the Holy Spirit. I have a wedding to attend."

Anne took Sophie's hand, and Sophie wanted just for a moment that they might keep winding their way through Old Town forever. Who knew her better? Who could she trust? Anne then looped her daughter's arm with hers, and said, "Your father would have loved this day, giving you away, and the specialness of being here in Tallinn."

"Thanks, Mom. I am pretending that he is here today, giving me away."

"I know." Anne nodded her head.

Arriving at the Church of the Holy Spirit, right under the feudal clock with its carefully painted yellow sun, mother and daughter got out. Someone held an umbrella to catch the rain as Sophie rearranged the gown she had bought in Rye. Sophie recalled the orange and yellow glass in the town hall, the wind and the river beside the chapel overgrown with saplings and thick-stemmed vines. Now, in a church weathered by neglect, she left Anne at the door and, once her mother had taken her seat inside, Sophie walked up the bare wooden aisle on her own.

Slipping in from a side door, Tucker met her at the altar, and for a second time, they heard an official pronounce them 'man and wife'.

At Tucker's newly opened Abbey Hotel, the wedding party danced and ate. Between courses, Sophie sat for a minute, thinking about her honeymoon: France, Monaco, the Côte d'Azur and their early-morning flight the next day. A tipsy, random young woman with waist-length, jet-black hair sat down beside her, lit a cigarette and exhaled with intent.

"Tell me," she leaned in, "you don't really intend to get pregnant, do you?"

THREE

Tucker waited patiently, parked outside Monaco's famous palace, enjoying the harbour view, the birdsong and the Mediterranean below. Sophie was running late. It had been an expected detour on their drive from Provence and along the *Corniche Inférieur*, the cliff road, from Nice to Menton. Ages ago, Sophie had sent out a number of applications to MBA programmes, hoping one had a hefty scholarship. When she came across the University of the Riviera she had laughed, as did Tucker.

"A university on the Riviera?"

"Maybe summer school," he said.

"Yes, better than an MBA in dark dank England or New England."

Surprisingly the University of the Riviera had called, asking if she could visit, and Tucker had insisted she take the opportunity while they were in the area on honeymoon as they would practically be driving past.

Sophie ran back to the car, out of breath, opened the door and got in. "You are not going to believe this!"

"What?"

"They've offered me tuition in exchange for helping with their marketing, market analysis, maybe online course development."

Tucker shook his head. "Well, hey, why don't I just drop you off at the Ferrari showroom and you can walk out with one?"

"Worth a try." She laughed.

Shifting gears, while Sophie tied a thin scarf around her head, looking for all the world like Grace Kelly in *To Catch a Thief*, Tucker whistled and wove their way back onto the lower cliff road.

In the morning, Tucker packed up the car and drove just over the speed limit to make the beach in Cassis. There he ordered two *matelas* as if he had been doing it all his life. No sooner had they settled than the weather decided it was on their side, becoming comfortably bright and breezy, with children squealing in delight, gulls spinning, and waves folding unevenly against the shore. Coconut-scented sun lotion vied with the smell of bread from the *boulangerie.*

"I like being married," he declared.

"Me, too," Sophie answered as they ate fresh mozzarella, tomato and pesto baguettes under their beachside umbrella. Sophie bought a white cable-knit sweater in Bleu & Blanc, and a pair of matching Capri trousers from a street vendor. In Les Olivades she bought Provençal table linens, and imagined a daughter, who might one day ask about her honeymoon. The tablecloth dotted with olive sprigs found its way into a shopping bag, along with a pair of slender-fit white jeans sprinkled with blue-grey *fleur-de-lis.*

"So, when do you get fat?" Tucker joked, slipping a hand into the back pocket of her denims.

"What?"

"When you're having kids?" he asked, putting their packages into the small trunk of the rental Alfa Romeo.

"I think you show around three months."

"Maybe you should have bought larger jeans."

"Maybe."

As they swam their way through a small group of children bobbing in the choppy water to the raft in the middle of the spring-fed harbour, Sophie thought with admiration about the man she'd married. He'd put himself through school, never gave up and had an uncanny ability to read her mind. He was making things happen in Estonia.

"You look a thousand miles away," Tucker said.

"No, I was just thinking about you." She wrung the seawater from her hair.

"You should take the university offer."

"I don't know."

"A chance like this doesn't come along every day, Soph. It's only nine months. Call the principal back."

"Okay, I will." She grinned as Tucker wrapped an arm around her.

After that, all the pieces fell into place. Over meal after meal, in rustic villages perched on mountaintops, and in open-air markets in busy town streets, Sophie and Tucker talked nonstop about how it would all work.

"Estonia is a stepping-stone. All of Eastern Europe is opening up."

"Are you planning world dominion?" Sophie teased.

"Yes," Tucker agreed playfully, drawing plans on the back of napkins, sketching out their plans, including what they had dubbed *Project Bébé*.

As they wound their way back to Nice Airport, Sophie felt reluctant to let go of the idea of returning to Tallinn. Where had the honeymoon gone? She reluctantly kissed Tucker goodbye. He was flying back to Tallinn and she back to New York through London, and then home to Rye. On the cross-Atlantic flight, sipping white wine, Sophie thumbed through *Milk*, her hastily bought French baby magazine.

World dominion.

Back home in her condo, reunited with her spaniel Daisy, Sophie wondered if she had gotten married at all? Had she really had a wedding, a reception, and a walk through an ancient manor house held together by errant saplings and waxy ivy? Had she really accepted a tuition-free place at a university for an MBA in Finance – in the South of France?

These thoughts ran nonstop as she met her mother in Brooklyn at the River Café.

"Want to make God laugh?" Anne Taylor grinned as she lifted her glass. "Tell Him or Her your plans."

"Yes. I know. Life is what happens, when you were planning something else?"

"Yes. Exactly. How's Tucker?"

"He's Tucker. Not bothered. Thinks an MBA course is perfect for a new wife. I, on the other hand, feel guilty. Shouldn't I be in Tallinn with him? But I'm happy too, Mom. I can't wait to get back to Monaco. I've already bought my Corporate Finance textbook. Is that weird?"

"No. The jury is in, my darling, and the verdict is: not guilty."

"Thanks, Mom."

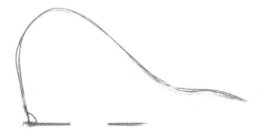

FOUR

"Here you are." The baggage handler turned to Sophie. "Friendliest dog on Air France." He set Daisy's crate down with care.

"Thanks," Sophie agreed. "She *is* a good dog."

France smelt of cypress, heat and Mediterranean salt. A black Mercedes drew up outside arrivals, ready to carry a dog, a kennel, luggage and Sophie; the driver motioned to her and called, "Taxi?"

"*Oui.*"

"I can roll down the windows," he offered, "for the dog, or maybe you want the air conditioner?"

"Fresh air, please."

Sophie held Daisy while they both took in the drive through Nice, along the Promenade des Anglais. Adults and children, some being pulled along by dogs, rollerbladed under tri-coloured flags that snapped sharply in the ocean breeze.

"What's it like here in winter?" she asked the driver.

"Compared to the rest of Europe? Paradise. But it does rain a little. Under grey skies those old buildings lose their colour."

Sophie refused to imagine drizzle, charcoal skies or pastel houses without the dazzle of sunlight.

"*Vint-cinq degrés* usually," he said.

"*Vint-cinq*," Sophie repeated.

"Through the mountains or by the sea? *Lequel préfériez-vous?*"

"The sea," she answered.

Couples walked arm in arm down the Promenade. While well-behaved dogs on leashes lured their owners forward, jagged white caps repeated themselves endlessly into the distance.

"Are you heading for Cap d'Ail?" the driver asked.

"Yes, Xavier Vacances."

Overhead signs warned of falling rock, while steel mesh held back large parts of the mountain as the Mercedes sped by. The road snaked ahead, with one sharp turn leading to the next, and through the chill of a dimly lit tunnel.

Once in Cap d'Ail, the driver pulled up at a roadside stand, shifting seamlessly into neutral.

"*Des tomates ou du melon? Très bien en ce moment.*"

"Thank you," Sophie said, getting out of the car and standing still for a moment to take in the fact that she had actually moved to France and was now shopping at a roadside stand.

The final crawl in the Mercedes to Xavier Vacances proved to be practically vertical. Pressed almost flat into the back of the seat from the steep climb, Sophie held on tight to her spaniel. Two smartly uniformed *gendarmes* at the side of the first bend saluted, and the driver nodded in return.

At Xavier Vacances, the driver took his payment, refused a tip and smiled. "Enjoy France," he said.

An infinity pool gurgled, but with no reception in sight, Sophie reread her paperwork from UR.

"Okay, self-service," she said to no one in particular, while she put Daisy on a leash, the crate and the luggage on a trolley, and her *American Baby* magazine under her arm. Up three flights, in an elevator, she found her one-bedroom studio unlocked and with a one-word message from management.

Bienvenue.

A narrow balcony with just enough room for two chairs and a table ran the length of the apartment and the Mediterranean ran the length of her view – as far as the eye could see. As she attempted to telephone Tucker, the wall phone fell apart in her hands. Through the static she heard him say, "Get a damn French cell phone. I can't hear anything. It's seven degrees here and f'ing raining."

"Not here."

"How's your room?"

"Sticky."

With her things put away, Sophie made her way with Daisy down the narrow steps leading to the main road. After a short downpour, which caught Sophie by surprise, and after a few feet on level ground, she found herself practically falling down a dizzying, municipal staircase that ran from the top of Cap d'Ail to the coastal path below.

On the path, she found portions of the concrete walkway, where it wasn't washed away completely, buckled and crumbled around deeply rooted palms, cactus and ground vines. Small coves revealed themselves one by one, while Belle Époque mansions rose up, still glowing in the late-afternoon sun.

Sophie slowly wound her way to the school, and was surprised to find it mostly empty. Everyone, except a Swedish exchange student who was manning the phones, seemed to be at lunch.

"Don't expect them back. It's *le weekend*," she huffed, "but glad you're here. I'm Abbi. I finished the programme last year but decided to stay. Who can leave Monaco?" She handed over the term schedule.

"Thanks. See you Monday?"

"You will. A number of new students should be showing up at Xavier Vacances, or maybe they're already there. Look out for Nadja Schmit. She's a fellow MBA student from the Cayman Islands, along with a couple of boys and a few mainland Chinese students. Yes, they're all at Xavier Apartments."

"Great."

"Sophie," Abbi called her back, "I forgot to mention that Gaspard Berger is no longer the principal sadly. He's left for family reasons."

"Sorry to hear that."

"The new principal is Pascal Dubois. I think the arrangement you made with Monsieur Berger is still in place, though." Abbi flipped through some paperwork. "Yes, that's fine."

On her walk from Monaco back to Cap d'Ail, pine trees and sea salt competed for Sophie's attention. At Mala Beach, she buried her toes into warm sand until a red sun sank into a deep blue sea.

No sooner had she climbed the final steps to Xavier Vacances, than Sophie found herself among a gaggle of students. They clustered just beyond the automated reception and parked trollies, by the pool. Together, they smoked, laughed and shared a bottle of wine. One rail-thin young woman waved her over to join them.

"I'm Nadja," she said, holding out her hand before the others could say anything. With a dark tan and salon-fresh hair, she appeared to be the ringleader. In spite of the afternoon heat, the evening had suddenly turned starkly cold. Nadja held herself sideways to the spaniel, sitting neatly at Sophie's feet.

"I'm Sophie."

"Where are you from?"

"The States."

"Obviously." Nadja rolled her eyes and drew on her cigarette. "Which one?"

"New York."

"I'm from Cayman. This is George and Klaus," Nadja pointed, "California and Italy. Although the names wouldn't suggest that." She heehawed. "Klaus from Italy?"

The infinity pool spilt over, into the night and seemingly into the villa lights below. As the stars began to come out, a cruise ship in the distance sounded its horn twice, and four Chinese students joined them, sitting a polite distance away.

"I plan," Nadja announced, "on being class valedictorian, and graduating Summa Cum Laude. Then back in the real world, I'm going to run the family fund."

Sophie patted Daisy and Nadja leaned in, whispering, "Have you seen all the Chinese? Stinky." She held her nose. "They're only here because they're middle-class and can't get visas into the USA. I'm not in Cayman anymore." She laughed.

"No," said Klaus, "we're in France, in a dump of a dormitory."

Sophie stood up, ready to take Daisy back to her apartment, and just as she turned to say goodnight, Nadja, lighting another cigarette, looked up and narrowed her eyes.

"Pretty sad," she smirked, "bringing a dog to school."

Sophie flinched.

"How the fuck old are you anyway?"

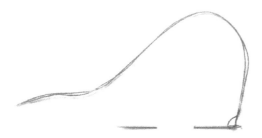

FIVE

When Alexis Alepoú showed up for the first day of class, Sophie relaxed. *Finally*, she thought, *someone my own age*. However, any hope of forming a demographic bond disappeared as she watched the divorcé with his salt-and-pepper hair doggedly zero in on two young women, who rolled their eyes and laughed when he wasn't looking. Nadja, on the other hand, stuck to him like glue. Alexis apparently already knew business inside out. Commandeering the favoured seat at the back of the room, he acted the pasha, or maybe the Greek tycoon that he actually was. *What's he doing at UR?* The Alepoú family had made their money in animal fodder, which Alexis referred to as horseshit.

Sophie sat in the front row, ready to learn, but began to suspect that readiness may not be highly regarded by the twenty-somethings and certainly not by Alexis Alepoú holding court at the rear of the classroom. The blond-wood desks around her remained empty. For a minute, she felt every day of her forty years and tried in vain to recall what it felt like to be twenty-five.

"*Va bene!*" their teacher began. In his well-cut black Ermenegildo Zegna suit, crisp white shirt and black tie, the Italian strutted slowly, confidently, preening, touching the back of his neck lightly, exuding European poise. "*Chi vuole imparare? Qui veut apprendre?* Who wants to learn?"

Sophie eagerly raised her hand. Laughter hit the back of her head in waves. Fifteen twenty-somethings smirked. Only the Chinese seemed, like her, to be out of step. The one and only Chinese male student smiled broadly and nodded at Sophie. Then, in very clear English, he said, "I, too, want to learn."

Professor Rossi nodded at the young man. Then he leaned in, putting an elbow on Sophie's desk and resting his chin on his fist. His thick, gold cufflinks and signet ring caught a glint from the fluorescent light overhead. He was so close Sophie could hear his watch tick and smell his Caron Poivre cologne.

"So... how badly do you want to learn?" Professor Rossi continued to lean on Sophie's desk, breath hinting of his morning Arabica.

Sophie held still, not certain what he was really asking. The room fell silent. Sophie might easily have slipped a hand behind his neck, just above his starched collar and pulled him close. She breathed carefully, not wanting to make a cultural mistake. *Not in Westchester anymore. What am I studying? Business? Money? Sex?*

"A lot." Sophie exhaled; Professor Rossi nodded and straightened himself up. He had all but dismissed her. *What was that all about?*

"*Bien alors*, good then," he said, rotating on the back of his heel. "*Mademoiselle—*"

"*Madame.*"

"All the better," he chuckled, twirling his Visconti pen, bouncing it off his thumb. "Lunch today?"

"Yes, thank you," Sophie responded, and a slight murmur ran through the rest of the class, to Alexis Alepoú and back again.

"You see," the Italian pontificated to the class, rolling his eyes, stretching and looking up at the mountains hovering over the small campus in Monaco, "you have to want it, really want it:

an education." He dropped his pose. "How many of you know anything about Socrates, considered the greatest teacher of all time?"

The class nodded.

"He had a student once, a young man who wanted to learn. Begged and begged. One day Socrates agreed, and took the boy to the river. At the river Socrates told the student to kneel, and when he did, Socrates shoved his head under the water. Thrashing and flailing, the student fought for air. Finally, Socrates released his young victim. 'What did you want most?' he asked. 'To breathe,' the young man gulped. 'Well,' said Socrates, 'come back when your longing to learn is as strong as your desire for air.'"

Professor Rossi paused, surveying the class with his dark eyes. "To receive an education," he said, "you have to want it."

Sliding his pen back into his jacket and tucking his sleek black tie into his trousers, he added, "That's it, class, for today. Except for you, Madame Mägi. I think we have a date, *si*?"

"We'll go to Graziella. You will love it," the professor said as he held the door for Sophie. "Not too over the top, but good food and a view of the harbour."

"I'm sure. Do you mind if I use your first name?"

"Thought you'd never ask," he responded with a chuckle. "It's Marco."

"So good to be with another adult."

"I figured it would be. By the way, I went to school in California."

"Whereabouts?"

"San Francisco," he said as he pulled out a seat for her and motioned to a waiter whom he appeared to know well. "Let me choose. Next time you can. Today is on me. Next one's on you."

Marco Rossi rattled on in Italian while Sophie enjoyed the vista of the harbour below and the looming cliff face and cathedral above. As the waiter served a dark red wine, Marco finally asked her, "So what are you doing in Monaco?"

"It's a bit of a long story, but I always wanted to get an MBA. I love business, but there never seemed to be the time or money to study it properly. When I was on my honeymoon recently, I popped into UR on a whim, really, and the next thing I knew, I was here instead of in Tallinn."

"So you have a husband?"

"Yes, we're happily married and only three thousand miles apart!"

"And you are not sure if being here is the right thing?"

"Exactly."

"It is."

"How do you know?"

"Because you are hungry," he said emphatically. "Now eat."

The two new friends dove into the *antipasti*, *primi*, *secondi* and *dolci*. Finally, after the *trio di gelati* they parted company, but while Marco now knew everything about Sophie, she knew next to nothing about him. He certainly hadn't mentioned a wife. Sophie was happy to have a friend who was over twenty-five, and glad to have found someone who shared the same theory about venture capitalists: that they had abandoned caution and a dot.com bubble was brewing. Everybody wanted a piece. Marco also clearly understood the potential of online retailing in Italy, especially for the luxury brands – Versace, Fendi, Gucci.

"*Arrivederci, bella signora*," he called out as she turned to take the coastal path back to Xavier Vacances.

A late-afternoon sun hovered over the sea. A breeze picked up and Sophie smiled to herself, thrilled to be living in the South of France, near Monaco, and working on an MBA. Lunch with Marco Rossi had been just what she needed. Knowing she had a spaniel to get outside and a husband to telephone, Sophie hurried back towards her small studio overlooking the Mediterranean.

"Tucker," she said on the phone that night, "it's all so different here."

"Fallen in love yet?"

"No, of course not."

"Not tempted by a rich Italian? Just kidding, Soph. I've booked us into the Monte Carlo Beach Hotel for the half-term long weekend. A special treat for your birthday."

"Amazing." Daisy whined and a last glimmer of light played on the horizon. The striped canopy snapped over the balcony. "I miss you, Tuck."

"Remember the goal: an MBA."

"Yes," she said, wishing for a moment they were in his turret flat, in front of the tiled stove, wrapped in a quilt, sharing an eggnog.

"Don't give up. It's what you have always wanted."

"What?"

"An MBA."

A baby.

After the call, with her feet resting on the balcony railing and with a cup of *verveine* in hand, Sophie felt relaxed, her mood lifted once again. She considered what she was grateful for: Tucker, Mother, Daisy and her new friend Marco, who would never ever get a job in New York or who if he did would be fired soon afterwards. Sophie laughed out loud. She was happy. So content, so deep in happy anticipation of Tucker's visit, and the what-if of a potential half-term pregnancy, that she almost missed the tapping on her door.

"Sophie? Are you there? It's Nadja. Do you want to get something to eat? Bottom of the hill. Klaus and George are coming. To-die-for pizza. At Aux Délices. You can't miss it."

"Okay," Sophie answered. *Why not?* "One minute. I'll meet you there."

Abandoning the sunset, she weighed up the prospect of cultivating her classmates. They were going to be together for nine months – she might as well make the effort. Try and forget.

How the fuck old are you anyway?

In the red-lit pizzeria, though, Sophie realised it was a set-up. Klaus and George, careful to exchange pleasantries, as if she were a professor or their maiden aunt, appeared to be ring-led by Nadja. The tomato salad and mineral water with lemon she chose immediately set her apart from her fellows, who ordered two large pizzas and two bottles of red wine. Nadja clearly did not intend to eat at all.

"Are you really forty?" Nadja asked, keeping her voice low and cajoling.

"No kidding," Klaus said, tugging at his collar and cuffs, "I never would have guessed." He brushed the shoulders of his cashmere sweater and straightened his Gucci belt.

"You look thirty at the most," George added, leaning in. "Really, my mother is your age and she doesn't look anything like you."

Sophie moved her salad around on the plate. "So, what about you three, how old are you?"

"Twenty-one," "Twenty-two," "Twenty-three," they answered in succession.

With the pizzas served, Nadja drank slowly, watching Sophie over the rim of her glass. George and Klaus talked endlessly about the bars in Nice and what they wanted to do after they finished their MBAs. Sophie listened politely when all she really wanted to do was snuggle up with Daisy and read her Corporate Finance book, refresh what little she knew about accounting and read Rossi's case study of Louis Vuitton.

"So," Nadja cleared her throat, "did you actually have lunch with Dr Rossi? Any info?"

"Info?"

"Yes. Married? Single? Kids? The class? Final project? Exam?"

"No."

"Well, what in the fuck did you talk about?" Nadja demanded with such force that the waiter came to the table. "Or are you just going to fuck him?"

Klaus and George stared in horror, then collected themselves.

"She's just kidding." Klaus laughed and lit a cigarette.

Sophie placed her napkin on the table and motioned for the waiter to bring the bill. Nodding at Klaus and George, she said calmly, "Thank you for the invitation. I have a bit of work to do and of course the dog needs to go out. It's a nice night. I'll walk back."

Klaus and George sat paralysed and Nadja remained silent as Sophie paid the bill and the waiter opened the door for her. Just as the walk up the hill to Xavier Vacances seemed momentarily insurmountable, so did her decision to take an MBA at forty, almost forty-one, in the foothills of the Alps, but then just as quickly, the smell of cedar and the salt air took her by surprise, turning things around. She had had a great first day. She picked up her step, remembering that she was twenty years older than most of her classmates and that patience was one of the gifts that comes with age.

Out of nowhere, Nadja's silver BMW convertible with the licence plate 'NOT YOU' screeched to a halt.

"If you'd waited," she chirruped out the window with the top down, "we would have given you a lift."

Sophie smiled, unwilling to make an enemy. "Thank you. I enjoyed the walk. Next time."

"By the way," Nadja said, pulling on the brake and lifting her hair away from her face, "if you want to make friends in this town, remember that being teacher's pet is not the way to do it."

The BMW squealed into the underground parking. While liquor-laced laughter ricocheted off the cement walls, Nadja sang: "Who let the dogs out?"

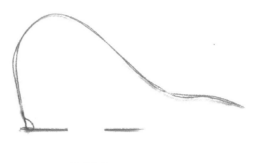

SIX

Sophie wondered where the sunsets and coastal walks went. When not buried in course work, she audited the school's online presence. In fact, unbeknownst to most of her fellow students, Sophie worked long into the night, trying to sort a way forward for the UR on the Internet. She contacted the University of California and MIT, where online was booming. Free education was becoming real. *Insane.* Get a degree from any university, no matter where you lived, from Siberia to the South Pacific – as long as you had access to the Internet, which it appeared would soon be everywhere thanks to wireless.

Stuff of dreams.

This morning she awoke early, dressed in jeans and a T-shirt, packed her bag with everything she needed for the day – accounting homework, finance case study, private banking comparative analysis, a PowerPoint presentation on world gold prices and her laptop. She slipped on sneakers, ready to walk down the mountain and pop in to see the local doctor on her way to school. From scalp to toes, she itched.

Without looking up from his desk, perma-tanned *Docteur* Francois nodded, amused because he had seen it before, ever since UR had been using the Xavier Vacances as a so-called school dormitory. The French students never fell for it, only the foreigners, especially the *Américains*.

"*Bien sûr* you itch," he said, "you're crawling with dust mites. It's Xavier Vacances, it's a holiday let, what did you expect?"

Ces Américains. He shook his head. The school had an attractive website and sent out lovely flyers, including among other things the address of his practice; the photograph of the apartments' infinity pool with a Mediterranean sunset in the background, but no one ever stayed past a week or two at Xavier Vacances and all of them visited him.

Word got out as usual, and all the UR students checked out of the holiday let-cum-dormitory, except for the Chinese students, who blasted their rooms with disinfectant. The French Riviera was getting real for them all. The sunsets, still amazing, didn't eradicate unkind classmates or dust mites. Nadja had moved out practically as soon as she'd moved in. She'd found an apartment in Monaco proper. Being class valedictorian and marrying the Prince were still at the top of her to-do list, which thankfully kept her too busy to bump into Sophie outside of class. Klaus and George rented extra rooms from Abbi, the receptionist who had a house in Fontvieille near the heliport. Pietro, the shyest and kindest twenty-something Sophie had met on the course, also found accommodation in a family home whose owners knew his Argentine father and who, without hesitation, put it at his disposal.

Despite the increasing workload and her efforts to improve UR's website, Sophie too managed to move. She remained startled by her own good luck, especially when she sat with Daisy on the balcony overlooking the palace and the sea. Who would have guessed Marco Rossi would know of an affordable flat within walking distance of school? Viewed from the balcony, the evening clouds, soft and pastel, resembled a Maxfield Parrish print. There were definitely no dust mites in Sophie's new studio on the Rock, right in the centre of old Monaco, overlooking the port of Fontvieille.

Sophie loved descending through actual rock when she took the almost vertical flights of stairs, or else went in elevators or on escalators that cut through the rock, to the shops below, where the nondescript University of the Riviera was based on three rented floors of an anonymous office block.

Despite the hustle and bustle of tourists that swarmed Monaco daily, there was a hidden, more leisurely pace of life in the Principality, hinted at in displays of startling white laundry hung out to dry high above the narrow streets; the distant barking of pampered lap dogs. Cobblestone alleyways opened onto exotic gardens and into the cool darkness of Cathédrale Notre-Dame-Immaculée. Sophie paused occasionally on the steps of the cathedral and thought of Grace Kelly, who, Nadja reminded her, must have had a shit time: people stepping on your crypt, locals pronouncing your name the same way they pronounced fat in French, *graisse*. Sometimes, Sophie caught sight of the Prince and the Royal Family.

Increasingly, in recent phone calls Tucker said the dark, cold weather in Tallinn, along with the poverty left from Soviet times, was beginning to wear him down. When he said this, Sophie would compare Estonia with Monaco, its weather and its untold wealth. It seemed a paradise. On the cathedral steps, with the subtropical perfume blowing off the sea and over the green San Martine gardens, Sophie felt she couldn't balance the equation.

Be careful what you pray for! she heard her mother's voice chiding her. *Dream anything.* Sophie had dreamt of an MBA and here she was. She made a note to call her mother. She missed both Anne and Tucker, but she felt she was in the right place, at the right time, doing exactly what she was meant to be doing, even if it seemed at odds with being married, with a husband miles away.

Often taking her Corporate Finance textbook to bed, working on her mini study table, Sophie would focus on advanced problems. Nothing came easily. Chapter after chapter, she forced herself to comprehend. She'd never studied like this before. *Is education truly wasted on the young, especially while they are figuring out life lessons and falling in love?* The moon came out, always with a cascade of stars. House lights, streetlights, car lights came on one by one over the foothills of the Côte d'Azur.

Sophie would put the textbook away, lean forward and watch through the porthole of a window in her studio high on her rocky promontory as *le TGV*, the high-speed train, illuminated its curving track. It reminded her of a miniature train set Anne surprised her with one Christmas. It too made its way around a mountain and through tunnels with its own special light. The sides of that model mountain too had tiny houses lit up, trees and mystery. Back then, in a flannel gown and robe, on her belly, with chin propped up in the cup of one hand, just as it was now, with the train barrelling through, she felt that all things were possible.

Even when her mother had asked, "A penny for your thoughts?" she did not say, "I wish I had a father."

Just as the *TGV* snaked out of sight, and darkness yawned with its slow-blinking lights and the steep sides of Maritime-Alps sloped into the black sea, Sophie closed her eyes; school tomorrow, and after that Tucker would arrive.

The next morning Sophie crashed back to reality. Gone was the euphoria of an MBA come true, sea breezes and *le TGV* at midnight. To her own surprise, she found herself on the cover of *Monaco Today*. Nadja waved the slick, oversized magazine back and forth in front of her like a banner as soon as Sophie walked into class.

"Cover Girl," she mocked, while a murmur filtered through the room along with the sound of flipping pages as the magazine was passed around. Everyone waited for Marco Rossi, who seemed to have made it his business not to show up with any particular regularity.

"What do you think, Cover Girl?" Nadja oozed.

Sophie didn't engage.

43

Finally, the glossy magazine made its way to Sophie. She stared at the image of herself, taken randomly while she walked from the Rock to school. She stood in the market, weighing a ripe, white peach in her right hand. Just as she prepared to respond, Professor Rossi walked in and snatched the magazine from her.

"Our own Grace Kelly." He smiled supportively and then barked at the class to sit down, shut up and circulate the handout he'd brought in. Sophie felt rescued just by having another person her age in the room, aside, of course, from Alexis Alepoú, who sometimes walked into class with a cigarette and a hangover.

Sophie half envied Alexis, Mr Horseshit, sitting at the back of the class, with a young woman on either side and a young male neophyte or two as close as possible. Whiling away his time in Monte Carlo, driving, gambling, drinking, he was waiting for his mother to die. His only job was to sit it out, here in Monaco, ready to take over the business when it became necessary. He was the family member designated a resident of Monte Carlo so as to render the Alepoú business tax-free. Nadja, with typical lack of taste, referred to him as a 'tax refugee'.

After class Sophie collected her books, repacked her bag, and set off to meet the new principal, Monsieur Dubois, to review UR's online presence – plus, she guessed, her own enrolment at the school. She'd had more than a hint or two that he regretted his predecessor's generosity to her. She also had a French lesson and a math tutoring session. She hoped for a quick meeting and then a salad on her balcony while reading the *Economist*.

Despite his erratic timekeeping Marco Rossi had turned out to be one of the better teachers, and in consequence Sophie fought hard to stay abreast of French, Italian and international news. While he didn't lay things out in the linear style of a textbook, a clarity Sophie appreciated back in the States, he had a way of teaching that engaged. Just as she was zipping up her bag, Nadja bumped her with one angular shoulder.

"Lunch?"

44

Sophie wanted to take care of business, go home, enjoy her rare, free Friday afternoon and maybe go shopping at Carrefour, the buzzing French supermarket built below sea level in Fontvieille. She wanted to rework a number of the problems she had not worked out correctly the first time around, but still she found herself saying, "Yes," from a sense of obligation. "I'd love to, when?"

"Now."

"Okay." Sophie hoped for the best but prepared for the worst. "Give me a few minutes. I need to speak with Monsieur Dubois. I will join you at—?"

"*La Salière.*"

Pascal Dubois popped his head out of the office, signalling for Sophie to wait. She nodded at the man who could be a stand-in for Pepé le Pew, a cartoon character she'd seen again recently when Ascent Magazines considered different advertising campaigns. Pepé, a skunk, travelled with an odour, just as Pascal reeked of tobacco and travelled in a haze of blue smoke.

Eventually calling her in, Pascal smiled slyly as if their meeting was a tryst. After telling her she should be discreet about her tuition discount, he said he would honour his predecessor's agreement as long as he saw results from her regarding the development of long-distance, online learning. He spoke in a whisper, even with the solid oak door to his office closed. Pascal liked Sophie's ideas, even if he didn't understand them, but he wanted results quickly or else, he said, throwing up his hands, "*Fini.*"

He wanted a new stream of income and the prestige it would bring. He held her back longer, asking after the progress of his nephew Napoléon, who was technically in her year group.

"Yes, he speaks English well," Sophie lied. "He should do well."

"Top of the class?"

Sophie nodded and didn't say he was never actually in class.

"How did you like the cover of *Monaco Aujourd'hui*?" Pascal asked, lighting himself another cigarette.

"Did you place it there?"

"Yes. I like the idea of a lead article on UR and you with your online knowhow – not the mature student stuff. I don't know what my predecessor was thinking. So, the focus is on your online learning, yes? I don't need a bunch of middle-aged women from New York flapping over here to study luxury brands. I need young bloods, all the kids who can't get in anywhere else. Not mature students."

"What?" Sophie was shocked at his sudden shift of tone and dismissive attitude.

"Yes. Berger was testing the mature female market. Getting you here for your Internet genius was just a bit of a ruse. He couldn't very well say, 'Yes, you are female and old, perfect,' could he? Your fees shouldn't be discounted. You shouldn't be here, but since you are, make it worth my while. Be brilliant or... *fini.*" He stubbed out his cigarette, but not before blowing a single, perfect smoke ring.

"Did you just insult me?"

"Yes," he inhaled, "*pourquoi pas?*"

"Why not?" Sophie fumed.

"You could always leave," he suggested.

"I don't think so," she answered. "I'm here to get an MBA and to put you on the map, whether you like me or not, whether I like you or not. I will finish the job like I promised your predecessor."

"We'll see."

"Yes, let's."

As she arrived breathless at *La Salière*, there appeared to be no space at the table, and Sophie considered just backing out quietly, but Alexis, catching sight of her, bellowed a hello and motioned her over. Klaus and George made room, while a waiter swiftly brought a chair.

"Cover Girl," Alexis imitated Nadja. "Our own Grace Kelly."

"Stop," Sophie said, as she tried to order lunch at the same time.

"So how did you get that cover?" Nadja leaned in. "That doesn't happen by accident."

"Actually, Nadja, I didn't know anything about it."

"Lunch with Rossi again?" Nadja drilled.

"No," Sophie answered, trying to translate the menu and not rise to the bait.

"Come on," Klaus and George said in unison. "Are you?"

Pietro discreetly motioned to the waiter, dissuading him from coming to take their order just as a confrontation was brewing.

All eyes were on Sophie, who gave up trying to read the menu. Horseshit leaned back on the banquette, one arm draped over a smirking Nadja's shoulders and the other laying claim to a young student from Norway. Sophie stood up; Pietro politely moved her chair back.

"Sadly," she said, "I'm not on the menu, today or any other day."

The restaurant fell quiet as she made her way over to the door, which Pietro was already holding open.

"I am sorry," he said, "for the behaviour of our classmates."

A small bell tinkled over the door, and that along with Nadja cackling was the last thing Sophie heard.

The cacophony of the lunch she had never wanted to attend faded behind her as she made her way back through the market and up the Rock to her apartment. At last, peeling the white peach the photographer had captured on the cover of *Monaco Today*, she managed to laugh.

Cover Girl.

"Surprise!" Tucker smiled, as she opened the door. "I'm early."

"Oh, it's so wonderful you're here," she cried out, hugging him and offering half of her peach.

"Good, then pack your bag, bring Daisy and lock the door, we're moving to the Monte Carlo Beach Hotel. The taxi is downstairs waiting."

Later, in their room at the hotel, they showered together, lazed in thick robes, and talked about the challenges they were facing. What would Tucker do with Pepé le Pew if he was in her situation? And Nadja? Tucker told Sophie to write Nadja off. Not worth your time, he had said.

"You know what I would tell her?"

"Yes," Sophie laughed, "I do, but she's younger, and I feel that she's been hurt in her life by someone, or something."

"Maybe she's just mean."

"Maybe."

They dined at the Chèvre d'Or, while Tucker told her all about another hotel he was opening in Estonia in partnership with a Danish entrepreneur. Over coffee he handed over her birthday gift, a pair of antique Baltic amber earrings. She ran her finger over the fossilised resin and along the intricate silver filigree. They appeared illuminated from within.

"They're beautiful. Thank you, Tucker."

"Thank *you*," he answered, taking the earrings from her and helping her to put them on.

Sophie didn't want the long weekend to end. She didn't want Tucker to leave and it had been so hard to say goodbye. As the weekend played over and over again in her mind, she refused to take the amber earrings off. *How can I live in two places at once?* The biggest wonder was Tucker babbling about babies, about whether or not she could get pregnant right now even, have the baby soon after graduation.

"Wouldn't that be great?" he had said.

"Oh yes." Sophie smiled.

"Twins?" he proposed with a grin.

"Okay." She laughed, charmed by his confidence.

"Happy forty-first," he had said as he slipped the amber earrings into her ears, "Mommy."

SEVEN

Just as Sophie calculated how fast autumn term seemed to be flying by, and how the pace of school and Monaco life had happily settled, with some of the other students' childish behaviour slipping into the past, Nadja made a point of coming to sit beside her in Organisational Behaviour.

Sophie's latest paper, clearly marked A+, lay on the desk between them. Nadja saw it, tapped it and simpered, looking up at Sophie.

"I can't believe how much you've aged," she said, "especially since that first day. Believe it or not, for a split second, I thought you were my age at first, until I looked twice."

Sophie toyed with her pencil. *Is this where I say fuck off?* she wondered, finding that she could not.

"By the way, does that horsehair of yours tie itself up?"

At this further provocation, Sophie moved seats.

"Something I said?" Nadja laughed. "Or was it my Clive Christian No. 1 Imperial Majesty Perfume?" She threw her head back and sniggered, as a wave of laughter swelled up across the back of the room.

Mr Ambrose swept into the room with the self-importance of a marketing guru who saw his specialty as the engine that ran any business.

"Okay, down to business, first things first," he said in his easy Australian accent. "Admin wants you to choose a group rep."

Sophie sat back. *No one's going to choose me.* Nadja put her hand up, Klaus volunteered Horseshit and Tengfei, the student from Beijing, cleared his throat and stood up.

"We would like Mrs Sophie to represent us," he said as he turned and nodded at Sophie.

The room fell quiet. The nominated candidates left the room and a vote was taken. Mr Ambrose counted twice, then asked the proposed contenders to return.

"The class representative," he announced without any fanfare, "is Mrs Sophie." He smiled at Tengfei and his contingent. While there was mild dissent, Sophie promised to do her best and thanked the class, in particular her Chinese classmates, who held a majority. *Why me?*

Mr Ambrose resumed his class, focusing on the need to monitor the market closely at all times. From that, he expounded, would grow a strategy, and ultimately the marketing plan.

"Marketing is strategy," he repeated before setting his class an assignment due next week.

Catching up with Tengfei and his girlfriend after class, Sophie thanked him again. They offered her a cup of tea from a thermos, while they sat on a wall, basking in the late-autumn sunshine.

"Tengfei," she asked, "why me?"

"Because you are the oldest."

Sophie took in the guileless fact from a young Chinese man, who accepted respect for age as a given. There it was again: *age.* And then, sitting on a wall with her cup of cooling Chinese tea, she felt pride.

Because I am the oldest.

Sophie packed her case, thanking the Monegasque government for the National Day of Monaco – November 19th, which meant a four-day break. She couldn't wait to fly to Estonia. How long had it been? It felt like ages. She'd written her marketing assignment, covered the extra math, and set up a meeting in Tallinn with the young Estonians who were developing the software that promised to allow voice calls between computers. She imagined herself working with them, or at least finding investors, or maybe even bringing the hot prospect to one of the top investment banks in London or New York, maybe even Ascent Magazines. If Helen Turnbull could do it in Finland, why not Sophie in Estonia? She tossed things into her bag, almost able to smell the cinnamon in her coffee, and called a taxi.

Sophie ran Daisy up the steps to the vet's practice, which wasn't hard to do, because Madame Duval, the ever-popular local vet, had a trick up her sleeve. She controlled her practice and her pet patients with the freshly ground beef she carried in her smock pocket. With her own dog, a Cavalier King Charles, sitting attentively on the exam table until she needed to use it, her office was a stage set for Dr Dolittle. Daisy felt perfectly at home and, without a second nuzzle, didn't look back as Sophie ran back down the steps to her impatiently honking taxi.

Her driver cursed as he drove furiously up the A8 and into Nice, finally making the airport in time. Once through security, Sophie breathed a sigh of relief. With a four-day break ahead in Estonia with Tucker, she felt she'd hit the jackpot.

She went in search of coffee and a croissant. Heading towards the newsagent, she noticed a large poster advertising the helicopter shuttle service between Monaco and the airport, and resolved to use that on her return to save time. In the shop she ran her fingers over magazines, French and foreign. It seemed just yesterday she was picking up bridal magazines. Now, she collected a copy of the *Economist*, but it was a wide-eyed baby on the front of *Milk* that stole her attention. At the register, the cover baby seemed to smile at her.

The gravitational pull of UR and France snapped the minute she boarded.

Au revoir.

She felt she could practically fly the plane herself by now, as she watched the sea, the mountains and Nice disappear beneath. Opening her Corporate Finance textbook, she stopped and thought instead about Tucker. He would be as happy to see her, as she was to see him. With that thought, she fell into a deep, much-needed sleep.

As the plane descended over a nighttime Tallinn, Sophie watched the airport floodlights bathe the Arctic firs in a white light that accentuated the already snow-dusted trees. Drifts lined either side of the runway, and yet everything ran as if it were a midsummer day. She could hardly contain herself. Waiting for her bag seemed an impossibility, and finally making her way through arrivals, she found Tucker wearing his usual heartwarming grin and holding out to her one deep red, almost black, long-stemmed rose.

Tallinn seemed so fresh, so new, so on the move. Even the first blast of frozen air was welcome to Sophie after the hot-house atmosphere of the school. As Tucker's old Russian jeep clung steadfastly to the road with its winter tires, Sophie caught Tucker up on the latest at UR and then he shared his own adventures. "Silly money. The Wild East," he said as she cradled her textbook like a baby, listened and bumped along in the jeep. "Real estate in Eastern Europe is blossoming everywhere, in every shape and size. The shopping centre, more like a strip mall, is underway. A hypermarket next, another hotel. Latvia, Lithuania, Poland. Might expand into Ukraine?"

As Tucker roller-coastered from one topic to the next, Sophie paid attention, impressed by his energy and enthusiasm.

"By the way, you'll love the new apartment!"

"I liked the old one, and the one before that. What happened to the turret apartment?"

"You know me," he answered unashamedly. "Always trading up."

In the new apartment, directly over his new offices, Sophie unpacked and they walked across the main road into Kadriorg for dinner in a restaurant that for all practical purposes looked like a cleanly cut Mies van der Rohe box. UR all but disappeared from her thoughts, until she mentioned the Corporate Finance project she needed to complete over the break. In three strokes of a pen, Tucker helped sort the outline on the back of a napkin, before sharing his latest dilemmas with the Tallinn city council.

"Bribery or a hit man?" he joked.

"That's not covered in my Organisational Behaviour class," Sophie quipped.

Wandering back through Kadriorg Park, arm in arm, catching the odd falling snowflake, they were two people in love; no one else and no other place else existed for them.

Up and out early, Tucker left a trail of his lemony aftershave. Breathing it in, Sophie roused herself finally, made coffee, pulled out her textbook, but then got sidetracked with her wide-eyed baby on the cover of *Milk*. She shivered. Even bundled in a goose-feather duvet, dressed in thick flannel pyjamas, and with a mug of hot coffee, the apartment was cold.

As she flipped through the magazine one article after the next caught her attention. "Breastfeeding," the headline read, "increases intelligence." Check; she would definitely breastfeed. Another article on ovulating offered a free, pullout temperature chart. Start charting? Check. Regarding 'How Fertile Are You?' she answered every question with a yes; very fertile.

Tucker had been right. If she conceived now, she could give birth not long after graduation. Could she do it? Finally, the Corporate Finance paper – governance in the computer industry – came to mind. Now warm at last, she stationed herself at the kitchen table and baby thoughts gave way to companies that had for all practical purposes no governance at all.

Tucker popped in twice, bringing yoghurt and fruit from the office fridge, while Sophie worked away, disappointed that she would not see him until well past nine that night, but at least it would give her a chance to complete a draft review of the marketing plan for UR.

When Tucker finally arrived home, standing in the doorway, at almost ten o'clock, he offered pizza and a bottle of red wine from Moldova. He kissed her before collecting glasses from the cabinet behind her.

"Don't stop. I'll put the pizza out."

"I can stop now," she answered, capping her pen.

"Don't you have some serious work to cover?"

"It can wait," Sophie said, picking up a slice of pizza. "It's amazing what I can accomplish on an airplane."

After a bottle of wine, a carton of Finnish vanilla ice cream and tales of corporate derring-do, they made love. Eventually, Tucker fell asleep, despite having claimed he wouldn't, and everything stilled as Sophie listened to him breathe, the hum of cars on the street and the hiss of the radiators. Snow flurries circled the halogen lamps outside the window and over the company parking lot. The room turned a soft blue, and there again on the floor lay *Milk* with her wide-eyed, cover baby smiling up.

Brushing the child's face, she counted backwards from graduation day. Tucker might be right. *Baby, right after graduation day.* She could do the final run to the Christmas break and then, thank God, she'd be back in Tallinn.

It will all fall into place, Sophie heard her mother saying.

All fall into place.

EIGHT

Four days later, Tucker once again embraced Sophie just outside airport security.

"Listen," he said quietly, "I hope you are pregnant. Be brave. Don't let those little fucks get you down. Time is flying and you'll be back here soon."

The phone in his pocket buzzed and he pulled back momentarily. "Sorry," he mouthed to Sophie, "office," and walked a few steps away.

"Thank you, *aitäh*, Tiu, you're an angel. What would I ever do without you? Twenty minutes. Show them the plans. You know the drill almost better than I do. Sophie's just leaving. I'll be there soon. You are a miracle, Tiu. *Aitäh*." He hung up and laughed. "Yes, I am learning the language! Russian, too. *Spasibo*."

They hugged once more before Sophie made her way through security.

"*Nägemist!*" he called out, before picking up his phone once again. With a quick look back and a wave, she smiled but he didn't see. The name echoed in her mind.

Tiu?

"Taking a degree in Finance?" a woman about Sophie's age asked as they waited to board Air Estonia. "I know that textbook," she added, pointing to the book that was half-visible in Sophie's shoulder bag.

"Yes, I am," Sophie answered, shifting her bag from one shoulder to the other. "At the University of the Riviera."

"Are you sure that's a real school? A university in the South of France?" The woman laughed as she and Tucker once had.

"I couldn't bear to take an MBA in dark, dank, cold North America, or even dark, dank, cold Northern Europe. UR's a real school and it is a paradise." They both watched through the daytime darkness two men de-icing their plane as sheets of snow still fell.

"I took my MBA at Harvard," her fellow passenger whispered. "Here's a tip: if you don't understand something, get a tutor. Don't struggle, or think you have to brain-fuck it. Just ask for help."

Sophie knew it was a three and a half-hour flight to Nice, and estimated that in that time she'd be able to fully flesh out the outline she'd drafted in Tallinn, review the math, especially internal rate of return, which tended to be her bête noire. In Helsinki Airport she bought a grey Marimekko shift, perfect for the warm winter in Monaco and the seeming cultural imperative that women should wear dresses. Despite her best efforts to resist, she bought a Finnish magazine, *Kodin Kuvalehti*, with a cover baby, of course, an infant dressed in a soft, light-blue vest nestled deeply into ample arms.

Cover babies.

Sophie recalled the fertility checklist, and felt smug. She never gave it a second thought; she would simply get pregnant. Didn't women do that every day? She vaguely recalled that a distant relative conceived an 'oops' baby at fifty-two. What was there to worry about at forty-one? Tucking the magazine and the thought away, Sophie pulled out the finance paperwork and left her wide-eyed French baby from *Milk* and the Finnish one in his blue singlet somewhere under her heart. As they prepared for landing, she congratulated herself: project done. Any finishing touches could be added in the morning.

Heli Air Monaco proved to be better than the terrestrial taxi, despite Sophie having to negotiate a weight allowance. As the doors were closed, she wondered, *Could I be pregnant now?* Maybe. They'd made love, of course, and according to her quick look at the fertility chart, it might have been a good time, spot on, even.

The helicopter pitched forward, the lift-off reminding her of her mother and the trips to Norway or Greenland, chasing glaciers. With the headfirst dip of the helicopter they would laugh, hold hands. Life was an adventure, if nothing else, her mother would say. Sophie left the orange earplugs in their cellophane packet, enjoying the din and drone of the blades.

The cold and dark of Estonia melted away in the soft white light of the Côte d'Azur. The helicopter hovered like a mechanical insect, nose down, along the coast, close enough for her to see the changes in the Alpes-Maritimes, the inlets and the promontories, then suddenly, sweeping bays.

After landing at the helipad in Fontvieille, Sophie took a quick taxi ride into Cap d'Ail to collect Daisy. It still amazed her that carrying a dog in a taxi in France was never a problem, and as they passed the *Jardin Exotique*, she pulled Daisy onto her lap and hugged her close. The air outside was intoxicating, and like it or not, for now this was home – even without Tucker – and Sophie loved it.

In the morning Sophie walked the ancient flight of stairs from her flat to give Daisy some exercise and to take in the beauty of the sunrise and the smell of the garden. The cobblestones, still wet from the previous evening's rain, might be the same age as those in Tallinn, she guessed. The pastel sky, a subdued blue, seemed sliced in half by a fine dramatic line of black clouds on the horizon.

Making her way to Professor Rossi's class, Sophie found that after her break with Tucker and her meeting with the smart

Estonians developing Kommune, the computer-to-computer chat program, she wasn't in the mood for immature twenty-somethings, for being a punch bag or negotiating the cultural differences between French, Italians and Americans.

The class was fully attended, with every student showing up after the national holiday. Sitting down in her usual seat in the front of the class, Sophie glanced up to see Marco Rossi, twirling his Visconti pen and looking down at her.

"Married life wearing us down, Ms Sophie? Or is it just being an American woman *avec tant de choix*? Too many choices?" He tapped the capped end of his pen on her desk.

Laughter ran through the class. For a moment Sophie looked straight ahead. *Perhaps he's right: too many choices.* She forced a smile; the professor smiled back.

"Now to the point." He turned to the class. "Who's done the paper?"

Sophie raised her hand slowly.

Scornful laughter rippled through the room.

"You see what I mean. Who will succeed in business?" The Italian professor paraded up one aisle and down the next, finally stopping in front of Alexis, who adjusted his Rolex. "And what did you do with your holiday, M Grèce?"

"I drove my Ferrari from here to Positano in five hours, four times."

Alexis bowed and acknowledged the ripple of envy.

"Next?" Marco Rossi demanded, pointing to a French student, then a Swede, then Klaus, then George.

"Skiing in the Alps."

"Boyfriend over from Sweden."

"Blue Boy every night."

"Not saying."

"Well, we know our Chinese comrades did their homework. What about you, Monsieur Silencieux – our Argentine friend?" Professor Rossi asked, turning to the young man who seemed by turn both younger and older than his years; who more often than not sat beside Sophie and who often thoughtfully saved her a place. Few of his classmates failed to notice his understated good looks.

Pietro stood when he spoke, lifting his gold, wire-rimmed glasses off his face. Impeccably dressed in a navy, bespoke Savile Row suit, with crisp white shirt and signature burgundy tie, he addressed Marco Rossi with that air of confidence that was the hallmark of an Oxford education.

What's he doing in Monaco?

"*Lavoro completato,*" Pietro said in flawless Italian, offering a folder to Marco Rossi with a respectful inclination of his head. "And in answer to your question as to who will succeed in this class, I can assure you it will be myself, most definitely Ms Taylor, and certainly our Chinese colleagues."

"*Touché.*" Marco Rossi nodded.

"Ooooh, so James Bond," Nadja cheeped.

"Books away," Marco Rossi commanded. "Now, answer this small exam question. It is the one and only time your work will be marked in my class. As in life, in business you sometimes only get one shot, one chance, to make an impression, to close the deal. Good luck, gentlemen, ladies. Define Internal Rate of Return – IRR – and how and why it is used. I want the formula from memory. You can create your own example. You have forty-five minutes. No calculators, no computers. When your answer is complete, put your papers on my desk and leave quietly."

What luck, IRR – the topic I've just been studying, Sophie thought. Pietro caught her eye and smiled. She smiled back. She had allies in the most unlikely of places. First the Chinese, who respected their elders and treated women as equal to men, and now a smart young Argentinian who claimed she was one of the ones most likely to succeed.

Sophie wrote out the definition of the IRR and worked her way methodically through Rossi's challenge.

Following this up with an example, she then mathematically, by trial and error, found the IRR. Then the weight of fatigue, the intensity of her four days with Tucker, the childish ridicule of some of her classmates and the strain of completing the assignment, all began to tell on her.

Why aren't I in Tallinn? Is Marco Rossi right, is married life wearing me down? Do I deserve to be in paradise while Tucker's in cold, dank, dark Estonia? And who's Tiu?

Sophie pushed back the thoughts and momentarily wished for a calculator or software that would perform the work for her. She worked through trial after trial, weighing the error, until finally she just stopped. This was as far as she could take it and for once the strength to remain poised escaped her. The rest of the class scribbled frenziedly, but she was done. She knew she'd got it wrong. How could she possibly be finished when everyone else was still writing away? She just gave up, gave in to the committee of voices in her head. She didn't care. The struggle was relentlessly uphill. She slid her pencil away, stood up, put the work on Professor Rossi's desk and left the room.

Hugging her books to her chest, she walked swiftly and pointedly towards the elevator, wanting to get out of the business school as fast as she could. She just wanted fresh air. She had failed, gotten it wrong, written a bunch of nonsense and felt she would never, ever understand. IRR? *What am I doing with my life anyway – at forty-one?* The clatter of footsteps sounded behind her. Was it Rossi calling her? She didn't care; she didn't stop. The elevator doors snapped closed behind her, and once on the ground floor, she stepped out into the warm Riviera winter sunshine.

Finding a small bistro on the *quai*, Sophie chose a seat overlooking the sea and ordered a piece of fish with sautéed spinach. Beyond her children still played on the beach.

Ridiculous. Did I think I could just waltz in and get an MBA? The French hate me because I'm American, my international twenty-

something classmates hate me, and Tucker – how long can we keep up this long-distance marriage?

She missed Rye. She inhaled the fresh air as children squealed, tossing a lime-green beach ball high overhead. Seagulls screeched as an unusually rough Mediterranean Sea broke against the manmade jetty.

Unexpectedly, Pietro appeared, towering over her. "May I join you, Sophie?"

"Yes," she smiled, coming back to her senses, "please. Please sit down."

"Rossi tried to run after you," he said as he hung his jacket over the back of the bistro chair and loosened his tie. "But you were too fast, so he sent me."

"Why?"

"To tell you, 'Full marks.' Only you."

Full marks?

Two young children ran laughing into the sea while off in the distance a builder wolf-whistled at someone who caught his fancy.

"Pietro, I need a minute," Sophie said, feeling her eyes starting to prickle with tears but holding everything in, holding everything back.

"By all means, Sophie," he said, reading the emotions on her face. "Here – take this."

He handed her a neatly folded linen pocket square and poured fresh water into her glass. They sat in silence while the waves crashed, the children roughhoused and the gulls reeled.

"I just got lucky," she said finally, grinning up at her new friend, catching the first tear in his neatly folded handkerchief.

NINE

Every time Sophie flew into Tallinn, she felt a sort of pride, a welling-up and a best-kept-secret sort of feeling, especially at Christmas when the whole place, covered in snow, radiated storybook magic, especially Old Town. She pictured Tucker and his long-stemmed, black-red rose, and his typical Christmas surprise, which could be anything from tickets to Dubai or Beethoven's Ninth in Symphony Hall with a sauna and dinner later high atop the Olümpia Hotel. Humming 'Ode to Joy' as she found a trolley, then barrelling her way through customs towards the arrivals hall, she couldn't wait to tell Tucker that she was, believe it or not, slated to be – or at least close to it – valedictorian of her MBA class.

"Hi, I'm Tiu." A tall young woman, with silken hair, waved and smiled at her. "Tucker sent me. I'm his right-hand man." She laughed at her own joke.

"Oh, hi," Sophie said with surprise, and passed over the cart to the younger woman, who already had her hands on the handle. "Where is he?"

"In a meeting," Tiu chuckled, "like always. And besides, I drive faster in the snowing than he does. Men… all toes."

With the efficiency of a woman on a mission for her boss, Tiu parked neatly outside the office complex, hauled Sophie's bags upstairs and announced that there was tea, coffee, yoghurt and *piparkoogiküpsised* – gingerbread cookies – in the kitchen.

"Thanks," Sophie answered, still puzzled that Tucker hadn't shown up at the airport or even called.

"Call me if you need anything." Tiu scribbled down her number. "Or just come down to the office. I am always there. Tucker will be back this evening."

Taking her bags to the still-spartan bedroom, Sophie relaxed at last, thrilled to be back, and kicked up the heating. After making a strong brew of coffee with cinnamon, she sat in the practically empty front room, listening to the muffled sounds of winter grow steadily deeper, along with the odd sound of heavy tires crushing snow.

After a pot of yoghurt to stave off hunger pangs, she pulled out the syllabus for the spring term, and started flipping through the new textbook for Accounting II – partnerships, corporations, manufacturing and financial statement analysis.

Intermittently, she called Tucker, but his phone kept going directly to voicemail, so finally, close to midnight, she rang Tiu.

"He's in Riga, stuck in the snow," she reported. "Isn't it brilliant, the snowing?"

"Yes, it is," Sophie replied.

"His battery is dead. He should be back in a few hours."

Sophie checked the radiators in each room. The whistling of the wind and the odd swoosh outside caught her attention and she forgot about anything else, except the fact that she knew Tucker had a pair of cross-country skis somewhere.

In the narrow closet near the front door, Sophie found not one but two pairs of skis, which surprised her for a moment, but then the incessant sound of winter outside resumed its call. Dressing warmly, she clipped on the skis, grabbed her poles and skied out onto the main road and into Kadriorg Park.

Not alone, despite the hour, she took her turn moving in and out and around local folk who also couldn't resist a winter wind and a pristine snowfall. Everyone smiled as they shared this other best-kept secret: cross-country skiing at night. The lights in the park and in the surrounding homes shone, and Sophie forgot everything except this wonderland she called her own. Who needed Monaco?

She slid easily over the snow and ice and even joined others on the Rocca al Mare promenade, covered in slick sea ice and uninterrupted flurries. Two and a half miles seemed like nothing, and watching a ferry or two come and go into the Port of Tallinn just fuelled her happiness. Who could spend Christmas anywhere else?

Finally, after skiing back to the office complex, brushing snow off and climbing the stairs, she expected to see Tucker. Instead, she found a note.

"Where are you? Are you crazy going out in this weather alone? Come downstairs. I'm in the office, finishing up a deal. Call me. Phone is back on. I found my charger."

With the fresh gingerbread cookies in her pocket, she bounded down the stairs and into Tucker's office, saying over and over again in what she considered her new language, "*Piparkoogiküpsised*, *piparkoogiküpsised*, gingerbread, gingerbread." The word tasted as good as what it described: ginger, cinnamon and cloves.

"Run, run, as fast as you can. You'll never catch me, I'm the gingerbread man." Sophie tossed the packet of ribbon-tied cookies across the desk, where Tucker sat.

"But I've already caught you," he said.

"Yes, I guess you have."

Tucker did have tickets for Symphony Hall, as well as for the ferry to Helsinki with an overnight stay. Before and after they circled Old Town on foot, by carriage and Soviet taxi, finding one new restaurant after the next. Everyone seemed to know Tucker and everyone enthused over Sophie, 'the wife who lives in France'.

In bed early on the morning of Christmas Eve, Sophie told tales of UR and Tucker spun stories about his growing empire, which he'd taken to calling Livonia, which he said was some mishmash of history that related to the south of Estonia on the border of Latvia.

"Livonia," he said, "back when my folks ruled the world."

"Get out often?" Sophie teased.

"Not much, Wife of a Thousand Years. I just love the fantasy of all of it. I'm having so much fun!"

"I'm happy for you, Tucker, really happy."

"Want to go to the manor? We can cross-country ski, if you're up for it."

"The manor?"

"Yup. I have a little surprise for you."

"Let's go, then," Sophie said, up, dressed and out the door before Tucker. "What else does anyone do on Christmas Eve?"

The manor looked practically the same. If any work had been done on it, it was not obvious, Sophie thought, as she skied neatly to a stop beside Tucker. The steady snow turned to ice and the wind picked up. Once inside, Sophie smelt fresh bread and coffee.

"Ta-da," Tucker said as he threw open a door that led into a small reception hall. "Merry Christmas."

The room spun with white lights, candles and a rocking sheep beneath a tree.

"What is this?"

"The first inhabitable room at Mägi Manor," he announced with a smile. "Sit down. I have something for you."

Sophie sat and, after introducing her to the security guard Heinrich and the housekeeper Maie, he rolled open the floor plans and drew a line from room to room with his finger, describing the manor as he hoped it would one day be.

"Amazing," Sophie said.

"For you, Wife of a Thousand Years."

She pored over the document the way she had once pored over

the obscure and faded documents sent by Gaabriel Mägi over a year ago. "Genius."

They ate black bread spread with onion jam, drank coffee with a hint of *Vana Tallinn* in front of an open fire. Finally, Heinrich reminded them of midnight mass, insisting he should drive them back, not only because it was late but also because the snowfall had now become a blizzard.

At mass, Sophie leaned against Tucker. As she studied the triptych behind the altar, her mind drifted to thoughts of a baby. She imagined herself holding an infant, beside the baptismal font, snow falling hard outside. Tucker took her hand.

"Next Christmas," he whispered, as if reading her mind, and kissed the side of her head.

Sophie met Tucker at Symphony Hall for the New Year's concert. As usual, he was running late, and would have to make the expected mad dash at the last minute. The concert started at eleven, so Sophie saved his seat, knowing he'd be there by midnight; he slid into the row just as everyone in their formal wear stood for Beethoven's Fifth, and then an encore.

Back in the apartment, as Sophie took off her amber earrings and Tucker unzipped her floor-length dress, she said, "Being here reminds me of living in another century, another time."

"Not me," Tucker said. "It is the end of the twentieth century, nearly the new millennium, and I plan to make the most of it."

"I know, but it feels like a pause in time. Tucker, I don't want to go back to Monaco."

"Yes, you do."

"I don't. I can finish my MBA here."

"I don't think so. You'd get bored in five minutes. You are on holiday now. You are not living the everyday reality... heavy metal in the water, electricity going out and I'm doing eighty hours a week. Trust me, you are doing the right thing."

"I am?"

"You are. Now, hold still," he said soothingly, holding her tight. "Happy 1999."

TEN

Where half of January, February and the first three weeks of March went Sophie did not know. Unusually, all had been quiet on the student and staff front since she returned, without one altercation with Nadja or anyone else. Sophie's friendship with Pietro had grown. They formed an informal study group, and often invited the Chinese, who seemed to know everything. Sophie even went out for dinner with Pietro and Marco Rossi on more than one occasion, overlooking the harbour, commenting on the unreality of the sunsets and the unequivocal beauty of the Provence-Alpes-Côte d'Azur planet, where they found themselves. Of course, they shared the odd bit of gossip, which always included what Pascal le Pew might be up to, and neither Sophie nor Pietro needed to wait long to find out.

As usual Pascal had Abbi call Sophie in the early hours to report that there was a meeting that she must attend.

"Be in his office at 8am."

"So early?"

"Sorry. Don't ask me anything, but be ready for big news."

"Okay. Thanks."

Without batting an eye, smoking and stirring his espresso at the same time, Pascal told her, "You will be partnering the heir to the throne at the Rose Ball this weekend."

"Me?"

"Yes."

"What about Nadja… or anyone else?"

"Oui, Cover Girl, it has to be you. Certainly not Nadja."

Pascal motioned for Sophie to sit down.

"But I'm forty-one. She's twenty-three and perfect for this. She would die for this."

"Yes, but we need someone who looks American. *Tarte aux pommes.*" Pascal waved his hands in the air. "Thin, not too thin, and blonde, not too blonde. You look a lot younger than you are. Remember, that's how you hooked us."

"*C'est ridicule.* I didn't 'hook' anyone."

Pascal ignored her. "*Le Palais* has requested a charming student to walk the heir in, maybe have one dance with him and then fade from view. Remember, he's the school's patron and you work for me. So… work."

"Get someone else, Monsieur Dubois."

"Mme Mägi, *insubordination*? Remember our deal…"

Sophie left the principal's office, knowing she had no choice. Leave at once and return to Tallinn, where Tucker made clear their life there was not a holiday, or dance with the heir apparent, who happened to be the patron of the school? What had she even been thinking, agreeing terms with UR?

No free lunch.

Later in the day, she took Daisy for a walk along the coastal path and noticed more signs of spring. As she sat in the late-afternoon sun, her phone rang. Picking it up as Daisy retrieved another piece of driftwood, she heard Tucker shout, "It's freezing and the heating's not working."

"It's perfect here," Sophie said.

"I'm sorry," he said, "I can't make this weekend. Moving offices, broken ground on the new hotel and closing the deal on the hypermarket. Hold on…" He shouted to someone, "Tell Tiu to keep the car running. I am coming."

"You didn't promise, but you were meant to be here. I am totally disappointed, Tucker. Can't it wait?"

"No. I'm sorry. I promise I will make this up to you."

"Look, don't worry, but you do owe me, and if Mom wasn't arriving this evening, you'd be in serious trouble. It's the only weekend she had free, and I was wondering how I was going to juggle my favourite two people at the same time anyway."

"Tell her I will miss her. Ask when she's coming back to Tallinn. I'm really happy she can be there if I can't. Love you, Sophie," he said, and then hung up.

"I love you too, Tuck," she said to the silent phone in her hand.

Sitting for a while on the small incline overlooking the water with the phone still in her hand and Daisy panting around a wet piece of bleached cedar, Sophie laughed out loud.

Dance with the Prince and fade from view.

A mild breeze complemented the sun, as Sophie closed her eyes, turning her face directly into the heat. *Okay*, she thought, as she walked Daisy back to her apartment.

One dance.

Anne Taylor beamed. Dipping low under the helicopter blades, she walked across the tarmac to embrace her daughter.

"So, Monaco and the famous helipad?" Anne said.

"Did you like it?"

"Yes, good trip, but not much room."

"Hungry?"

"Yes, let's drop my things off at the Hermitage first. Is Tucker here yet?"

"No, I'm afraid he's too busy."

"So, no Rose Ball?"

"Well, yes and no. I have to accompany the Prince – just into the room and then the first dance."

"Good, you escort him. And I," said her mother, "will escort you."

"Thank God it's just one dance."

Sophie kept hold of her mother's hand. It was soft, warm and familiar to her touch. Sophie admired the attention Anne commanded wherever she went. While her mother checked in at the hotel, Sophie watched. It never ceased to amaze her. Anne Taylor would know what to do with Nadja or Pascal, anyone for that matter. How did she do it?

Smooth as silk, strong as iron – and lovingly, deeply sympathetic.

With maternal pride, Anne escorted Sophie to the Rose Ball and smiled on while Pascal introduced her daughter to the heir apparent, and as they made their entrance into the great hall, both of them embarrassed by the pantomime but warm-hearted enough to carry it off. The famous royal proved to be less stiff and more charming than she had expected. Knowing it was both for a good cause and for her job, as le Pew had reminded her, Sophie knew the paparazzi snaps wouldn't hurt anyone. Sophie even felt a bit of empathy for the Prince, who was just five months younger than her.

Hopefully he would soon find a bride.

For Anne and Sophie, two of the most elegant women in the crowd, the ball became a private party and afterwards Sophie was more than happy to share her mother's sumptuous hotel room, where Daisy was already happily tucked up between the two beds.

In the morning, they breakfasted on the balcony, overlooking the harbour. The yachts anchored there gave the tiny strip of coast a sense of robust affluence. Sophie sipped her coffee and pulled apart a warm croissant. *Le Rocher*, her Rock, stood triumphant in the morning light, across the harbour. Tired from having stayed up so late, enjoying her mother's company and the Rose Ball, Sophie had to prop herself up on one arm, while she admired her mother, sitting across the table. Freshly showered, hair still wet and smelling of Diorissimo, Anne appeared to have slept well and now was bright-eyed and alert, relishing her breakfast.

"I live over there," Sophie said, pointing over the yachts. "It's just a tiny place, but my roomy terrace overlooks *le Palais.*"

Nodding, Anne looked out over the water. She smiled at Sophie. She not only adored but also admired her daughter. After private high school, Sophie had never asked for or taken a penny from her. She'd won a full scholarship to study at college, then went straight to work. She never once asked to use any of her mother's contacts, and Anne knew better than to offer. They sat in happy silence.

"So, what's the problem?" Anne finally asked as she finished her cantaloupe and poured a fresh cup of coffee.

"Problem? None," Sophie answered.

"Yes, there is. I know you," Anne said, lifting her coffee. "Tell me."

"I'm married," Sophie started, "and thought I should just be able to handle everything."

"Problems?"

Sophie sipped her coffee and sighed. "Well, things are falling into place, but not exactly the way I'd imagined. I love Tuck and keep wondering what I'm doing here, in Monaco. Do I really need an MBA?"

"What does he think?"

"He's okay with it, but I'm not sure I am."

Anne didn't say anything for a while, looking up at the palace and then back to her daughter. "There's only one more term to go, Soph. You can do this. An old teacher once said to me, 'You can quit when you're finished.' What do you think?"

"Yes, I suppose so."

"June is not so far away. You can do it."

"I guess I can."

"Are you worried about Tucker?"

"A little. His office is like a Ford modelling agency."

"Darling, have you ever met a short Estonian?"

"No, but he's got a right-hand man… or rather woman. Tiu."

"Soph, my mother gave me a suggestion when I was a young bride. Your father travelled a lot, as did I, and of course the idea of him straying occurred to me as well. I used to laugh, thinking, *Just my luck*. Who would ever be able to have an affair on a glacier in Greenland while investigating erosion? He did have people he relied on more than me. But your nana told me, 'Anything you need to know will eventually come your way. Until then, consider any misgivings you may feel as just your imagination and forget about them.' That served me well. I never again muddied the water for more than two seconds with my fears. Trust Tucker. What are your options otherwise?"

They spent the rest of the weekend walking through Monte Carlo, going to Cap Ferrat and Nice. In Nice, they strolled the market and the Promenade des Anglais. Anne shared the complexities of funding for her most recent project, mapping ice sheet limits, while Sophie's enthusiasm for the Internet, the potential of online courses and the Estonian video chat software spilled over as they tested the black olives, the flat, chickpea *socca* and afterwards the lavender ice cream with thyme, lemon and honey.

On Sunday afternoon Sophie and Daisy took Anne to the helipad. Sophie never wanted to say goodbye. As with Tucker, she felt loved and respected whenever she was with her mother, to whom all the answers came easily. As Anne turned back to wave, Sophie smiled. Her scientist mother, ever graceful in a V-necked sweater, soft blouse, dark jeans and ballet flats, dipped neatly and disappeared inside the waiting aircraft.

Sophie told a puzzled Daisy, "That's it. You can quit when you are finished."

73

Anne's visit kept Sophie going. Nadja's absence meant things were much calmer at school. Rumour had it she was in rehab or working feverishly in the family business in the Caymans, which was under government investigation. Even Alexis, the arrogant Greek, warmed to Sophie now and occasionally they had lunch.

While Sophie had intended to use the short Easter break to finish the prototype for UR's first online course and the marketing strategy for Pascal, when Tucker showed up unexpectedly in an Aston Martin Volante, she didn't know what to say.

"I have work to do," she argued, all the while throwing a week's worth of clothing into a canvas bag, "but I guess I can do it on the road."

"Honeymoon again?"

"Yes," Sophie said gleefully, pulling out her tortoiseshell sunglasses, "I can do that."

"Le Long Weekend." Tucker imitated the French. "We can hide out in Aix and maybe make a trip over to Cassis? You can work while I sleep."

The flowers, the villages, even the gusting Mistral, seemed to conspire with them: the perfect holiday. Each room, more a private apartment, in the hotel in Aix looked out onto a square, with its own fountain to the front and lavender fields to the back. Except for a quick wander into the market for fresh bread or coffee, they ate, slept and talked.

"Do I need to propose again?"

"Maybe."

"Okay, so what's next?"

"Lunch. Lunch and more lunch."

They sat on the limestone cliffs, overlooking the sea at Cassis, nibbling cheese, a baguette and perfectly ripe grapes.

"Are we closing in on a year?" Tucker asked.

"We are."

"What are your highs and lows?"

"Being with you and being without you," Sophie answered.

"Well, that can't go on forever. We have a little plan, you know."
They grinned.

Project Bébé.

ELEVEN

Marketing, the first class of the last term, Monday morning, proved less than dazzling. Once again Sophie, her Chinese classmates and Pietro presented, while most of the other students claimed not to have had time to complete the assignment over the Easter break.

The Australian professor clapped his hands. "Into groups, everyone," he announced. "These are the groups you will remain in for this last term, the one you will make your final presentations with. Choose well. People you like, colleagues with different skills. You will be presenting to a number of local and international bankers, who will give you your final grade, maybe a job if your idea is fundable."

Sophie started to wonder if she should just perform alone, when a hand rested on her shoulder. Fenfang, the eldest – maybe twenty years old, if that – of the Chinese female students, spoke to her.

"You will be in our group?"

Sophie nodded. "Thank you, I'd like that."

"We thank you, Chairwoman."

"Chairwoman?"

From the corner of her eye, Sophie caught Pietro sitting alone and motioned him over. Fenfang smiled, but only after scrutinising him and conferring with her comrades, which seemed to take an eternity, did they break ranks and welcome Pietro too.

"Group think," he said to Sophie.

Tengfei would serve as group speaker. This was not open to debate or vote. Who were the two class loners to argue? Biyu and Changying, also from Beijing like Tengfei, and longtime friends of Fenfang, made up the band of six.

Just as they were starting to discuss project options, Sophie noticed another East Asian student, a petite young woman who for most of the year had remained a shadow, practically invisible.

"Tengfei," Sophie asked, "what about Khulan?"

"No, she can find another group."

"Why don't we vote on it?"

"No."

"But she's Chinese and doesn't have a group to join."

"Not Chinese. Mongolian."

"I'm not Chinese. Neither is Pietro. Please. I wouldn't have a group without you and neither will she."

Another long huddle and finally Fenfang agreed.

"Great. Let's take a break and meet after lunch," Sophie suggested.

Walking quickly to get to her apartment, Sophie left the building. Two blocks away, four students brushed up against her. Klaus, George, Nadja, who had arrived back for the last term, and Alexis blocked her way.

"So, you got the Chinese?" Nadja carped. "It won't help you, no matter how hard they work."

"Actually, no," Sophie said, slipping past, "they got me."

"You won't win."

"Win what?"

"Class valedictorian."

"Nadja," Sophie said, "I'm really not interested in being valedictorian. I want you to win. Enjoy your group, enjoy your lunch. Maybe I'll see you this afternoon."

"Not if I can help it." Nadja laughed.

Sophie sailed past, catching a clementine tossed by the fruit vendor who by now knew her well.

"Hey, Cover Girl," Alexis shouted behind her, "you know who you really remind me of? Hillary Clinton."

It wasn't a compliment. "Funny!" Sophie turned back, surprised by Alexis' change in behaviour. "I was about to say the same thing about you."

As the elevator shot up through the million-year-old boulder to *le Palais*, Sophie grinned. *What an idiot, Mr Horseshit. Class valedictorian? Why not? Okay, Hillary, what do you say? Let's rock.*

The phone rang as Sophie unlocked the door. Tucker's name lit up the LED, and she dropped everything.

"I've got my first investors, from Lebanon," he launched in immediately.

"I'm so happy for you."

"The European Bank for Reconstruction and Development can go..."

"Congratulations, Tucker! You are amazing and this is just a sign of everything to come."

"I wish you were here. Sophie, I owe you. I couldn't do any of this without you."

"You could. And I wish I was there too, but I have my final group presentation," she said. "Four Chinese students, one Mongolian, Pietro and me. We're presenting to bankers, and there's potential for jobs."

"You will ace it," he said. "Sophie, if you don't watch out you just might be class valedictorian."

Sophie laughed.

"Look, I love you. Tiu has sorted a party for the Lebanese, and we have to get going."

The afternoon buzzed. Sophie thought momentarily of New York City and Ascent Magazines. She pushed Tiu to the back of her mind.

We have to get going.

The team tossed around ideas. Active inertia... zone of death... Internet security... virtual office... financial terrorism.

"We are presenting to bankers," Tengfei interrupted. "They're only interested in where they can make a buck. I suggest the banking industry in emerging markets."

Fenfang agreed, and her female colleagues Biyu and Changying nodded in unison.

"That should be easy," Pietro added. "I already have data for Latin America, Eastern Europe and most of Asia."

"I'm okay with that, considering the adjudicators are all bankers," Sophie added, "but maybe we should narrow our focus – one country, one sector? Or that might be too niche. Analysis seems a bit safe, but I think we're on the right track."

"I think we also might add impact on people," Khulan said shyly, "corporate responsibility."

Tengfei dismissed this with a wave of his hand and his three mainland Chinese colleagues turned their backs on the Mongolian woman.

Finally, the group decided on the topic of emerging market banking, focusing on competition, consolidation and stability. Each chose the part that worked best for them and got to work. While quietly confident that they would do well, Sophie encouraged them to redouble their efforts.

"Make this the real thing," she urged, as she sorted a number of backdrops for the presentation, including a set of Tang dynasty chess pieces. Sophie would open and then close the presentation, but Tengfei would serve as primary speaker, with other members speaking on particular topics.

Four mad weeks of research and practice presentations took them through May. Although exhausted, Sophie proved an able chairperson as usual, making sure everything ran like clockwork and that everyone still remained friendly. She coerced them into rehearsing over and over again, and no one refused. They appeared to be the only group taking the assignment seriously.

Sophie had struck gold with the Asian students. Diligence and long hours were a given. Khulan turned out to be the most original, practical and insightful of them all. Pietro, already destined for great financial success as the scion of his Argentine family, provided deep intelligence and a sense of fair play.

The mock, student-faculty presentations started on June 5th. Sophie's group would present last on the final day of the three-day schedule. Were the cards stacked against them? Would anybody show up on the last day? Would the stand-in judges, bored by then, have seen it all?

While this was not the real presentation to the German, Italian and French bankers, which would come next week, it gave the students a chance to practice. Sophie continued to think that something was missing. Weren't they, in fact, pitching themselves? Weren't they really, in the end, all looking for jobs?

Sophie opened the presentation with an eye-catching image of the world turning in space with the highlighted countries of Central Europe, Latin America and Asia animated and accentuated. French subtitles enhanced every PowerPoint slide. Khulan and Biyu handed bound, multilingual copies of the presentations to the faculty and staff. Other students stopped fidgeting.

"The banking industry worldwide is being transformed," Sophie opened. "Global forces for change include technological innovation, deregulation of financial services at the national level and opening up to international competition, as well as – equally important – changes in corporate behaviour, such as growing disintermediation and increased emphasis on shareholder value. In addition, banking industries in Central Europe and Latin America have been transformed by the privatisation of state-owned banks that have dominated in the past."

Their audience settled in, attention caught by Sophie's opening sentences and the seductive images. Tengfei then took over, commanding attention, and one by one introducing Fenfang, Pietro, Biyu and Changying. Finally, he introduced Khulan, who brought her contribution to a robust end before Sophie returned to the stage.

"Thank you, fellow students, faculty, staff and my group." She led the applause. "If you have any questions, please join us in the student lounge."

The audience roared and clapped their appreciation as Professor Rossi stood up.

"Bravo."

The standing ovation continued for a few minutes. As Sophie surveyed the room, she realised Pepé le Pew, who had definitely been around for the earlier presentations, was missing.

"You came, you saw, you conquered," Marco Rossi declared, hugging Sophie and shaking the hands of the rest of the group. "*Molto bene.*" He put one arm around Pietro and gave him a squeeze.

The Chinese Group, as they had come to be called, took the preliminary prize from the run-throughs, and Sophie couldn't have been more proud if they had been her own children.

My own children.

What Sophie wanted most now for her group was a job offer for each. For herself, she wanted to wrap up her MBA, get back to Tucker and to meet this little bébé who kept appearing at the oddest times in her thoughts and in her dreams, something she had not shared with a soul, not even Tucker.

Choosing a magazine from her stash beside her bed, Sophie whistled for Daisy, who happily joined her on the terrace. Together they waited for night to fall, as Sophie thumbed through the most recent issue of *Femme Actuelle*. Scanning an article on pregnancy and the danger of hair highlights while pregnant, and sipping a cup of *verveine*, she caught sight of that same cheeky baby who liked to take her by surprise.

While she had had some hope of being pregnant by graduation, none of her visits with Tucker had resulted in conception. But Sophie didn't mind; lovemaking was not all about baby-making.

She reflected further on the half-day's presentation. Everyone had performed to their strengths and had spoken clearly and confidently. There had been no technical glitches, and the bound handouts stood out – elegant, simple and to the point.

While she had celebrated everyone's research and hard work, they all acknowledged the real-world experience she brought to the party. As she watched the last of the daylight fade and the stars come out, she laughed out loud: what was this feeling? It went beyond professional delight. It had hit her as each of her team had taken their turn at the microphone, stayed with her afterwards as they shared a meal at Song Qi and remained with her now.

Mothering.

"Daisy," Sophie ruffled the top of her Springer's head, "it's time to make that baby."

Tucker picked up the phone as soon as she called.

"It's so beautiful tonight, Tuck. I wish you were here. The presentation went well, and I just wanted to say thank you. It seems just yesterday you said in Cassis that I had to do this, and I have, and it has been the right thing to do. Who do you think is rumoured to be the class valedictorian?"

"Mrs Mägi."

"Mrs Mägi."

After the call, Sophie listened to the TGV circle the base of the sheer mountain face below her apartment. She would be forty-two in October, not too late for *Project Bébé*, she reasoned. Tucker would be here soon, with graduation not far off. She drifted into sleep, thinking of her husband, Tallinn and the fact she had finally gotten her MBA.

TWELVE

"Sorry to bother you, Sophie, but Pascal asked me to call you."
Abbi spoke clearly. It was early; Sophie was still sleeping when her
cell phone rang.

"No worries," She shook off the slumber. "Is there a problem?"

"No," Abbi hesitated, "he just wants to see you and your team."

"Okay, thanks."

No sooner had she hung up than Pietro called. "We have to
present again," he said. "Pascal claims he's heard so many good
reports, he wanted to see it for himself."

"They videoed it."

"He wants to observe first-hand."

"Why?"

"I have to warn you," Pietro said, "there's been an insinuation
that you weren't up to the job. Meet me for breakfast."

They both ordered a brioche, juice and coffee at the small café
outside *le Palais*.

"What is le Pew up to now?"

"I don't know, Sophie, but be careful."

"I will."

Pietro took the bill, as Sophie rushed off to meet the others. "I'm right behind you," he called out.

Assembled in one of the conference rooms by nine o'clock, Sophie explained what little she knew.

"We did a good job. Pascal just wants to review it."

"He wants to remove you and the other women," Fenfang said without hesitation.

"Why do you say that?"

"Because it is true. Didn't you see him speaking with his nephew, and leaving just before our presentation?"

"I don't want to think about what that might mean. Let's just do our best and present professionally."

"I have the scripts, the laptop is loaded," Pietro confirmed.

At ten thirty precisely, Pascal arrived with his nephew Napoléon, whom no one had seen in ages. Had he ever attended class? Term after term, he remained at the top of the class, with seriously high pass marks in every subject. Referred to as the masked man, *le fucking fantôme* or *Le Neveu*, the Nephew, no one knew anything about him.

The performance ran on autopilot. The Chinese Group remained the best UR had to offer. Pascal blew smoke rings and conferred with *Le Neveu*.

"*Je vous remercie. Bien joué.*" Pascal clapped his hands, holding his cigarette in the side of his mouth. "Good job. Sophie, Pietro, the rest of you."

Presentation day came, and Pietro was the first to discover that not only were they not the lead group, but they had been scheduled for the early-evening slot.

"It doesn't matter, Sophie," he said as he packed up the equipment after their early-morning rehearsal. "We can all go home and come back later to set up."

"It does matter. You may not need a job, but I actually would like one, and Tengfei, Fenfang, Biyu, Chinyang and Khulan all came here at too much cost to leave without an offer. They are all trying to find a way to get to America."

"I know, but I trust good things will happen if we just continue to do the best we can."

"Did you see who has the prime, morning spot?" Sophie asked.

"Yes, *Le Neveu*. He's been shoehorned into Nadja's group with George and Klaus."

"Good luck to them."

"Somehow I don't think you mean that."

"Considering their presentation is entitled 'Emerging Market Banking: Competition, Consolidation and Stability', most probably not."

"You are kidding me?" Pietro asked.

"No. Look at the schedule."

"*Merda.*"

Sophie and the team shared a quick bite to eat and agreed to go home, have a rest and meet again later in the afternoon. They would not change a thing. Even if there were no one in the audience, they agreed to present as if they were before the CEOs of every major bank in Paris, Milan and Berlin.

"We all know," Sophie said to the practically empty auditorium and her team, "the best is always saved for last."

A commotion ensued in the back of the auditorium, and Nadja's voice rang out. "Fuck me. Best for last? The last will come last – isn't that the way it usually goes? 'Emerging Market Banking'? Didn't you hear that was already done? Guess who got jobs? Not you, Cover Girl."

"Losers." Klaus and George's sarcastic laughter trailed behind them as they all clattered out of the hall. "Who wants to stay for this shit? Copycats… get a fucking life."

"Continue," a gentleman in the back of the room said, ignoring the interruption. He leaned forward in anticipation.

As before, Sophie stood in front of the dazzling image of the globe turning in space, with the countries of Central Europe, Latin America and Asia vibrantly brought to life. Khulan and Biyu stood by with bound copies of the address to hand.

"The banking industry worldwide is being transformed…" Sophie didn't miss a beat and each member of the group presented their area of expertise as convincingly as before.

"Bravo." The same sober gentleman who had quelled the interruption earlier said as he came forward. One of the only two judges left, he stepped up on stage. "The best presentation I have seen all day."

He introduced himself as Alexander Köhler and asked a few probing questions, which the members of the group answered eagerly in turn. This turned into a longer conversation and even a debate about the Internet and dot.coms. Noticing the time, Herr Köhler invited the group to join him for dinner.

As they sat in the splendour of Le Louis XV in the Hôtel de Paris, Khulan continued right where the conversation had left off in the school's auditorium.

"Value increases with the number of actual Internet users. Business as we know it will change in ways unimagined, not just banks, at a speed unimagined. The more people who understand this, the wilder the betting will become – actually already is. I think we're seeing a classic bubble."

Fenfang piped up, "Rational becomes irrational." She highlighted Netscape's initial public offering in 1995 as the trigger that initiated the craze. "A company with no profits – a web browser," she laughed, "and an unparalleled first day of trading."

Biyu then took up the theme. "Netscape's IPO informed Internet startups, investors, the news channels and investment bankers that Internet stock was hot. Did a new market exist? Were the old rules out? Was a company now valued by website page views rather than its balance sheet?"

"Who created the buzz?" Alexander asked.

"Analysts," Sophie answered.

"Exactly," he said, nodding.

"There's an obvious conflict of interest," Pietro added, waving for another bottle of wine. "Once an analyst was just an analyst, but the lines between retail and investment banking have disappeared."

"Analysts are mixing with the money," Tengfei commented.

Chinyang broke open a bread roll. "Some analysts predicted rises in Internet stock, while more traditionally minded colleagues forecasted a drop."

"And the latter were fired." Biyu chuckled.

"A field day for sellers," Pietro said. "The only-say-buy guy is now a superstar. It's a bubble and it has got to burst."

Sophie smiled at her group. They could be discussing green bananas for all she cared. Here they were, talking freely and convincingly to the most influential judge ever to have agreed to judge an MBA class at UR. And he seemed more than happy to listen.

Alexander asked if anyone wanted dessert, and as no one wanted to go home, they all said yes, including Sophie, who was hoping Tucker might appear after saying he would do his best to make the final presentation.

"Objectivity was lost a long time ago. Analysts aren't clairvoyants. Can a business forgo profits for speedy growth? Promise sky-high profit with no earnings?" Pietro interjected.

"The point is," Sophie added, "whether analyst- or media-driven, the market has lost touch with reality. It's falling. The big question now is: where are the new opportunities?"

"Exactly," Alexander said, taking a second look at Sophie, "a few companies will survive. There will be loads of failed dot.coms. Cheap buys. If you develop these with realistic fundamentals, *voilà* – long-term gains. Who's first out of the gate?"

"Amazon," Sophie shot back.

"Who's in?" Alexander asked.

Everyone at the table raised a polite hand.

"Well, welcome to the New Economy," Alexander smiled, "the New Gold Rush."

Just then Sophie spotted Pascal across the room, first blowing a smoke ring and then sauntering over to their table.

"Herr Köhler," he said, thrusting out his hand.

The lean banker stood up. "Pascal."

"I see you've met our superstars, and they've met you – Alexander Köhler, star Westcox Brown partner."

"Westcox?" Tengfei only just repressed an excited squeal.

"Have you met *mon neveu* Napoléon?" Pascal asked, wheeling Alexander Köhler away while staring venomously over his shoulder at Sophie.

She and the rest of the team looked at each other, smiled and this time no one suppressed the burst of excited chatter and speculation that broke out.

The question on everyone's lips? *Who's in?*

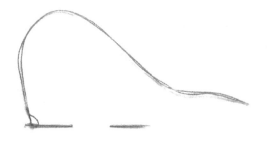

THIRTEEN

It was awards night at the *Grande Salle du Paris*. "Who needs an f'ing job with JP Morgan or Westcox Brown?" Nadja threw back her head and roared, pointing at the Chinese Group. "I'm getting back to the Caymans as fast as I can. Tomorrow morning. Thank God! Can't wait to get out of this flea trap. Who needs a New York-based banking firm when I own Rule, the best offshore money-laundering subsidiary Deutsche Bank has ever known?"

"She's joking, of course," George said, as he and Klaus pulled their drunken friend away from the table.

"They're coming with me," she managed to slur before they walked her outdoors for some fresh air.

Pascal had punctuated his comments with smoke rings as he swivelled lazily in his chair earlier in the day.

"Class Valedictorian," he said to Sophie. "You must stay on as our poster girl. There's a sizeable demographic of women of a certain age who'd like to come to Monaco and take a business degree, especially in luxury goods, *n'est-ce pas?*"

Professor Rossi and Pietro had intervened when Sophie at first declined the valedictorian honour, convincing her that she deserved it.

Sophie, watched proudly by Anne, who had flown in to share

her daughter's triumph, stood up to make her acceptance speech. In her fitted shift, with upswept hair, she felt a million miles away from Rye and her old job at Ascent Magazines. "It's all about teamwork, about only quitting when you finish…" Sophie spoke simply and to the point, acknowledging her team – the Chinese, Pietro, Khulan. Anne smiled up at her from the audience. "So, embrace it all," she told her classmates, "one step at a time. Never give up. That way you won't miss the dream."

After the awards, the University of the Riviera MBA class of '99 met at the Salle des Etoiles at Sporting Monte Carlo for the graduation ball. Under its open skylights, with stars shining overhead, Alexis held forth.

"*Oui, mes amis*. I am staying on for another degree."

Everyone laughed.

"You're just staying to guard your tax-exempt status," Nadja retorted, back for round two.

"Yes," he shrugged, "and to drive my graduation gift, a McLaren F1."

"Why not come to us?" She raised her glass to him. "Rule specialises in 'try to hide the pie', right, boys?"

"Right." Her faithful henchmen George and Klaus nodded along with her.

"What about you-hoo?" She pointed to the Chinese students at the far end of the table, where Fenfang sat quiet and erect beside Tengfei.

Fenfang announced, "We are all going to London, in the morning, to work for Mr Köhler at Westcox Brown."

"No change for me." Pietro smiled. "I'm carrying on the family tradition, running our home office in London."

"What about Cover Girl?" Nadja turned her attention to Sophie. "Looking for a job with *Vogue*? Or maybe riding Köhler's tail, or whatever, into the Great Anglo-Saxon financial capital of the world?"

Sophie smiled enigmatically. "Just deciding."

Making a baby, she confirmed to herself silently.

Alexander Köhler had tried over lunch, dinner and a sail along the Côte d'Azur, to convince Sophie to work with him, to move to London and stick with the team. There was money to be made in all the fallen or falling dot.com stars, he assured her.

"Commuting to Tallinn would be easy. You could get back once a week. More if you wanted," he promised, but Sophie had held firm.

Now she fidgeted impatiently in her seat. *Where's Tucker?* It wasn't easy making the connections into Helsinki, then Paris, Nice and helicopter or taxi into Monaco. *Will he miss everything?*

The ball began with a traditional tombola as the orchestra played its first notes. As Sophie was choosing her ticket from the small revolving drum, Tucker slipped in to sit beside her.

"Sorry," he whispered in her ear.

"Thank God! I thought you were dead. How was the flight?"

"Bumpy, delayed, but at least I'm not dead." He laughed as he took a ticket of his own. "Ready for our cross-country extravaganza? I've rented a convertible – Porsche 911."

"So that's why you were late. Did you drive to the Italian border and back?"

"Maybe, but I opened it up between Nice and here, and it's amazing."

"Luggage?" she asked.

"None. We travel light. You, me and Daisy."

She beamed at him. "It's a date."

Dancing with Tucker for the first time since the wedding, Sophie could not stop smiling. It seemed longer than a year since they made their decision that she should accept the UR offer while they sat on the beach at Cassis. All eyes were on Sophie, now changed into a strapless gown, especially Anne, who watched her daughter and her son-in-law with pride. With her head resting on Tucker's shoulder, Sophie relished the memories of the last nine months but couldn't wait to escape.

Project Bébé.

"Monaco to Tallinn," she whispered, "via Italy, Switzerland, Austria, Germany, Poland, Lithuania and Latvia."

"Perfect. Beats NYC to Rye."

Anne interrupted their dance, kissing and congratulating Sophie once more before leaving for her hotel.

"I couldn't be prouder. Enjoy your big adventure. Call me when you reach Tallinn. I'll get myself to the helipad in the morning."

"Thanks, Mom, we will. I love you."

Tucker swept his wife around the dance floor, half showing her off and half thrilled to be embarking on the road trip from France to Tallinn, but startled into an abrupt and unexpected halt when he noticed Sophie staring at Alexander Köhler, formally dressed in tails. He was standing in one of the floor-to-ceiling ballroom windows, both arms pressed against the frame, as if he were holding it up and at the same time readying himself to swoop.

"What's wrong?" Tucker asked, but before Sophie could answer, Alexander had walked up to them.

"May I have this dance?"

Before either Sophie or Tucker could respond, he moved her gently away, pressing his face so close to the side of her head that she pulled back.

"I'm sorry," he said, loosening his grip. "Tell me why you are not coming to London? It's the chance of a lifetime. You are brilliant and the team needs you. *I* need you."

"Because I'm taking a road trip to Tallinn, where I'm making a home, and if the skies part and luck is with me, I'm starting a family."

"A baby?"

"Yes."

"Why not do that in London? You can travel back and forth."

"Because I'm married, and you already have the rest of the team. They are all so talented. They will make you a fortune."

"I already have a fortune."

"I know," Sophie said, "but I think you really want something else from me."

"I do."

Tucker broke in just as the dance ended, and Alexander Köhler bowed out politely. "Thank you," he said. "Perhaps next time in London then." He nodded.

Sophie dipped her head ever so slightly as he left the ballroom. At that moment, Khulan appeared by her side and presented her with a small gift. Grinning, she folded Sophie's hands over the rectangular sandalwood box tied with a white linen ribbon.

"*Xièxiè māmaā.*"

"No, thank *you*, Khulan," Sophie said.

Thank you.

"Let's get this show on the road!" Tucker ticked off the countries they would see. "Italy, Austria, Poland – ah, yes! – Lithuania, Latvia and Estonia. Let's go."

"Okay."

"This feels good. Just me and you."

"It does."

"All packed?"

"I am. Everything was shipped to Tallinn last week. It's a tiny bit hard to leave this beautiful place, though, Tucker."

"Once you hit the open road, it will all be behind you. Hands on the steering wheel and you will let go, I promise."

As Tucker went to collect the car from the underground garage, Sophie looked around her. She would miss the narrow alleys, the cobblestones, the sky-high bleached laundry snapping overhead, descending *Le Rocher* to the garage, UR, the sun-drenched terrace and her view of the slippery, silvery Mediterranean.

You came, you saw, you conquered.

Sophie called Daisy and then picked up the small gift from Khulan. Pulling off the ribbon, she opened the delicately crafted box. A hint of sandalwood filled the air, while inside, nestled between folds of white silk, lay a delicately carved wooden fan. The pleats contained the image of an Asian woman, head in profile, slightly smiling, self-assured and happy. A note written in Mongolian and English read:

By letting go it all gets done. The world is won by those who let it go. But when you try and try, the world is beyond the winning.
                                                                            Lao Tzu

Sophie called Daisy again and left the keys on the kitchen counter before closing the door one last time. Tucker gunned his Porsche in the lot below.

June rolled out in various shades of green and ochre as they snaked their way through Italy and into the summertime Swiss Alps. At night Sophie and Tucker slept soundly, nestled together. Luck and fortune, they agreed, were onside. When she took her turn at the wheel just over the German border, Tucker surprised Sophie with a pair of monogrammed driving gloves.

"Better grip." He laughed.

"Critical."

On the autobahn, they challenged each other, and in the end Tucker won the 'who could drive the fastest' at two hundred kilometres an hour. They splurged on a two-night stay at a quiet chalet far from the motorway. There they roamed the countryside and talked about everything. Back on the road, they sped through Poland, wishing they had more time to see the country, especially around Krakow.

"I'm going to come back. It's where Spielberg decided to make *Schindler's List*. Or so they say."

"Who knows? I might have offices there one day."

Anything is possible.

As they crossed into Lithuania, Tucker grew quiet. His face flushed, and Sophie took over the driving again. Daisy barked incessantly.

"Relax, put your seat back. Do you want some water? Maybe sleep. I can drive from here," she told him.

When a short while later Tucker's face turned ashen, and he mentioned stomach cramps, Sophie refused to carry on.

"We're not going any further. We've got to find a hospital." She touched his forehead. "You're on fire."

"I am not going to the hospital in f'ing West Jesus, Nowhere."

"You're not going to die in a rented Porsche either, Tucker."

Following the highway signs straight into Vilnius, Sophie found her way to the local emergency room. By then Tucker was speaking gibberish, and it took her best sign language and the medics' broken English to get them to the car and him out of it.

"Appendicitis?" one young doctor said to another and Sophie before motioning to her that she should wait outside in the hall or go down to the cafeteria.

After what seemed like hours, the same smart, young Lithuanian doctor appeared.

"You were lucky. He's not out of the woods, but he should make it. It's an infection. We need to watch for that now. Why didn't you bring him in straightaway?"

"I did," Sophie said.

"You almost lost him, Mrs Mägi. He's sedated now. The surgery was a bit more complicated than expected. The appendix burst on the table. It happens sometimes. You should get a hotel room, wait and call in the morning."

Lost him?

Sophie sat back down on the plastic chair in the waiting room.

"I'm not going anywhere."

She held on to the cold coffee she'd been given hours ago. Looking down at the polished cement floor, then up at the green cinderblock walls, Sophie only wanted to see Tucker.

"Mrs Mägi, would you like a private room for Mr Mägi or a ward?"

"Private," Sophie mouthed.

"He'll be alright." The red-headed nurse smiled. "Our young doctor is dramatic, a bit self-important. Would you like to see your husband?"

"Yes," Sophie answered.

"I can count on one finger the number of times a beauty like you arrived in a sports car with an almost dead man in tow. He probably thought you were Russian."

"Russian? I'm not Russian."

"I know. But he hates Russians, and you arrived in one of the very few sports cars this town has ever seen. Usually only Russians can afford them. Let's go see your husband, who is not dead."

But, whiter than white, Tucker did look to be in a bad way. While humming machines monitored his vital signs, Sophie pulled up a chair by his bed.

"You should find a hotel," the nurse said. "He will be okay here."

"I'm not leaving."

"It's not allowed." Then on second thoughts, the nurse looked around. "Let me find you a blanket. The desk will need your car keys."

Sophie fished in her bag.

"Do you want anything to eat?"

"No. Nothing."

"He will be fine." The nurse knelt beside Sophie. "You need something to eat. I'll be back."

In the half-light of green displays, Sophie dropped her head onto the bed and against Tucker's shoulder. Everything paled except her need for him to survive. She pushed back the 'what ifs' and the thought of her father having died before she was born, but could not help wondering if a baby had already been conceived in a remote chalet in Germany.

Before she could pick up her phone to call Anne, a steady beep from the monitors brought an emergency team running. She was told to leave. In the hallway the nurse distractedly handed her a sandwich and pointed back to the waiting room.

"I'm afraid it's a coma," she said. "I don't know why. Be brave. Someone will speak with you soon."

Sophie couldn't move. Frozen, she cradled Tucker's belongings and the plastic-wrapped sandwich. Then she recalled Daisy and made her way to the hospital entrance.

Where is she?

The fresh air hit her just as a security guard stopped her, asking about the green Porsche.

"Yes. It's mine."

"I have your dog. She's at my house with my wife, who came to collect her. Don't worry. We are a small country, like a single big family. We take care of everyone."

"Thank you."

"You need to sleep."

"No. I'm going to wait for my husband."

"Okay. When he is safe, you see me. I will help you find a place to stay."

Back inside, Sophie's phone lit up with a text: *Are you okay? Thinking of you. Are you in Tallinn yet? Love, Mother.*

Sophie couldn't get hold of Anne fast enough. When she did, the story tumbled out as if someone else were not only telling it but also living it. Hadn't she just been waltzing around a ballroom in Monaco? Telling tall tales in a German lodge?

"Listen to me," Anne said, "history is not repeating itself. First, you don't know if you are pregnant and Tucker is not going to die from a burst appendix. You are going to eat and you are going to rest. Find a hotel close by. Tucker is in a hospital with people who know more about appendicitis and comas than you do. I love you. Check on him then go to a hotel. Promise?"

"Yes."

After being reassured that Tucker's condition was temporary, a result of trauma, they said, Sophie left the hospital and found the small hotel suggested by both the night nurse and the security guard. With stiff white curtains, fresh flowers and a votive candle burning, Sophie dropped to her knees on the floor beside the bed, overcome with fatigue and the kindness of strangers. She prayed.

Lost him?

For the first few minutes she recalled childhood prayers and then found herself just begging God, Whoever, *Please keep Tucker safe. Return him to me.* Drifting in and out, she roused herself. Anne was correct. Tucker was in good hands. All that she needed was a plan. He'd come to, and she would sort lodgings for herself, him and Daisy. They would stay a week or two until he could travel and she was perfectly capable of managing the drive to Tallinn. It was just another project, and she could see a clear trajectory. She could manage easily.

As the sounds of birds and cars floated in, a light knock sounded at the door. On her knees all night, praying as if that alone – remembering every minute of their time together – would keep him alive – and of course planning the future, even jotting notes, she had fallen asleep with her head on the quilt.

"Mrs Mägi, the hospital called. You are to come right away."

"I am coming. Five minutes."

At the hospital, Sophie dashed to Tucker's room. He sat upright in his post-Soviet pyjamas.

"Hey," Tucker grinned, "I guess that was five miles of bad road?"

"Yes. Five miles of bad road, but all in hand now."

Sophie found a small country cottage not too far from Vilnius, where Tucker could recuperate, where she would take care of him, and Daisy could have space. The security guard put the small house at her disposal in return for a few expeditions in the Porsche.

By the end of week two, Tucker felt his old self again, more than ready to hit the road.

"Where is Tiu?" he barked into the phone. "Yes… I almost died," he shouted. "Tell her that. Who's running the shop?"

"Easy does it," Sophie mouthed.

"Do you know what two weeks… actually more… means to the business when there's no one at the f'ing helm?"

"You have an able team. And Tiu is fine. I called her once you were out of the woods. Didn't want to alarm anyone."

"Tiu?"

"Yes. It seems she's gone to Sweden. On a scholarship or something. Stockholm School of Economics."

"News to me," he said.

Whatever you need to know, Anne had said.

With a bag full of antibiotics, painkillers if necessary and fresh gauze for a change of bandages, they got back on the road. Slipping on her driving gloves, Sophie smiled at Tucker and patted Daisy.

"Better grip," she said as she flexed her fingers.

"Thank you."

"For what?"

"For saving my life."

"It was nothing," she said. "Let's drive."

Deciding to break the seven-hour trip, they checked into a roadside hotel in Riga. Still bearing all the signs of the Soviet occupation, the hotel proved to be spartan, but with the arrival of bread, borscht and bacon on the threadbare tablecloth, Sophie celebrated Tucker's newfound appetite and their close shave.

What can't a little sound project management achieve?

"To Tallinn," she pledged.

"To Tallinn," Tucker echoed, holding up his own glass of Latvian white from the northernmost winery in Europe.

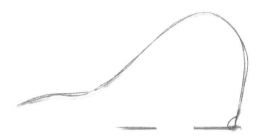

FOURTEEN

"Where are we going?" Sophie asked when Tucker told her to take the leafy drive into Kadriorg Park, rather than the freshly paved and familiar turnoff into the parking lot outside the office complex.

"Just wait." He winced, turning to look ahead.

"Tucker, I'm bushed. I've done all the driving. I want to unpack, relax."

"You will," he said. "Turn here."

Sophie stopped the Porsche in front of what could only be called a dream come true, a page straight out of the leather-bound book of fairy tales she cradled as a child.

"It's yours."

Carl Larsson might have painted it himself. The pale green, wooden house, surrounded by a picket fence, held captive a wild rose bush and an apple tree amongst the white birch. Pink shutters framed window boxes full of billowy red geraniums as summer clouds sailed by.

Before entering the house, Sophie used the brass pineapple knocker just to hear the echo sound.

"Beats over the shop?"

"Beats over the shop," she agreed.

"Enjoy your new home, take a nap, take Daisy for a walk. I'm going into the office. Show off my scar and let them know who's who and what's what."

Sophie kissed her husband and let Daisy loose into the garden.

After exploring almost every nook and cranny of her gingerbread home, Sophie took a shower and had just enough of a nap to feel rested. With Daisy in tow, she went for a walk around Kadriorg Park to remind herself that she was, after what seemed like forever, finally 'home'.

Tsar Peter I's palatial gardens brimmed with children, dogs, bicycles, a huddle of grandmothers, all embracing the sun as only an Estonian could after a long, dark winter. Sophie relished each child as they raced by, as if they were her own.

She did double-takes around the rose garden and the Swan Pond, looking into prams, waving to complete strangers' children, who waved back happily. Daisy stayed close as they made their way past the promenade leading to the president's house and then to the sea wall. She couldn't wait to have her own baby.

Walking the entire length of the esplanade from Kadriorg to Pirita and back again, she envisioned the steps as if on a logic network chart scribbled across a freestanding whiteboard, from step one, one night in a small German chalet, to the final step, the end goal: a newborn baby Mägi. Skipping stones over the calm Baltic Sea shallows and throwing driftwood for Daisy, Sophie acknowledged *Project Bébé*.

Underway.

At a small 'grab and go' just off the park, she took a personal delight in how fast the shops in Tallinn seemed to be filling up with Finnish, German, Spanish and Israeli goods. She felt a part of the surge towards freedom, independence and a free market. Guessing at a number of items with unreadable labels, she finally settled on penne pasta, which clearly looked familiar, and Fazer mints, which filled her with the delight of memories and her flights into and through Helsinki. At home, as she sunned herself in her small garden, she took a call from Anne on the first ring.

"He's fine, on the mend. The drive was uneventful. Beautiful. South Estonia's the potential breadbasket of the world, Mom."

"What about work?" Anne asked. "Have you considered Helsinki?"

"I'll try Tallinn first. Oh, and Mom, you were right. There was no Tiu. A real figment."

"Didn't think so, sweetheart. Tucker will not risk losing you."

After the phone call, Sophie once again opened and closed every door in the house, looked in every cupboard, thinking, designing, considering where her things might go, which room would be the nursery and which would be her home office. In the kitchen, she danced to the local rock and roll station, and finally upstairs, set up her laptop not far from the room she intended to be for the little one.

End goal.

The phone rang.

"Tucker said he is late so eat without him. Or go to Old Town and he will meet you there."

"Thank you, Aytama. I'll meet him in Old Town."

Tucker's new secretary, handpicked by Tiu, might have been her actual mother, maybe even her grandmother. Tucker liked to say that she was probably the one splashed across the old newspapers, driving the Soviet tractor straight up until Independence Day, then threw off her scarf, hopped off and never looked back.

"Capitalist through and through," he said. "Can add, subtract and find the mean faster than a machine."

As Sophie sat brainstorming a list of options for work in Tallinn, she put video chat at the very top of her list, then, running a bit late, she dashed into Old Town to meet Tucker at The Donkey's Stall, where he was not only seated but already eating.

"I am sorry to make this so rushed. So much to catch up on. Two weeks is a century with what's happening in this country now. I have to eat and run."

"No worries," Sophie said, as she served herself a blini from his plate, with Russian caviar and mushroom soup from the tureen. "Thanks for ordering."

"Remember," he laughed, standing at the door without any sign of having had a life-threatening appendectomy, "eat for two."

"Yes." She nodded. "Black Forest gateau is on the menu."

Sophie felt pregnant, as if she carried a new life, and hugged that secret close. Despite Tucker's emergency in Vilnius, things were taking shape. After lunch, she strolled past the shops, the Opera House and Symphony Hall, and went straight into Apotheka, where she bought a pregnancy test, with instructions in three languages.

"Negative," she said aloud to Daisy, who whined by the kitchen table. "No worries," she added, fighting back the disappointment, "just warming up."

At almost midnight, Tucker slipped into bed beside her, making just enough noise to wake her up.

"Sorry," he said, "nature of the job. Good day?" he whispered.

"Brilliant." She spoke softly, wrapping her arms quietly around her husband.

The next day, Sophie grilled everyone she could think of about a job – bankers, software developers, business startups. Tucker handed over all his contacts and said to use his name.

"You need to be bilingual, at least," one banker said. "I have candidates fluent in not just Estonian, which isn't easy, but Russian, Finnish, German and English."

"I'm learning," she said.

"So, call me back when you've learned."

Dinner after dinner, Tucker commiserated with her.

"Competition is stiff." He shrugged. "Estonians and Estonian descendants are flocking to Tallinn. It's a bit of a gold rush."

"You don't speak Estonian."

"Different story."

"How?"

"Numbers. I speak numbers. And with the rest of the returners, even those with rusty Estonian, I am a member in good standing of the Club."

"What Club?"

"The Club of Estonia."

"Okay. I don't want to do translation, write a memoir, teach English, work at the US Embassy. I want to use my MBA. What was the point? It's been eight weeks, Tucker. Should I worry? Start thinking about Helsinki?"

"Or London?"

"London? That's a three-hour flight away."

But Project Bébé?

Pietro called one quiet Sunday afternoon to ask how Sophie was doing and if she was coming to London anytime. He let her know she and Tucker could use the small garden flat attached to his family's London home.

"It's virtually empty and we don't mind dogs."

"Thank you. Let me speak with Tuck and maybe see you soon."

"You sound tired."

"No, just a bit bored. Can't find a job."

Sophie shared the invitation with Tucker, who said without hesitation, "Let's go."

The next weekend they were on Estonia Air, and in short order curled up in a jewel box of a garden flat on Eaton Square, surrounded by historic gardens, just a few steps away from the famous King's Road. After attending a service on Sunday at St Peter's Church just minutes away from the small flat, Sophie had to admit to Tucker she was missing English, even if it wasn't American English, and maybe London might not be such a bad idea.

Pietro had met them from their taxi to hand over the key. As she hugged him, she looked up and in the doorway of the main house above stood a relaxed and smiling Marco Rossi, leaning against the doorframe while he gave a lazy, one-handed wave. Pushing Pietro back while holding on to his forearms, Sophie smiled.

"Pietro," she said, as he turned to look up at Marco as well, "are you two an item?"

"Yes," he said with a grin.

"I see," she said, happy for them both.

With its own private garden and a separate entrance just off the main road, the flat was perfect for Sophie and Tucker. The imposing property at one of the most prestigious addresses in London felt almost too comfortable. With security patrols day and night, they could easily walk to the shops, Harrods or Sloane Square. Even Sean Connery and the odd prime minister were rumoured to have lived around there once upon a time.

Tucker surprised Sophie with a meal at Harry's Bar, which he knew was her favourite. They ate mostly in silence, both thinking the same thing – that she should actually stay in London to look for a job – though neither of them wanted to say it. No one wanted to mention a baby either. Finally, over a shared lemon meringue, Tucker broke the silence.

"Sophie, you've given Tallinn your best shot, and I think that you and Daisy should move to London. You know as well as I do that it will take Estonia a few more years to hammer their way through their economic restructuring, their emergence onto the world financial stage. You belong here; where you can find a job, speak the language. You're wasting your talent. I'm not far away. It's a fairly cheap flight, back and forth. We can do this."

Sophie put down her fork. "No."

"Think about it."

106

"No."

"You're wasting your time and skills?"

"Something will turn up."

"Sophie, I want you to have the same chances I do."

"I'm not giving up."

"It's not giving up," Tucker said.

"It is."

"Well, just think about it."

"Maybe."

.

After the tenth job interview and the tenth banker suggesting Sophie learn Estonian before coming back, Tucker bought the aeroplane tickets for London, including one for Daisy.

"It's a bitch of language, Soph. I told you so."

"You did. Back in Rye, I remember."

"So, you may learn how to get by in Estonian in six months, where to put the odd umlaut, but fluent?"

"Never."

"Ever. So how about London?"

"Okay, you win."

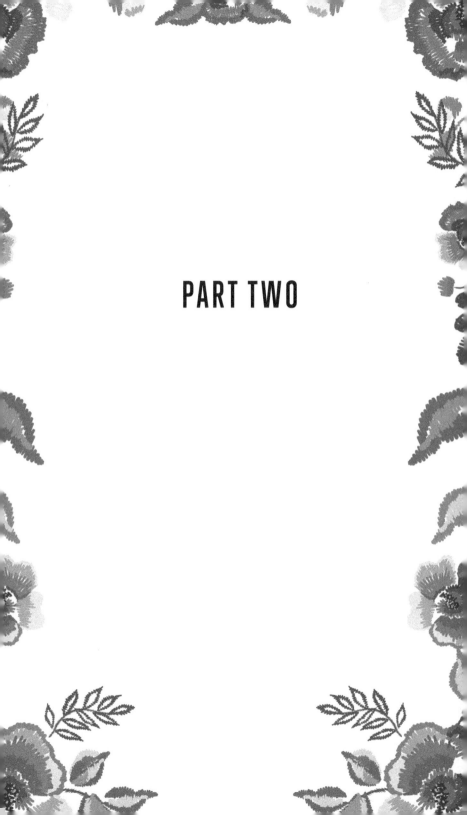

PART TWO

FIFTEEN

Despite the prestigious address, the private garden, the architecture, the history and the London buzz, Sophie walked forlornly around Hyde Park, sheltering beneath an umbrella. What would she do without Tucker, and now without Daisy, who'd had to be quarantined? Even the odd breakthrough in her job search couldn't take her mind off the out-of-date British quarantining of dogs.

Is rabies really still a threat?

Rain pelted ceaselessly and Sophie counted the days until Tucker would arrive. Despite wet walks and dank journeys on the tube she refused to give up anything – *Project Bébé*, finding a job or being with Tucker, even if they were now separated by 1,625 miles. Seeing Daisy through the imposed and outdated isolation became a priority. From her first trip from the airport to the kennel, she found the system abhorrent, especially for a country supposedly full of dog lovers. She had found her spaniel quivering, frightened, sitting most unusually for her on top of her kennel. Dogs barked, woofed, yelped and howled, right and left, and a plume of smoke blew incessantly from a building at the perimeter of the grounds. Daisy, terrified and ready to burst, finally urinated over the roof of her refuge.

Shivering, she stayed close to her owner as Sophie took in the austere, cold, concrete enclosure; and Sophie stayed equally close to Daisy, staying for as long as possible. She had asked the kennel receptionist if she could place newspaper on the barren floor. Outside, she forced herself to breathe evenly as a French couple, escorting a bounding, yellow Labrador, came up beside her.

"Do you need help?" they asked.

"It's all so medieval," she said, waving her hands in frustration. "I'd like to take my dog straight back to Estonia, France or even America. Anywhere. I don't understand. Rabies? Who gets rabies in this day and age?"

"*Argent.*" The Frenchman rubbed his fingertips together.

"Money," his wife said. "It's not cheap; has nothing to do with rabies. But you can do it!" She fluffed the back of her Labrador's head. "Time will fly by – you will see – and *animaux* are like people. Adaptable. Put some photos on the wall: you, husband, children, birds, animals – big eyes, and, of course, a little money for the staff, the kennel cleaner – not so much, a decent bottle of wine, *chocolat*, biscuits – and he will take your little dog with him *pour une petite promenade*. Remember, big photos of the children. *Les enfants. Très important.* Time will fly. You will see. *Bonne chance.*"

"*Merci.*"

"Kidney failure," the caretaker said dolefully as Sophie passed by, "that's what you need to worry about most. These cold floors."

Sophie sat back down, cross-legged, holding Daisy in her lap. "Excuse me," she called out to the same caretaker, "what's the incinerator for?"

"Dogs and cats," she answered without looking back, and then paused. "Miss, you'll get through this and so will your dog. Not many actually die in here, you know."

"Any other options?"

"No. This is as good as it gets, and no matter what, it's six months, even if you flew back to wherever you came from today. Dog's goin' nowhere."

On the underground back into Central London, Sophie gave herself a pep talk.

You can quit when you're finished.

She finalised a list of banks to contact, and then reread on her laptop the reference Pascal had fallen all over himself to write. He supposed it would look good for UR's online magazine when she got a job: "Older woman graduates University of the Riviera and lands job in Finance in the City of London."

Sophie felt that even if she and Tucker spent an hour on the phone every night, she still might falter for the first time. However, remembering Khulan's sandalwood fan and her inspiring note, along with the memory of sun-bleached laundry under a stark blue, warm Riviera sky and her newly minted MBA, Sophie had hopped off the tube in South Kensington, took in the rainy, grey, London sky, and smiled before buying a bouquet of tulips, a bottle of water and a shiny magazine entitled *Mother & Baby*.

"London makes sense," Sophie told her mother down the line as she walked away from the tube station. "So many opportunities. Trading, investor relations. With my age, experience and an MBA I can skip the trainee programme. It's exciting, bit hectic. I'm meeting as many people as I can, as fast as I can."

"Are you sure you don't want me to make a few calls?"

"No, Mom, I'm doing fine, but thanks."

"It will work out. Think. A year ago you were just beginning an MBA." Anne waited. "Now, about dinner? I'm in London shortly. I'll text the dates."

"Great. I love you."

"Love you. See you soon."

"Mom? Thanks."

"For what?"

"For just being you."

Sophie slipped into the meet and greet at the American Women's

Club in South Kensington, just as everyone announced their names one at a time. Monaco might as well have been a decade and a million miles away. Gone were the slim, tanned young women from her MBA programme, but nevertheless, Sophie felt an immediate bond with the red-headed woman sitting next to her, as she introduced herself to Sophie.

"Robin. From France now, but originally from Texas. Like art and archaeological digs."

"I'm Sophie. From Monaco, and most recently Tallinn. Formerly Westchester County, New York. Likes banking and babies."

"Enjoying the rain?" Robin snorted.

"Daily," Sophie quipped back.

Just then a busty blonde from Arkansas leaned into them and said, "I always tell the new girls – 'just off the boat' – to buy a nice, thick, long scarf and no matter what – rain, hail, sleet, snow, grey or not – go out. Wrap that big, woolly thing around your neck and go out, or trust me, you never will, and that can be a very long time in England."

Sophie waved the wide end of her cashmere scarf, demonstrating. "I've got it."

"Me, too." Robin waved hers.

Oh, England.

After the meeting, Sophie passed through the same slick, wet streets, making her way home. She wanted to rewind, be trotting up the mountainside to *Le Rocher*, sitting on her terrace, overlooking the sea, enjoying another sunset, or mostly to be wrapped up in a wool blanket sitting in front of the fire, in her own snug, gingerbread home in Kadriorg waiting for Tucker. As the gas flames in her garden flat guttered, she cupped her tea in her hands.

What next? And what about Project Bébé?

Within two minutes her phone buzzed.

Pietro, sounding breathless, started straight in. "Look, Sophie. I've been mandated to find the smartest person I know to help with the European media effort at Westcox, and you, in my opinion, are just that person."

"What are you doing at Westcox?"

"Tengfei roped me in. My family thought it would be good experience and Westcox respected the money my family would invest."

Köhler.

"The Chinese have gone back to Shenzhen. Khulan to Ulaanbaatar. They were, as you can imagine, very homesick."

"It's not working with Köhler himself, is it?"

"Not directly. You'd work with me. Can you start now?"

"Now?"

Pietro met her the next morning in the lobby as soon as she came through the glass doors. Excited at the opportunity facing her, she shook hands with Gregory Dean, Head of the Department.

"Well, I've heard great things about you." He laughed. "Is it Taylor, Mägi or Taylor-Mägi?"

"Taylor-Mägi," she responded.

"Okay, Ms Taylor-Mägi."

"Call me Sophie."

"Sophie, follow me."

Pietro smiled and took his leave, as Gregory Dean led Sophie upstairs, through a variety of typically corporate corridors and into a small office.

"What do you think?" he asked, motioning as if he were a realtor to the small office with its thin slice of the City just visible through the window and the buildings next door.

"I think the tech bubble—"

"About the office," he interrupted.

Sophie stared at him. "Look, the office is nice, but I'm here for an interview."

"You've just had it. Take it or leave it, this is your office."

"I'll take it." She smiled. "It's a start."

115

Pietro popped back in with a black binder, annual reports and his own research.

"Good," Gregory said. "Pietro knows the drill. I need the pitch book by tomorrow noon." Gregory walked out of the office, looking back over his shoulder at Sophie, who had already made herself comfortable at the desk and spread out the binders Pietro had placed there.

"Welcome aboard!" Pietro said.

"You must have done some sales job."

"Not me, it was Pascal, with a little shove from Marco."

"Marco?" Sophie smiled. "Okay, let's get started."

Sophie continued the research Gregory Dean had requested, as well as studying Westcox, the City and media. She authorised an antibiotic for Daisy, who by now did have an infection, and waited, intermittently put on hold, to register for a kennel visit for the weekend.

"With my husband," she said.

With the French woman's advice in mind, Sophie organised images for the kennel walls: *National Geographic* clippings of wide-eyed jungle animals and reduced-price 1999 calendars showing endangered British birds in flight. She bought a silver heat reflector for the floor, a box of dry dog biscuits, a bottle of Cabernet from Waitrose, as well as a box of Cadbury's Roses for the tractable kennel staff.

While out shopping for Daisy, as well as a smart two-piece suit for herself, Sophie slipped into Waterstone's on King's Road and bought *What to Expect When You're Expecting*. Job or no job, dog or no dog, *Project Bébé* was still underway. After drafting a quick bulleted list of weekend ideas, from early Christmas shopping at Harrods to a dinner at Harry's Bar, she reformatted a fertility chart, took her temperature, entered the data, noting viscosity of cervical mucus.

Popping from baby site to baby site, she sat back, amazed. The online resources and advice seemed to be growing every day.

She searched, researched, figured things out and weighed the odds, made projections. Would having a baby at forty-two be an issue? Her vital signs seemed to say not. They were casebook, practically perfect – menstrual cycles that ran like clockwork, PMS, clear discharge, good flow, hormones balanced, no pelvic pain, no health issues, a good diet and physically fit.

Wrapped in Tucker's old bomber jacket, Sophie sipped Earl Grey tea in front of the fire, while she computed. Over forty, even with IVF, it seemed like statistically the odds might be against her, but she'd beaten the odds before, hadn't she?

An MBA? In Monaco, even? Who'd have guessed? Why don't you just walk into the Ferrari showroom, and drive one out?

Sophie mused, *Should I have done this twenty years ago?* But what about Jane Seymour? Not so long ago, hadn't the actress given birth, and she was definitely older than forty-two. An online search agreed; at forty-four years and nine months, *Dr Quinn, Medicine Woman* star Jane Seymour had given birth to twin boys in late 1995 with the help of in-vitro fertilisation.

IVF.

Sophie shut down the laptop and closed the lid.

In-vitro?

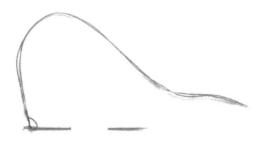

SIXTEEN

Knightsbridge, Chelsea and South Kensington glittered with Christmas. Store windows displayed stripy gifts under snow-flocked trees with mammoth candy canes while twittering robins wore miniature scarves and tiny top hats against a background of rosy fires beneath marble mantelpieces adorned with fir and cedar branches.

Sophie and Tucker strolled, hand in hand, happy to be together, taking it all in – the great city of London. Tucker surprised Sophie with a private fitting at Harrods, where a floor-length cashmere coat trimmed in faux fox proved the perfect gift, just in time for the unexpected snow. They skated at the rink in front of the Natural History Museum and sipped hot chocolate, as they made plans for Christmas in Tallinn.

"A blizzard in Old Town."

"Rose and apple, kringle…"

"Cinnamon, sugar…"

"*Piparkoogid.*"

"Gingerbread."

Tucker and Sophie fell into a rhythm, seeing each other every other weekend and speaking nightly on the phone. Robin, who Sophie had started to see outside of Women's Club events, referred to him as the Lone Ranger, the masked man.

"I'll see him soon enough," Sophie told her when they met up a few days after Tucker's most recent visit. "I'm going to Tallinn for Christmas. I negotiated a decent holiday package, by virtue of having a husband almost two thousand miles away."

"And they actually bought it?"

"What's to buy? It's the truth, and perhaps, Robin, whether I like it or not, I think I have a friend in high places."

"What?"

"Never mind. Bit of a long story. Alexander Köhler—"

"Not *the* Köhler?"

"Maybe."

"Never mind. You know I've actually been to Tallinn. I did an extensive ultrasound on the *Danse Macabre* by Bernt Notke in St Nicholas' Church. And it turned out to be the real thing. Fifteenth-century."

"Really?"

"Yes, Death sweeping us all along – the weak and the strong."

"Chin up," Sophie chided her friend. "How about Life sweeps us along?"

"Good weekend with Tucker?"

"Yes. Shopping, eating, sleeping."

"Lovemaking? Charting?"

"Yes. Just started charting. I think I'm ovulating."

"What are your odds?"

"Don't know. Charts are easy, I can manage that. It's just… I don't want it to feel like a project, and yet it is, isn't it, really? A Project. And of course, after France, I'm feeling *mon âge*. You can't imagine how many times that came up. I didn't feel old in America. Do you think forty-two is too old to have a baby? Do you think I'm daft?"

Robin stirred her tea. "Sophie, I'm forty-two. Same age as you and I'm trying. Everything seems normal. I don't want to believe that Eli and I will not be able to have a baby. He has a grown – adult child, and it has taken me so long to find him. He is *the one*. He adores me, looks after me, and is my partner. I know everything about him, and he knows everything about me. We are in synch. We'd love to have a baby."

"So, let's do this together!"

A waiter in tails set a tiered cake stand of sandwiches, scones and pastries in front of them, and then refilled their fragile teacups.

"Another pot, ladies?"

The tearoom buzzed with mostly women chatting in every conceivable language, from Russian to Chinese and Arabic. Sophie leaned in to hear Robin, whose voice had gone unusually quiet and whose eyes welled up.

"Shortly after I met Eli, I got pregnant – totally unplanned and unexpected – and because his wife was on her deathbed, we made a quick decision to terminate. It was totally the wrong time. The pregnancy happened so easily, I assumed it would happen again – just as easily."

"I'm so sorry." Sophie touched Robin's hand. "At forty, Robin? You didn't think…"

"I didn't think. I didn't know how we would have a child anyway. We move around a lot. His family business is in New York, his son is in San Francisco, and I fly everywhere for art restoration, archaeological digs."

"Look," Sophie said, keeping her hand folded over her friend's, "other women our age, and older, get pregnant all the time, right? It's just a project. Get the critical path modules up and running! Let's give it a shot. Why not? Have you looked at IVF?"

"Never."

"Why not?"

"It happened once naturally, and if it is meant to happen again, it will."

Sophie released Robin's hand. She wanted to say, 'Yes, but that was two years ago.'

"Yes, it might," she said instead. "But I'm looking into IVF. Why not? We're in England, home of the test-tube baby, right?"

"I'm *not* doing IVF."

"How are you going to run a project if you don't run the odds? Look at all the options?"

"Split the last scone?"

"Yes."

The Finnair descent over Tallinn, now as familiar to Sophie as the train once was from New York City to Rye, relaxed her. With fast-falling snow, a steady wind and white lights, what most countries would designate a blizzard, Estonia called Christmas. Business as usual, planes de-iced, went on their way, to the steady din of indigenous snowploughs.

Row after row of Arctic pine signalled a very different landscape than England, with its perfectly squared farms and only ever thin dusting of snow. The six-foot drifts below teetered at the top of Sophie's *Christmas Wish List*, along with, fingers crossed, a baby boy or girl, blond, blue-eyed, brunette or green-eyed, and to be home again in Tallinn, despite the deadweight of a briefcase full of Westcox work. In that moment, in that peaceful descent, anything and everything seemed possible, from a baby, a two-country marriage and clearly another magical Christmas in Tallinn.

Rushing through the remaining, yet to be renovated, mud-coloured, brick corridors, always a reminder of Soviet design, then beyond passport control, baggage claim and out two swinging doors, past two armed guards with one German Shepherd each, Sophie found Tucker holding a bouquet of roses so dark, so red, so rich that they might as well have been frosted. All the waiting men, young or old, appeared to grasp roses, some in bunches and some a single stem. Chivalry may have died out across Europe and the rest of the world in the fifteenth century, but here in Tallinn, it lived on.

"For you," Tucker said, taking her bags in exchange for the frozen roses. "Dinner?"

"Yes."

"This is serious weather, even for Estonia," he said, as he lifted her bags into the back of his Russian jeep.

"I love it!" Sophie cried, listening to the jeep's engine turn over neatly and begin to hum.

With visibility at practically zero, the snow still continued to fall heavily and unabated. The cadence of tires crunching, muffled engines and muted silence suffused the landscape, and Sophie treasured it as a blanket, as if it was life itself.

On the top-floor restaurant of one of Tucker's new developments, Sophie smiled. Everyone seemed to know Tucker, and by default her, Mrs Mägi, who lived in England.

The menu featured reindeer, a Witches' Casserole and, of course, blinis with caviar and forest mushroom soup. Over coffee, they laced fingers.

"I missed you," Tucker said.

"Me, too. However, Tuck, the upside is that every time we meet, it feels brand new."

"It does," he said. "No old pair of slippers here."

She laughed and kissed him lovingly.

Finally back in Kadriorg, in her gingerbread home, Sophie smiled as Tucker put logs in the stove.

"I think I could do 'old slippers.'"

"Yup, me too." He lit a match.

"I feel safe here, Tuck. Don't you?"

"I do."

The snow fell quietly, stealthily burying the apple trees, whose topmost branches still batted the night sky, while the wild rose bushes lay already still, blanketed. Within the soft blue, painted walls of her wooden home, she listened to the storm's muffled angst. As she padded across the cream-coloured floors, with flurries racing past as lace curtains might, she felt for an instant as she once did as a child, embracing a leather-bound volume of Hans Christian Andersen fairy tales.

"Why am I living in London?" she asked.

"Because," Tucker responded, "Estonia is just figuring out which way is up, and it was impossible for you to find a job here. And you now have a job in London, a good one. Stop worrying; let's go for a walk."

"Now?" she cried. "You just lit the stove."

"Yes. Right now."

Jumping up, pulling on layers of clothes, snowsuits and boots, they raced each other. Then Tucker playfully pulled out a long-tailed, woollen cap, and placed it over Sophie's long, blonde hair.

"And matching mittens." He grinned, handing them to her. "I bought them from the old women selling along the Old Castle Wall. Christmas present. Everyone's into the game: commerce. What could be better? A bustling economy in a free and independent country? But there's still the language factor. How's your Estonian coming along?" He laughed out loud.

"How's yours?" she retorted.

"I don't need it for my business. 'Yes', 'no' and 'show me the profit' are the same in any language."

Arm in arm, they walked through Kadriorg, Tsarina Catherine's Park, as the snow began to let up. They stopped for the odd snowball fight, with Tucker waxing on about everything from a new office complex to a strip mall, interspersed with titbits about Tsar Peter the Great and the park he built for his Estonian wife. Together, they tested the ice, walking across the frozen Swan Pond to the green-domed gazebo, now buried in snow, with its glittering Christmas lights still struggling to shimmer.

Tucker hustled Sophie into Café Katharinenthal at the corner, and they both giggled, as he ordered a vanilla coffee and one still-warm kringle.

"We didn't have dessert, did we?" he asked, knowing they had.

"Don't remember," she concurred.

The world seemed to still, as Tucker shook snow from his jacket and brushed snow from her hair. They pulled apart the circle of sweet bread, licking the chocolate and powdered sugar from each of their frozen fingers.

"Ready to have a baby?" she asked.

"Since the day we met," he said, tucking a strand of hair behind her ear.

At home, they fell into bed, and between the warm flannel sheets, with the remnant glow of old coals in the stove, they kissed, for all the world tasting of cinnamon, vanilla, chocolate: a thousand-year-old recipe for a buttery Estonian kringle.

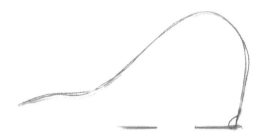

SEVENTEEN

The first two weeks of January flew by, and Sophie was thrilled Robin had called.

"You shouldn't jog," Robin cautioned.

"What? No? I'd die!"

"You said this month you were 'textbook perfect'. Temp steady at ninety-eight degrees – I mean, thirty-seven – then popping up half a degree. Raw egg-ish, cervical mucus. Great sex with Tuck."

"Is this Miss 'I'm Just Going to Let It Happen' talking?"

"Sophie, you have a chance here. It feels a bit like if you get pregnant, I get pregnant." Robin paused. "Do you know, someone told me I reminded them of their nan today."

"What's a 'nan'?"

"British for grandmother."

"You're kidding me. You? How old was this person?"

"I don't know. Late teens. I did the math. I am old enough to be her 'nan'. Just."

"Oh right. If you were in some Third World country. Just. Forget about it. They look older in this country anyway. Look, you forget and I will meet you halfway. I will walk around Hyde Park? No more jogging."

"Deal," Robin agreed.

Sophie did hope. She wanted to run, jump, punch the air.

I might be pregnant!

She laughed out loud as she power-walked around the Albert Memorial across from the Royal Albert Hall. Had she actually stood on her head after sex, just to make sure the sperm knew which way to go? It would still be two weeks before she could check, but she bought the pregnancy test kit anyway and decided to make an appointment at the Dodd Fertility Clinic.

Just for information.

Trotting down Walton Street, Sophie stopped at Itsu for sushi and her favourite boiled spinach salad with sesame sauce. Across the street she spied an antiques shop full of curios. A rocking horse, maybe twelve inches tall, slender, caught her eye. It appeared that it might keep rocking if tipped on its blade-like runners. She bought it, carrying it home as if it were a sighting of land, a possibility, an act of faith, something for her baby. She placed the horse tenderly on a shelf beside her bed.

I'm ready.

The online, pop-up, checklist of barriers to fertility provided a small footnote about previous abortions. Sophie noted it, thought about Robin and committed to never ever mention it. Robin had as much a right to wishful thinking as she did. They were both perfectly healthy.

Two years earlier, during a routine exam, at forty, Sophie's doctor in Rye suggested a blood test to check her hormones for fertility, to evaluate her ovarian reserve.

"Plenty of eggs left," she said when reporting the results. "Nothing to worry about. FSH – your follicle-stimulating hormone – is seven."

"Not sure what that means," Sophie had said.

"You're ovulating, still have eggs to harvest for a good time yet – no guarantee of quality, though, just quantity. If you run into trouble, go to West University's Human Reproduction Department. They even have a catalogue. Sperm or eggs, you get a full dossier. Design your own baby. No problem. They even have photos of the donors."

Sophie continued to read down the pop-up checklist. Strong sense of smell. Yes. Egg-white consistency, super glue cervical mucus. Yes. Extra amorous. Yes. Saliva change. Yes. Bigger breasts. Yes. Regular menstrual cycles. Yes. Partner's sperm up to scratch.

Partner's sperm up to scratch?

Hadn't Tucker mentioned a terminated pregnancy in the past with an old and long-forgotten girlfriend? Weren't men fertile forever? Didn't Charlie Chaplin have a baby at seventy-three? Robert De Niro at sixty-eight? Picasso? Sixty-eight, too?

"I'm sure he did," Sophie mused aloud.

Two weeks flew by in no time. Sophie and Pietro put their many pitch books together in record time, and requests for even more poured in. Gregory Dean couldn't have been more pleased.

"This one is on the move," Gregory sang out every time he passed Sophie in the corridor.

"The next pitch book is for a company called Topple Ltd, a broad-based conglomerate with at least one division having something to do with pianos," Pietro said, dumping boxes of files onto her desk.

"I don't know anything about pianos."

"But you are good at research?"

"I am." Sophie laughed, and immersed herself in all things piano, roaming the Internet and even interviewing the head of piano at the Royal Academy of Music and the Royal College of Music.

Pietro identified four piano companies that might be worth something to Topple. Together they massaged the math, the statistics, the graphs, which mostly made the acquisitions attractive, and later when she watched Gregory Dean dazzle the CEO of Topple with their beefed-up pitch book, she sat back pleased. They had closed the deal; they had secured Westcox another very nice, very lucrative consulting job.

Sophie met Anne for lunch at the Capital on Basil Street. "I think you have the Midas touch," she said as soon as Sophie was seated. "I have two old school friends at Westcox and they've asked if you were my daughter."

Sophie listened, twirling her spoon in the chamomile tea. "Really?"

"Apparently you are making a name for yourself."

"I doubt that, but thanks, Mom."

"Anything else new? How's Tucker?"

"He's brilliant. I can't wait for Easter when we'll have longer together. And..."

"And?"

"And – I think I might be pregnant."

Sophie went for a long walk over to Battersea Park, knowing she was in fact putting off the pregnancy test. She didn't want to call Robin and confess that sinking feeling. Her lower back ached, and she felt bloated. PMT.

Premenstrual?

As she walked, a light breeze spiralled leaves around the base of an old chestnut tree.

Could be; could not be.

Not able to put it off one more minute, Sophie popped out of bed just after midnight and broke open the heavily sealed test kit. She peed on the stick and held it up to the dim light in the windowless bathroom. Squinting, she saw a blue line; she turned it one way and then another.

Does the line connect? How dark should it be?

She read and reread the instructions, then took a second test.

Maybe the urine was too weak.

Sophie tossed the second plastic stick into the trashcan with the first.

"Not pregnant," the twenty-four-hour customer service operator said in a Gaelic accent. "Yes, that reads not pregnant."

"Thanks," Sophie said, and clicked her Nokia closed, looking up at the slender rocking horse she had purchased on Walton Street. She imagined Marco Rossi's voice along with a whiff of his peppery cologne.

Don't give up too soon.

Sophie printed off a few more monthly ovulation charts, filling one in with the current date with her fine-point pen. Only when a small number eight burst into a perfectly formed, midnight-blue splash did she realise she was in fact crying. She blotted the stain with a tissue and straightened the edges of a stack of charts, much the way she would neaten the pages of her now well-respected pitch books.

'Here, let me take that one,' she visualised Pietro saying, remembering the day he had followed her to the *quai*, to the bistro, and handed her his perfectly folded handkerchief.

She thought about calling Tucker, but it would be the wee hours in Tallinn, and she knew he wasn't interested in eggs, temperature and cervical mucus. He hadn't seen the blonde toddler who visited Sophie's dreams.

Sophie pulled out the small, sandalwood fan Khulan had given her, and traced the finely carved, oriental women. Snapping it opened and closed, she fanned herself, feeling much the same as she did on the day when Pascal had made an issue about her age.

She recalled his voice as she slowly fanned herself, and for the first time in a long time, she let herself cry until the whole ruined chart filled up with splashes of tear-sized ink stains.

Sophie chose to hibernate for the weekend, drinking copious amounts of green tea, and redoing work for the office that didn't really need a second look. After letting the setback take her as low as she felt she could possibly go, she wrapped her muffler around her neck and went out.

Just go out.

Happy to have Daisy released from quarantine, Sophie put a new leash on her dog and stepped out. The local dog walker had told her about the best routes in Hyde Park and Battersea. Seeing Daisy at the ready, nose down, lifted Sophie's spirits. The sighting of spring blossoms might do it too; any February plant in bud would suffice.

Sorting things out in her head as she walked, glimpses of a winter honeysuckle bush, a snowdrop and a bed of purple crocuses made her smile. Life seemed to push through, no matter what, despite her disappointment, in the carefully tended beds of Hyde Park.

Too old to conceive.

She played through a call she might have had with Robin; she didn't really want to see her friend just yet because she knew the first question would be: 'So, are you?'

'Am I what?'

'Pregnant.'

'What was I thinking? But I feel healthy, Robin, really fit. How many times do you hear about older moms having twins? Are they all IVF or donor eggs? How do I have a child without being with Tucker every night? Do I store the sperm? Is the distance between London and Tallinn an issue? What are the options? Give up my job?'

She visualised saying, 'Yes.'

'What kind of marriage do I have anyway? Who can afford to jump on a plane at a temperature surge, while having to pump out the next assignment-winning pitch book?'

Again, she saw Robin agreeing.

'I need to know more about IVF, talk with someone, have a fertility test.'

One red-letter day Sophie spotted daffodils for sale.

"From the Isles of Scilly, where it is a bit warmer," the flower seller said as he took her change, handing her the bright bouquet, while Daisy tugged on the leash.

"Just thinking of you."

"Finally," Robin cajoled. "Am I not on your call *now* list? I've been calling. I thought you'd never answer. You call me wailing, then disappear. I came by the flat twice, heard Daisy and figured you'd gone for a run or just wanted to be alone. Or disappeared into the mechanical, maniacal jaws of Westcox Brown."

"No. Sorry. I just wanted to be alone. I'm not pregnant, Robin. I just needed a bit of time to take that in. But I have my scarf now and a brolly. Ready to go?"

"Yes. South Ken? We can walk to the meeting together. I'm sorry, Sophie."

"Don't be. I have eggs left and if I can figure out how to get Tucker and me in the same place at the same time… But guess what?"

"What?"

"The chances of conceiving at forty-two?"

"Do I want to know?"

"Less than five per cent."

"I don't want to know. Guess what?"

"What?"

"Another person, doing my hair, said it was like her gran's!"

"No?"

"Yes."

"It's a British thing," Sophie explained. "They do the lifecycle differently. They drum it into their kids, from tadpole and egg to slumped, pot-bellied and bald in forty years."

"It's shepherd's pie and all that beer."

"Fun-ny. Hey, have you ever gone to the Tuesday afternoon fertility group, the International Women's Club group?"

"Are you kidding me? I told you, if Eli and I ever get pregnant again, great, and if not, so be it. I'll see you in ten."

"Robin, wait. The nan thing, gran thing – it's just British branding. Nothing to fear. Forget about it."

131

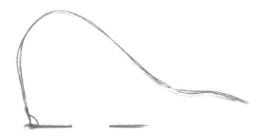

EIGHTEEN

Sophie finished opening her Ameritrade account online just as Gregory Dean called.

"You are moving to Media. The next grunts to join get the pitch books. Congratulations!"

Happy at her promotion, Sophie called Tucker and Anne. While they both congratulated her, she felt lonely. She wanted a dinner, a celebration, someone to say 'well done' in person.

Instead, Sophie made a cup of tea, sitting with Daisy and watching the rain pour. She admitted to herself that she had thought 'the biology rules' didn't apply to her. The truth was that she hadn't even thought about it, taken it fully on board. Who did? A twelve-year-old in biology class? So while she did know her ovaries might be packed with more eggs than she would ever need, they obviously didn't last forever.

On paper, she doodled, weighing her best- and worst-case scenarios – not necessarily in any order. 1) No children ever. Tucker would go with the flow. Lots of people did that, claimed no kids afforded them a good lifestyle. 2) Artificial insemination.

3) IVF. 4) ICSI – actually forcing the sperm into the egg. 5) Donor eggs. 6) Donor sperm. 7) Surrogate mother.

Sophie studied the rain through the windows at the front of her apartment as it hit the pavement and splashed back. She continued to arrange options like daffodils in a vase. 8) Adoption.

Adoption. A child who needs me as much as I want her. Or him. Just for the joy of it. For me. For her, for him. For us.

Who didn't know someone who had been adopted? Sophie recalled a childhood friend, years ago. Nothing wrong there. If anything, her parents had doted on her too much. But couldn't the process be long, never-ending, fraught with obstacles? Which country? America, Estonia, England, China? Male? Female? Could she justifiably raise a child from another culture? Korea, for instance. How would that work? Was it true that sometimes adoption triggered a pregnancy of one's own?

"Adoption," Sophie said clearly over the phone to Tucker that night.

"Okay," he responded without a second thought, "if that's what you want."

"Seriously, you are alright with that? I am not so sure."

"Sophie, we are in this together. I know some men want to clone themselves, but I don't. I wish I was there with you."

"Me, too."

"Okay, I will make some enquiries here, see how it works, but I need to sign off now." Tucker broke off to shout to Aytama, "Yes, tell them I'm coming."

"Wait!" Sophie caught him before he hung up. "Your sperm. We need to check it out. Can you do that?"

"Yes. I can do that."

She sat for a minute before finding her jacket, scarf and keys.

Adoption?

Daisy relished the high winds pounding London. They crossed the Albert Bridge, which seemed to sway and give way in the wind, and circled Battersea Park. Mothers and young children with strollers dotted the park. Fiddling with her lunch, feeding half of it to Daisy and the rest to the swans, she tried not to think the obvious. She watched the swans drift.

No child? Ever?

Back home, with Daisy curled up in front of the gas fire, Sophie spoke with Robin, who was off again, this time flying to Panama to authenticate pre-Colombian pots. If she were not married to Eli, she'd be living in the Caribbean. She'd given Sophie a small terracotta fertility figure believed to be from Ecuador. They called her 'good luck Luli', who now sat on her wide buttocks beside the slender rocking horse with her outstretched arms and legs framing her fruitfulness.

"The trip was totally unexpected." Robin laughed.

"It's brilliant. Made to order," Sophie said, while deciding not to propose the options she'd considered: adopting together, maybe a brother and a sister, or IVF twins from a surrogate mother or splitting eggs from a donor.

"Take care of yourself, Sophie. I have a good feeling about your visit to the Dodd."

"Thanks. It's supposed to be the best in London. Forty per cent success rate… for forty to forty-two-year-olds."

With her favourite scarf wound around her neck, Sophie walked to the Dodd.

Just for information.

Ushered from room to room, producing her passport multiple times, she finally found a seat in a cheery waiting room with various couples and the odd single woman, drinking tea from plastic cups. Women dressed in pastel hospital gowns walked into one consulting room, and out another. Sophie made herself tea at the oversized machine, then juggled the hot cup, as she stirred the scalding liquid with a flat wooden stick.

After an hour of watching the BBC, taking quiet phone calls

from the office and Pietro, who was sworn to secrecy about her mission, and another two cups of tea, Sophie finally met the famous Dr Grace Carroll.

If anyone can get you pregnant...

The British doctor looked Sophie up and down.

"Thirty-five?" she guessed.

"Forty-two and a third," Sophie offered.

The doctor laughed with Sophie and then narrowed her eyes. She studied Sophie's thick, long hair, her clear eyes, the energetic attitude and healthy nails.

"You *look* younger."

"Thanks."

"No thanks required. Age matters in this case."

She came out from behind her desk, then leaned onto the front of the desk, flipping her PC around while at the same time managing the mouse.

"Look at these numbers," she said. "At thirty-five you have a chance. Forty-two? Forty-three? Even with IVF? The success rate is maybe four per cent in general. We have a higher rate for forty to forty-two, but you are just past that, really."

"Yes, I read that."

"My suggestion? Forget it. Live a good life. Do you really need kids?"

"Maybe I'm in the four per cent."

"Doubtful."

Anger forced Sophie to breathe, rejecting the information.

"So, it's just down to stats?"

"I am afraid it is. We have the best fertility stats in the UK."

"Because all your patients are twenty-two to thirty-five?"

"Yes," the consultant confirmed, unabashed. "Look, I'll take your blood, but even if your FSH – your follicle-stimulating hormone – is less than nine this time round, your age is important. I'm guessing yours is probably fifteen at your age, give or take, and if you were younger, I'd say let's go, but you are over forty-two."

Then the clinician softened a bit, understanding that she was delivering bad news to the umpteenth woman who had come to her too late, who was going to have to understand that for her most probably the answer was no children. "I'm sorry."

"Can't we just give it a go?"

The doctor sat back on her desk, cradling her computer. "Look at the numbers."

"I see the figures and there appears to be a small chance. What if I feel lucky?"

Grace Carroll got up, looked at her watch and then briefly into the waiting room before closing the door. "Sophie... may I call you Sophie?"

"Yes."

"Sophie," Grace began in the ringing tones of a British girls' school, "you do not want to have to take these drugs. They are serious. I promise you. You do not want to do them. There are side effects, especially if you need more than one cycle, which you would. I've been doing this for more than ten years. Younger women only see success rates of twenty to thirty-five per cent per cycle, but chances of success go down with each cycle. Costs go up, and even with three full cycles chances – with a younger candidate – only go up to forty-five to fifty-three per cent. Want to talk about ovarian hyper-stimulation syndrome? Uterine cancer?"

The two women sat in silence. Sophie took the information in, and then stood and shook Grace Carroll's hand. At the door, she paused, turning back.

"May I ask you a question?"

"Yes."

"Do you have children?"

"No."

"Why not?"

"Don't want any. Never did."

"Okay," Sophie said. "Thank you for your time."

With her knees buckling momentarily, she managed to walk

to the elevator. She couldn't get out of the Dodd fast enough. Before heading towards Sloane Square, she stopped at the Phases, a dress shop next to the clinic, where she thought she might find something for Tucker's investor dinner that night at the RAC. He would arrive in a few hours. The sales assistants seemed to be speaking underwater, and Sophie's limbs felt dead.

Chances of having a child? Zero.

She chose a black satin shift patterned with tiny white roses, a silk black wrap and a pair of black strappy sandals. The assistant wrapped the package in pink tissue and handed her the slick shopping bag.

Side effects? Serious drugs. You don't want to do this.

"Have a lovely evening," the young woman behind the register said in a thick, rich Pakistani accent. "Something special tonight?"

"Thank you. Just dinner," Sophie said, "with my husband."

"Amazing things happen, you know," the woman offered, having seen many women walk in to buy themselves something after they came out of the Dodd.

"They can," Sophie said.

"If you never get your heart broken," she said in her melodic voice, "you will never learn to love. That's an old saying from my country."

"Thank you."

Not broken.

With tears brimming, Sophie wanted to get home. She wanted her garden flat, Daisy in her arms, a cup of tea, a chat with Robin, even if long-distance, and Tucker, who would put one strong arm around her, pull her close and say over the top of her head in a clear, calm, voice, '*Fuck it.*' That is exactly what he did the minute he arrived in the flat when she shared the facts, as well as before he boarded the plane back to Tallinn, kissing her goodbye one more time.

Fuck it.

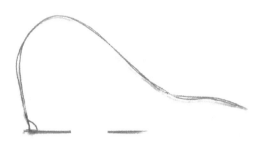

NINETEEN

Pale narcissi lined the walks and climbed the knolls of Hyde Park. Swans chased tourists from one side of the Serpentine to the other, while children watched the Queen's Guard drill in the arena not far from their barracks.

"Not giving up," Sophie said clearly.

She still could sometimes see 'her' baby, a toddler, barely old enough to walk, holding herself up to the side of the bed, her head resting just inches from her own. Then just as quickly the toddler would disappear, be gone. Sophie often practised opening her eyes softly, slowly, and sometimes the glimpse of this small child would last just a bit longer.

Wasting time, wanting to be alone with her thoughts, Sophie circled St James's Square communal garden and passed the East India Club. The scent of cut grass filled the air, buoying her up. For whatever reason, she felt lucky. Hadn't they gone from zero to one hundred per cent on the UR presentation? Hadn't the Topple pitch book been completed overnight? She thought of Khulan, Biyu, Fenfang and Chinyang. Hadn't they, in the end, won?

Against the odds.

Pietro seated Sophie and then himself in the small café. "I'll order."

"Thank you."

"So, tell me all about it."

"My odds aren't brilliant."

"I'm sorry to hear that, Sophie."

"I'm not giving up, though."

"You wouldn't be you if you did, would you?"

"No, Pietro, I wouldn't." She took a sip of Evian. "So, Media now!" She beamed.

"Media." He grinned. "Can you believe it? We are so lucky."

"Yes, we are, aren't we?"

Sophie never tired of Westcox's streamlined offices in the Express building on Fleet Street. She loved the buzz, even the busy taxi rank and the art deco treasure trove inside. Tucker had been right. A job like hers would have been impossible in Tallinn.

Gregory Dean bustled in just as she also made her way into the conference room.

"How does it feel to be in Media?" he asked. "Sophie, I admire your drive. I really appreciate what you both did with Topple and the rest. You know you made my year, my bonus, my promotion. I hate to lose you."

"It's teamwork. Always has been and always will be." Sophie paused. "So, who's the new manager for Media?"

"I don't know him, but he's coming from Frankfurt, maybe? This is a big company. He's a partner, and his family, I am told, has been connected to the firm in one way or another for ages. His specialty is media. Apparently making the firm a fortune. Out of my league. Not that—"

Before Gregory Dean finished his sentence the conference-room door was flung open, and Alexander Köhler walked in, immaculately dressed, smelling of pine and open spaces. Sophie rose in disbelief, just as he put a hand on her arm and kissed her on both cheeks.

"What a surprise," he said, before turning to Pietro and shaking hands. "I'm sorry to be later than expected, may I take everyone to lunch?"

Gregory made his excuses and left as if his mission had been accomplished. Pietro equally made excuses but agreed that Sophie could fill him in later that evening by phone.

"Yes," she said, "I am famished. Lunch would be perfect."

Hopping out of the taxi in Mayfair, strolling the last twenty minutes to Harry's Bar on South Audley Street, they passed the Ritz, dodging traffic and milling pedestrians.

Feeling a bit heady, taken by surprise, Sophie's last remaining thoughts about Dr Carroll's prognosis disappeared. After all the rain, a hint of a spring day, talking media and seeing Alexander Köhler with happy memories of Monaco rushing in, made it feel like a new day, a hopeful beginning.

"Media," he started, as they ordered and sampled the *crudité*. "I'm waiting imminently for the market to fall – could be any day now, even today – boom to bust. This is just a continuation of the conversation we had with your colleagues in Monaco. You and Pietro will work with me. A lot of companies will fall flat, but a few will work in the long run."

"Yes," Sophie said without demur. "I agree."

"Aren't you surprised to see me?" he asked.

Tucker came and went the following weekend, agreeing once again to have his sperm tested.

"It's not an issue."

"I'm sure," Sophie said, bringing his coffee into bed along with the Sunday paper, "but just in case. You know, thirty per cent of all infertility is triggered by an issue with sperm – its volume, count, quality and motility."

"Sophie, look." He put down his coffee. "If you want to keep trying, okay, I'm happy to give it a go. If we're lucky, we're lucky. If not… But remember, I've made it on better odds than four per cent, and so have you."

"That's true," she said before stirring the organic honey into the last of her French *verveine*.

"Enjoy the civilised world, Soph. Tallinn at the moment is not First World. We made the right choice – you here and me there. I love London."

"Me, too," she said. "We will get there in the end – same country, same house, same bed."

"Same pillow?"

"Yes. That's what I miss: pillow talk."

"Speaking of which," Tucker said, "I think your new boss is a snake."

"What? Where did you get that idea from?"

"Your graduation dance in Monaco."

"You don't even know him. You met him once."

"I don't need to know him. I can just look at him."

"He wouldn't be at Westcox Brown if—"

"If what? His family wasn't loaded. You think partnerships come for free? Good work? No, he's been dealt in."

"Are you jealous, Tucker Mägi?"

"Does the sun rise in the morning? Who wouldn't be? Handed a billion dollars at age thirty-three and a rock-solid trust if you happen to, oops, excuse me, blow through a billion before that."

"You don't know that."

"He's from the Köhler family, for fuck sake. What are they not into? Steel, diamonds, oil, global real estate portfolio. Mills in ancient times. Cotton in India. They own more real estate in London than any British property tycoon. In fact, more than anyone else holding property in London. Am I jealous? How'd you like to be handed that? And now Media – the Internet. Licence to make money."

"Tucker," Sophie said, "I like what I have, who I am. Who cares about Alexander? He's just my boss. He's not a bad guy. I just wanted to catch you up on what's what, the irony of ending up with Köhler as a boss."

Calming down, Tucker slipped his arm under Sophie's head. "Sorry. I'm glad you have this chance. It's just… what I wouldn't do to have been handed a billion bucks, and it does seem a bit odd Köhler has surfaced in London… as your boss?"

"Tuck, the truth is we don't really know what anyone else has or hasn't got, right? And what would you do if you didn't have what you've got, what I've got? If life'd been handed to you on a silver platter?"

"I'd have doubled it."

"Ready to Hoover?" Alexander Köhler asked as they met for coffee Monday morning in her office.

"Hoover as in Hoovering up? Cleaning up? Making money?"

"Yes. The bust is looming. I'll see you at lunch, Friday. I want to know which companies you and Pietro have on the radar."

Meeting at Harry's Bar, they enjoyed a typically good meal of veal and spring vegetables, and finalised their strategy.

"Toast?" Alexander asked, as he lifted his glass.

Sophie lifted hers.

"You know," he said, focusing on his glass, "this winery takes into account the phases of the moon, uses only Chardonnay white grapes. What do you think?"

"Buttery," she answered.

"Not the wine. The Hoovering."

"Yes," she raised her glass, "I'm in. Hoovering."

Parting company after their late lunch, Sophie made her way back through Mayfair, too late to go back to the office, past the Ritz and through Green Park. She watched the sun sink while she crossed the Mall and went to feed the swans in St James's Park. As she sat on a green bench facing the water, a single large female swan left

142

the Serpentine and came straight to the bench. Sophie tapped seed onto the ground and the grateful bird pecked about her feet. Just when Sophie thought she couldn't feel more thankful for a good husband, a great job and a decent boss, she felt a tiny flutter in her stomach. The streetlamps came on as she stood up, locking eyes with the mute swan.

Ovulating?

She smiled, assuming so.

TWENTY

"Dream come true," Robin said as she and Sophie strolled through St Luke's Gardens. "The Caribbean is to die for and, fingers crossed, another assignment appears to be coming through."

"You are going back?"

"Yes. If I can."

"You know, I don't take time off work for just anyone, Robin."

"I know, thanks. It's very good to see you."

The spring weather enticed wild primrose and crocus plants out in the well-turned flowerbeds; even tulips were pushing through. Spreading their blanket out under flowering cherry trees, they drank up the surprising sun and continued to chat.

Children from a local, private nursery filed by hand in hand, with girls wearing striped pinafores and straw hats, boys in flannel shorts and striped jackets. Spellbound, the two women failed to notice the bounding Labrador that came out of nowhere, halting on their blanket. In the distance, a dishevelled, desperate mother holding a broken leash wielded a double stroller bearing two small children over the uneven ground towards the two friends, who were now standing up and trying to get the young animal under control.

"Grab his collar," the dog owner shouted in an American accent. "Or he'll be on the King's Road."

Sophie watched the twins, who seemed to think their mother and the runaway dog hilarious, while Robin managed to corral the black Labrador and all three women collapsed on the blanket, laughing louder than the children. Whining, the dog strained at his newly knotted leash, while the ginger-haired twins clapped, ready for more. The not-too-young mother introduced herself, breathing heavily and resting a hand on a pregnant midriff.

"Thank you, ladies. So sorry to bother you. My name's Louise."

They compared notes on a whole variety of topics, where they were from in the States, what brought each one to Merry Olde England, when they were each going home, if at all, what did each think of the UK, until the topic finally came around to fertility.

"These," the woman said proudly, "are my Clomid babies."

"Clomid? You aren't old enough," Robin said.

"Older than you think – or than I look, I hope." She chortled. "I'm thirty-seven."

"That's not old," Sophie said, "I'm forty-two."

"When I had these two, I was thirty-five, with my chances slipping away. Another woman suggested Clomid and – *voilà*. My Clomid babies. It explodes your ovaries. Like shooting fish in a barrel. Husband can't miss… unless, of course, he's shooting blanks."

"Really?" Sophie sat up.

"Down, girl," Robin said, grabbing her friend's wrist.

"What's Clomid?" Sophie asked.

"It's a low-level fertility treatment. It's cheap and, if you're still ovulating, then why not? Clomid helped me ovulate. It works like oestrogen – does something to do with the pituitary to increase FSH and – the real gunpowder – LH, which helps to produce more eggs in one cycle. Both times for me, it worked like a charm. I went to a real Clomid guru. Nice man. Bit eccentric. Look, here's my number. Call me and I'll give you his details. I warn you, though, he's very eccentric. Think monocle."

145

"It's England," Robin added. They all laughed.

Walking home, Robin tried to dissuade Sophie from using Clomid.

"She's five years younger than you. That's her success factor. Look, it's okay if we missed the boat. Don't wreck yourself over it."

"I'm not missing the boat. I'm swimming after it! It's in my bones. I am a mom. Maybe I missed basic biology somehow, somewhere, but I know, Robin, I know it. I *am* a mom."

"Okay," she answered. "Anything can happen."

"Yes, anything. The funny thing is, I don't feel too old," Sophie said.

They parted company, Sophie to review notes on the conglomerate Alexander wanted to buy and Robin to work on her Panama research. Suddenly, Robin turned around. With the late February wind now whipping at her back, she shouted, "N-O. She was thirty-five. You're not!"

Monday morning, after pushing back all her morning appointments, Sophie sat in a basement consulting room on Harley Street. Seeing her right away, the Clomid specialist conducted a pelvic exam, analysed a blood sample and confirmed Sophie's hormones to be perfect, low enough at FSH nine, and gave her the prescription, a dosage requirement of fifty milligrams.

"Take it between the second to fourth day of your menstrual cycle."

"That's perfect. Today is day three."

On her way to the office, Sophie bought a bottle of Evian and swallowed the tiny white tablet triumphantly.

"C-l-o-m-i-d." Sophie spelled it out for her husband from the back seat of the black cab as she raced to Fleet Street.

"What? Clone Me?"

"Sort of. No. Like shooting fish in a barrel, apparently. We have to have sex when I'm ovulating."

"Happy to oblige!"

"Can you get to London?"

"Yes. But, Sophie, one favour please: no more facts and figures. I failed science."

"Okay."

As Sophie snapped her phone closed, and the taxi pulled up to Westcox Brown, without warning a rush of light exploded from the base of her skull. Blinded, as if a hundred cameras had snapped at once, she leaned back on to the taxi's headrest.

"You okay, Miss?"

"Yes," Sophie said, "I just need a minute."

"That's the Big Pop," Louise said when Sophie called her, with her twins chattering in the background. "That's it exactly. A massive white blast. Flash!"

Sophie closed the office door and carried on the call. "Why didn't you tell me? It's like crashing cymbals in the middle of a Debussy."

As if the orchestra just went haywire.

"Congratulations! It's a small price to pay. You'll see. Happy hunting. Fish in a barrel, remember." Children squealed in the background. "On the naughty step," Louise shouted, "now."

"Initial public offering," Alexander said. "The Communications, Media and Technology Group, are responsible. No pressure, Sophie, Pietro, but all eyes are on me – you. Understood?"

Alexander narrowed his focus and dropped a thin slice of lemon rind into his and Sophie's espresso, while Pietro made himself a cup of tea at the other side of the conference room.

"Sophie, I want you to staple yourself to an analyst and learn the business. I suggest a woman I've known for a while now – she's a top analyst, top scholar. First degree in engineering from Imperial College London. You're meeting her today. She's with us on Hoovering. You need to dazzle her with this IPO."

147

"How did you find her?"

"I didn't," Alexander said. "She found me. She's on point. How to clean up during the bust. She agrees Amazon is the first carcass."

With the Clomid still strobing, Sophie steadied herself. "There's a profile of Caterina on your desk."

"Thanks, Alexander. I'll get onto it right away." Sophie left the room, with Pietro following behind.

Pulling out her Evian, after first placing the coolness of the plastic bottle against her forehead, then the back of her neck, she took a long drink. "Pietro, will you read the profile out to me?"

"Are you okay?"

"Yes, I think so. Baby drug."

"You sure?"

"Just read."

"Ms Caterina Sciarra. Internet analyst. Imperial College London. Harvard MBA. Cambridge. Superstar. Unstoppable. London-based. On everyone's GPS."

"When do we meet her?"

"Today, late lunch apparently."

As the small CMT team pored over the menu, and Alexander motioned to the waiter, an Italian woman – dressed immaculately in Versace – entered the dining room at Harry's Bar.

Alexander stopped speaking, as did the others in the dining room. "Caterina," he greeted her as he stood up.

"Alessandro."

With a light kiss on either cheek for Alexander, and a handshake for Sophie and Pietro, Caterina pulled her smooth black hair back over her shoulder and sat down slightly too heavily for her small frame.

"I'm so sorry to be late," she said in perfect English. "With three and a fourth on the way," she placed her hand on her abdomen, "I think I am finally slowing down. At forty, this is going to be my last. I'm old enough to be a *nonna*."

"*Ne dubito*," Alexander said, rattling on in fluent Italian while Sophie asked the waiter for more water, trying to keep the pain in her lower back in check.

"Sophie," Caterina leaned over, touching her arm, "I understand we are working together. Your first job is this supernova IPO, and then once your name is gold-plated, we start the Hoovering?"

"I'm still a bit unclear—"

"Don't worry. It will all be made clear. *Molto chiaro*. You and Pietro will be stars when I'm finished." Caterina then turned to Pietro. "So, you must be Italian?"

"Argentine, but yes, Italian originally – my great-great-grandparents were from Sicily."

When a German colleague arrived, Alexander left, making his excuses. Caterina filled Sophie and Pietro in on the current status of the public offering, as well as what she and Alexander hoped would be the trajectory, then brought them up to speed on what she thought would be the demise of the tech bubble.

"The Federal Reserve is about to announce a rate hike. Then slowly but surely the party is over."

"The economy is overheated," Sophie added, "the markets need a correction, investors need it."

"Maybe," Caterina responded. "Depends on which investors you are talking about – the common man?"

"You've already made a fortune, haven't you, Caterina?" Pietro asked.

"Yes, but not just me. It's now round two: cleaning up. When they fall out of the sky we catch the ones that have growth potential, that are real companies with a future."

Caterina filled her water glass, and Pietro asked, "When?"

"Now," Sophie answered.

"Correct," Caterina responded, "the demise might even be happening this precise moment."

After she'd ordered a sugary *sfogliatina*, Caterina asked Sophie, "How can you stand to be away from your husband and children in Estonia? I could never do that. I want them in my pocket all the time. I'm so lucky to be here, in London, where my entire extended family works. We go to Italy to play."

"As a matter of fact," Sophie answered, "my husband is coming over this afternoon, and I don't have children."

We go to Estonia to play.

Caterina paused incredulously, licking sugar from her fingers. "How old are you?"

"Forty-two."

"No."

"Yes."

"You look ten years younger – much younger than me. That must be why." She laughed. "*Niente bambini.*"

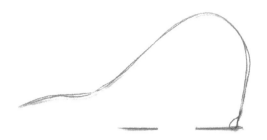

TWENTY-ONE

Niente bambini.

Sophie ran the meeting with Caterina backward and forward to herself as she waited for Tucker to arrive.

"Oxford?" Caterina had said when Sophie mentioned the weekend drive she was planning with Tucker, the getaway to the Cotswolds.

"If you are in Oxford, you have to meet Dr Vizemon. I'll make the introductions, the arrangements."

Feeling more than a little bulldozed by Caterina, Sophie felt relieved when Tucker barrelled through the arrivals doors, briefcase in hand and his hair just this side of too long.

"You cannot imagine, I…" he said, before Sophie finished his sentence.

"Almost missed the plane; they had to hold it for you; left your passport in the office, and they had to race it to the airport. Thank God it was Estonia, that's all I can say. They held the plane."

"Exactly."

Arm in arm they found the Hertz counter and collected the keys to the rental car.

"Do you know what *niente bambini* means?" Sophie asked as they pulled out of the airport.

"Nine something?"

"No, it means 'no children'. It's a question Superstar Internet Analyst Caterina asked me, incredulous. '*Niente bambini?*' As if I should have any."

"Who cares?"

"I do."

"Okay. Take it easy. You know, Love of My Life, I'd lay down my life for you, but I'm not going to spend the weekend bemoaning fertility. Let's try to keep it in check. So, she's pregnant, the font of fertility. How many kids did you say?"

"Three. With another on the way."

"The only thing you need to know is that I am behind you, a hundred per cent. I don't care about anything else. Kids, no kids. Doesn't matter. *You* matter."

Sophie squeezed Tucker's hand on the steering wheel.

"And, remember, hold off on the science. Not my strong suit. On the other hand, sex I get."

With her back aching and her abdomen swollen to twice its normal size, Sophie shifted, readjusting the seatbelt, making herself comfortable. During the hour and a half trip to Oxford from Gatwick, Tucker entertained Sophie with news from Tallinn, Latvia and Lithuania. While on occasion his vision veered towards happy delusion, his humour over proposals that rose to the top of the city council's pile only to fall, then rise again against the odds, gaining planning permission, kept things in check.

"Blenheim Palace," Tucker said, "is one thing I want to see. Churchill's ancestral home. Amazing, isn't it? Us here in England? Long way from Rye."

"Long way."

Unexpectedly, the manager at the Old Vicarage in Oxford upgraded their reservation to the wedding suite.

"The bride got cold feet." He laughed as he unlocked the door to the light and airy room, with a balcony overlooking one of the world's oldest universities.

"We like the room," Tucker said, dropping his briefcase to the floor, diving onto the bed, wrapping himself around Sophie, who yawned and had already tucked herself in.

"Let's sleep for three days," she said.

"Okay," he agreed, glancing out the window. "Look at those spires."

"There's a buzz here," Sophie said. "Can't you feel it? Maybe the students?"

"Reminds me a bit of Old Town, Tallinn." He placed one hand on Sophie's hip. "Forget about Caterina. Probably office politics. And look, if you really want to talk science, I will do my best."

They rode a bright green, tandem bicycle into and around the centre of Oxford, with Tucker doing the heavy pedalling, bought fudge on Broad Street and visited Balliol College and Christ Church Cathedral, where they lit a candle.

The next morning, after breakfast, Tucker walked into a real estate agent with Sophie.

"Anything going in the city centre?"

"We're just looking," Sophie emphasised to the realtor.

They stepped into an apartment not far from the hotel, a rabbit's warren of small rooms with rolling wooden floors from God Knows When. While Tucker discussed the price and local planning permission, Sophie shook her head.

"Hey, Soph, you're spoiling the fun. I like real estate, even pretending." He smiled at the agent, who smiled back. "It's just a game. We are not buying anything in Oxford. I promise."

In a local café, Sophie put her hand over his. "Okay, I really don't want to buy or rent another place where you are not. I'm still trying to figure out the Tallinn-London thing. Don't you think it's a bit odd we don't live in the same place, same address, yet we're married and trying to have a little one?"

"Merchant marines do it," Tucker suggested.

"Yes, they do, but I think they store the sperm."

"Or maybe they're lucky, or young."

"Or maybe somebody else is the father?" Sophie proposed.

"Maybe," Tucker agreed.

The last thing Sophie wanted to do was to meet Caterina in Oxford on her weekend away with Tucker, but as she had consented, she did. Having left Tucker with yet another real estate agent, Sophie took a taxi to a private home in Summertown, North Oxford.

Caterina's assistant profusely apologised on her boss's behalf. Something had come up; the assistant would make the introduction and come back to collect Sophie in about an hour, sooner if she wanted.

"Remember, he's a Nobel Prize front-runner," she said plainly, as if Sophie could forget.

How many times had Caterina said it?

Sophie frowned. Alexander Köhler had mentioned the name so many times that Dr Vizemon might as well have been on the Media team, sitting at every conference table, calling all the shots. Alexander had even sponsored Dr Vizemon's research, paying for many of the publications himself.

With a warm handshake, practically an embrace, Dr Vizemon welcomed Sophie into his snug study. He mentioned Alexander with respect, and only referred to Caterina as 'that analyst'. Sophie found herself enraptured, not because he had written the book on market bubbles and understood the ecstasy of the speculation that drove them, but because she found him a genuine and caring human being, who might be teetering on old age but had the spirit of youth.

Perhaps it was the genteel fire, the hot chocolate or the schnapps, but Sophie felt lulled into listening to a genius who explained everything she had been studying.

"The Internet bubble… ignoring traditional investment metrics…

the ratio of a company's current share price versus its per-share earnings..."

"Yes." Sophie felt a chorus to this gracious gentleman's speech.

"It's branding and market share. Low interest rates, technology."

"Yes."

"IPOs are fuelling the exuberance."

"Yes."

"Is the dot.com bubble bursting? Tell me what you think."

"Yes. We've got an eye on the fall-out – maybe Amazon and Google."

Taking Sophie by surprise, Caterina's assistant bustled up the walk, and straight through the front door. "Ready?"

"Yes," Sophie answered, rousing herself from the warmth of Dr Vizemon's study.

"Miss Taylor. Come back to see me at any time. Please give Herr Köhler my very best."

Sophie stretched her back as soon as she slipped into the taxi beside Caterina's assistant. She focused on breathing, while her lower spine spasmed and her belly pushed against the tight band on her dress jeans.

Had she just listened to a learned man describe the dot.com bubble as if it were just one more episode in the profound and expanding nebulae of history, as if it were something beautiful and with both precedent and future expectations? Patterns. Dutch tulips, the South Sea and South America, Japan and the value of the Imperial Palace. Now the superhighway and its dot.coms, and maybe even on the horizon a housing bubble.

"The Old Vicarage," Sophie said, while the assistant pulled a bottle of water from her bag, passing it over.

"Are you pregnant?" she asked boldly.

"Pregnant?" Sophie repeated, swallowing the water.

"My older sister is, and looking at you I just thought—"

"No. I'm not."

Clomid backache.

Tucker couldn't get enough about Dr Vizemon.

"He's a genius," Sophie said, "and a storyteller. Very down to earth, but it was hard to listen sometimes when my ovaries are exploding."

"Sorry about that." Tucker embraced Sophie. "Good news, though. I've pushed back a few meetings and can stay a bit longer."

"Thank you."

"Why thank me? We're speculating, aren't we?"

"We are," she said.

Gambling.

After Tucker flew back to Tallinn, Sophie discovered she wasn't pregnant, and decided to call the Clomid specialist.

"Why didn't you tell me how painful Clomid is? I was totally disoriented."

After a silence on the other end of the line, the doctor measured his words.

"That's it for you. I'm only authorising one cycle, not three."

"What?"

"Mrs Mägi, you need to have a husband in residence, and you have to want this baby more than anything else in the world."

"I do."

"I don't think so."

"Why? Because I am too old?"

"No. Not at all. It's simply because I'm afraid you find it impossible to let go. Having a baby is not a science project."

Robin took Sophie to lunch at the Sloane Club and commiserated.

"I don't want pity, Robin. I want to know what to do next. I've got to deal with this. Time is short."

"Or over?" Robin swirled her latte.

"Not funny. I know you are okay with no kids, and mothering

Eli's grandchildren—"

"Hey, that's below the belt."

"Sorry. I'm struggling. You know, I managed to get Tucker to have his sperm tested."

"And?"

"Disaster. They grade sperm on motility and quantity. One to five, with one being the best. His quantity is good or average, a three, but motility is – let's just say, in Tucker's case, his sperm is doing the backstroke. The options, according to the urologist, are artificial insemination using Tucker's centrifuged sperm, to see if a few can swim straight, or go straight to ICSI, which I don't know anything about."

"Did you try the fertility group?"

"It's on the list." Sophie paused. "The urologist also suggested donor sperm."

"Oh my God, where do you stop? When do you know when?"

"I don't. The Clomid was hard enough. Do I get off at the ground floor or do I go to the basement?"

"Maybe."

"Yes, but here's the kicker. My ovulation is perfect. Casebook. When Tucker left the examining room, the sperm specialist asked with a wry smile, 'Why don't you take up with someone else?'"

"Was he trying to be funny?"

"I don't know. Maybe practical. That's exactly what the woman who cuts my hair did. When her husband had zero chance she went silently raging out of the room, and when the walls began to spin, she went straight to the local pub, got smashed, picked up the best-looking guy, who happened to be a South African rugby player, and got pregnant. Turns out now, three years later, he's a decent guy, supports the kid. She also went straight to the divorce courts."

"Is that an option for you?"

"No, absolutely not."

"So, promise me you will at least check out the Fertility Club and investigate the ICSI clinic."

Surprised, Sophie looked up from her research, "Alexander, your private plane, whenever I want? That's a bit extreme, and not necessary. Estonia Air flies direct from Gatwick."

"How else are you going to get pregnant, and work for me?" He smiled like a brother.

"First, I work for Westcox Brown, and second, how do you know I'm trying to get pregnant?"

"Would it offend you if I said that once upon a time you appeared not to have a care—"

"I've got to go." She stood up, shaken, as if he had opened her desk, reviewed her fertility charts or, worse, seen every appointment with every consultant. "Pietro is up to speed. I'll meet with Caterina. Everything is ready to go. If I need to fly, Alexander, I'll fly Estonia Air."

Sophie excused herself from her own office, and left Alexander staring at an empty desk, studying the sliver of the City beyond. As Sophie pounded down the hall, then the elevator, taking herself for coffee, and then as far away from Alexander Köhler as she could get for the moment, she realised she had been spending more and more time with him, most of it unnecessary and certainly more than what she had ever understood or agreed from Pietro or from Gregory Dean's original job description.

Did I discuss fertility with him? Is it an office joke? A concern among senior management?

Even Anne Taylor had now mentioned that she thought Sophie was perhaps devoting more time to Westcox Brown, or was it to Alexander Köhler, than to herself or Tucker. Bold enough now to reserve lunch for them both without any prior discussion, Alexander had demanded Sophie's presence at even dinner too, all on the pretence of work, client service.

By now Sophie knew Alexander didn't need to work; he did it for sheer entertainment. He didn't work for wealth. In fact, his office nickname among the staff secretaries was RT – Richer Than. As Sophie took time out, had a coffee and considered her options, she knew for sure that, whatever Alexander was or was not, she was not at Westcox Brown for his amusement.

Contrite for being unprofessional, for leaving her boss sitting in her office talking to an empty chair, Sophie called Alexander, apologised for her abrupt departure and agreed to dinner. She did want to celebrate before she left for her quick break in Tallinn. The IPO had been a success, with her presentation and marketing playing the pivotal role. Even Caterina sang her praises, and from New York, the word was 'damn as in damn well done'.

As they settled into their seats at Mark's Club in Mayfair, Alexander leaned in. "Even if you are hard pressed, you still look beautiful."

"Thanks," she replied, caught off-guard by this unexpected compliment.

"Tell me," he said, "why did you marry Tucker?"

"He's my best friend," she said, "and he makes me laugh."

Alexander sat back, and then he roared, slamming a fist down on the table so hard that several waiters came running. "He makes you laugh?"

"Yes," Sophie said, startled, "he makes me laugh."

"You married someone because they make you laugh." He boomed. "What about sex?"

"Alexander," Sophie responded, "I don't know what this is all about, but I am not having this conversation with you, now or ever. I think you are taking advantage. You put me on your team as an analyst, which I have been happy to do, but you seem to want more, and that is not going to happen."

He reached over without any forewarning and pulled Sophie towards him by the back of her head, just above the neck, before kissing her directly on the mouth. For a second, her body went slack, but then, taking a second breath, she put her napkin down and placed the menu back on the table.

"*That,*" she said, "wasn't funny."

"No," he said, "it wasn't meant to be."

"Count me out. I'm not hungry. I'm going home."

"Wait."

"Grow up, Alexander. This is not a game. I'm a work colleague, and a good one. I respect you, and our friendship. I expect you to do the same."

Back at home in her garden flat Sophie tossed her key and bag on the kitchen table, with Daisy chasing after, and made her way to the bathroom. There, she splashed cold water on her face.

Why don't you take up with someone else?

Not only did her ovulation chart read perfect, but the ovulation test kit also demonstrated that her LH surge was on. From tonight through the next few days she could get pregnant. She needed to get to Tucker now.

A South African rugby player.

She picked up the phone.

Why not?

"Alexander. I will need your plane after all, if the offer still stands. I'll send it back from Tallinn."

"As you wish," he answered, unfazed. "Will I see you back in London?"

"Yes."

"Sophie, I apologise for this evening. I don't know what came over me."

"Apology accepted. We both know what came over you."

"It won't happen again."

It won't.

"Impressive!" Tucker said as he took Sophie's small bag, looking back at the midsized Cessna. "Is he leaving it running for you as well, or will you be sending it back, and you taking public transport like the rest of us pukes?"

"Don't be ridiculous. Of course it's going back. It was a nice gesture, and," Sophie smiled, "I'm ovulating."

"He lent you his private jet because he knew you were ovulating?"

"Yes, Tuck. That's right. Alexander Köhler knew I was ovulating."

After dinner in Old Town, Sophie and Tucker curled up in front of the fire at home. In her bag, Sophie had plastic cups and a plastic syringe. The urologist had suggested that she should ask Tucker to ejaculate into a plastic cup, load the syringe with the contents and then place it as close to her cervix as possible before emptying it. This might help a bit with the lack of motility, he had said, and Sophie wondered how to spring that on Tucker as she heard him singing in the shower.

When he came out of the shower, lobster-red, Sophie stared in disbelief.

"Did you just take a sauna?"

"No, a hot, relaxing shower." He dried his hair with a small towel, with another wrapped around his waist.

"Tucker, don't you remember what the urologist said? No scorching showers, cold if possible, no saunas and no drying your scrotum with a hair dryer. Your sperm is probably dead now. It will take another ninety days to regenerate when we are already dealing with sperm that doesn't go anywhere."

"Okay," he said, hopping into bed.

"Okay?"

"Okay."

"It's not okay. That's three months before you have decent sperm again! How old do you think I am? I only ovulate once a month, and look how hard it is for us to be in the right place at the right time, or even the same place at the same time."

"Don't give up," he said, snuggling close. They made love and afterwards Sophie, half-jokingly, again, did a yogic handstand against the headboard, leaving the plastic cups and syringe in her bag.

In the morning as they walked in Kadriorg Park, under the ancient elms, Tucker told Sophie about 'Artz Frankenstein'.

"He's a local fertility doctor. I don't know his real name but the secretaries call him 'Artz Frankenstein' because apparently he has this amazing track record of making babies, primarily multiple births. He's called the *kauboi*, cowboy, because he tries anything, doesn't give a hoot about statistics."

"Isn't that dangerous?"

"Only game in town, Soph. A few celebs from London and LA have visited his clinic. His website regularly shuts down with so many hits for egg donors. Estonian girls are in big demand."

"You're kidding me?"

"Nope."

"Why do they do it? There are side effects, you know."

"Probably to pay tuition or help their families out." He paused. "I also met with the Director of Children Welfare about adoption."

"You didn't."

"I did."

"What did they say?"

"She was about to throw me out, said she didn't set up adoptions for single men."

"You mentioned you had a wife?"

"Yes. So she said, 'Good. Come back with her.'"

"I'm not giving up, Tuck, not yet. I could be pregnant right now, as we speak."

"That's right," he laughed, "as we speak. I place my money on your handstand technique."

Travelling back into London on the Gatwick Express, Sophie recalled her morning in Tallinn. Tucker had already disappeared to his office, leaving a trace of his lemony cologne, while a spring snow tapped on the frosted skylight, waking her slowly. Her towheaded toddler had appeared at the head of the bed, placing a beautiful, almost luminescent face ever so gently close to hers.

"Soon." Sophie had almost reached out.

Soon.

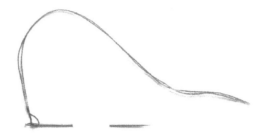

TWENTY-TWO

At Pizza Express on the King's Road, Sophie pushed a half-eaten Greek salad around, secretly studying two brown-eyed twin girls, who had instantly captured her heart. Their mother, tapping her shoulder, had asked in the overcrowded dining room if they could sit at her table, as it was for four. The girls had giggled, bringing out their glitter pens and sparkly notebooks.

Before they had a chance at much of a conversation, a waiter approached Sophie.

"There is a gentleman waiting for you outside."

Taken aback, Sophie paid her bill, said a quick goodbye to the family, and went outside. There she found Alexander's driver and the familiar dark blue Mercedes. However, it was Alexander at the wheel and the driver, after opening the rear door for Sophie, got in beside his boss.

"What's this?" Sophie asked.

"The sky is falling."

"What?"

"NASDAQ peaked on Friday at 5,049. I'm sure of it. That's a two-year increase of 226 per cent and a four-year gain of around 390 per cent. Caterina agrees. What do you think?"

"Exactly the same. Did you buy up Amazon? Ebay? The prices are low enough; if not at the bottom, close enough. Where are we going?"

"To see Dr Vizemon."

With a light rain falling on the windshield, Sophie found it odd that the stars still shone. Maybe it was just the magic of the Cotswolds. Buoyed up by Alexander's passion for the markets, she also grew excited, unable to resist his will.

Caterina met them at the door, with her eldest child in tow.

"He's in the study. This is my eldest daughter Bella."

The housekeeper served tea, as the small company pulled up chairs. Bella held Caterina's hand, both excited.

"Okay, my little banker friends," the professor said, "this is how it is going to play out over the next year. Alexander, Caterina and Sophie, you are correct. This didn't start yesterday. Most probably five years ago – 1995. Think tulips, South Sea Bubble, and now dot. com… all the same cycle. Where would we be without our human nature, our greed, our fear, our panic, our patience, our chancers?" He laughed.

"Go on." Alexander kept Dr Vizemon on course.

"You made your money on the frontend, with IPOs," he waved his hand, "but now you're going to clean up by buying the 'stars' as they fall right out of the sky. Long term this is what will pay off. By December this will be over, but just as the tulip bubble left an industry in Holland, this technology will leave behind its own truism: eventually no company will not be an Internet company – digitised, even."

Caterina squeezed Bella's hand as they shared a grin. For Sophie, that was worth the drive alone – to see that, Caterina and Bella, the mother-daughter love they shared.

"Start buying," Vizemon advised.

"Yes," they all concurred, returning cups to saucers.

As the driver took the wheel of the Mercedes on the trip back to

London, Alexander slipped in beside Sophie. If he had been her husband, she would have taken his hand, she felt so relaxed. There was nothing that needed to be said. They quietly reflected on what lay ahead. They savoured the moment as the sedan wound its way smoothly through the early-morning countryside.

Are we the lucky ones?

Sophie inadvertently touched Alexander's hand, and he folded his fingers around hers.

"You know," he finally said, "it's okay to have a friend."

"Yes." She exhaled, letting her eyes fill with tears, releasing the struggle of the last few months, maybe longer. Maybe there would be no baby, and certainly she would never have a real-life father of her own. Had she ever even thought that? Said that? Certainly she had never said it aloud, never even shared it with Anne, who always strove to be both father and mother. The early-morning sky spread out. *Like eternity itself*, Sophie thought, as she reflected on Caterina and Bella.

Mother and daughter.

Alexander pulled Sophie close, and she didn't resist as he rested his chin on the top of her head.

"Just friends, Sophie," he said. "You don't have to worry. I will never try anything again. Let's have a coffee, before we start working like dogs. What do you say? Let's go to my place."

"Okay," Sophie said. "I trust you."

New day, new dawn.

Welcoming Alexander by name, the doorman of his apartment block nodded at Sophie, who smiled. In the elevator, Alexander threw his jacket over his shoulder.

Alexander flung open the doors to the wide, almost 360-degree veranda overlooking the City. Light crawled further across the sky. Early church bells began to peal. The city air, fresh now, would soon be tainted with the descent of traffic and tourists in a few hours.

"A gin and grape juice?" Alexander asked, as an ice dispenser dropped moon-shaped cubes.

"Just grape juice," she responded.

Sipping in silence, the last bit of night sky retreated. Yawning, they both lay back on the double lounger, staring through the plate glass.

"Future at hand?"

"Future at hand."

Their heads came together and he held her hand once again.

As a friend.

She imagined again who her father might have been, then closed her eyes just for a second, before they both fell into a deep sleep.

Unembarrassed, like old friends, they ate breakfast, and agreed to see each other in the office shortly.

Sophie took Alexander's car back to her apartment in Eaton Square. She was drained from the trip to Oxford, her visit to Tallinn and the realisation that, no matter how engaged Tucker might be in baby-making, the chances of parenthood for them were slim to none. Refusing to be overwhelmed by the success of their guesswork on the NASDAQ, the work ahead and Alexander's warmth, the possibility that if they had made love, she might have conceived, Sophie smiled to herself.

I will not now, or ever, be seduced by anyone other than Tucker Tõnis Mägi.

TWENTY-THREE

Caterina, Alexander and Pietro were precise and methodical as they lined up the liquidations, well aware that all the tech company owners had cashed out for millions weeks ago.

Sophie didn't feel tranquil as she watched Caterina fling back her hair, feeling no responsibility for any of the *sar-din-ay*, as she called them.

Sardines.

"Well, I'm a sardine, Caterina," Sophie said, as all heads turned.

"Just for now." Caterina laughed. Neither Alexander nor Pietro joined in.

"I don't like what's going on here," Sophie continued. "She is listing these companies as a buy when they are clearly not. She's advising brokers across the company who represent those 'sardines' and are looking to us for advice."

Caterina jumped up and slammed down her phone in the same instant. "What are you? A *simpliciotto*." She put her hand on her pregnant abdomen.

"No, actually, I am not." Sophie stood up.

"Alexander, where did you find this one?"

"That's enough," Alexander said, standing up too. "Pietro, why don't you and Sophie take a break?"

Sophie walked through the office and then with Pietro on to the elevator.

"Let me get a cab," Pietro suggested. "We can have lunch."

"Thanks, but I'm not hungry. I'm going to walk. I thought the point today was to save the tech companies that we could – for future profit – not screw minor investors who depend on their investments. I don't get it. She's on a multimillion-dollar salary. The bank makes at least seven million on a hundred-million fundraising exercise. Why can't they just tell these companies that it's impossible to raise money for them? Tell them the truth. Switch gears and look at other companies. It's a blatant conflict of interest."

"You're right, Sophie."

"So why are you involved? It may have taken me a while to figure it out – but I don't want to be complicit. I love business. I took an MBA because I wanted to analyse and advise, not cheat people."

"Sit down." Pietro motioned her to an outdoor table at a café they were passing. "I apologise. I take full responsibility. I got you into this, and I will help get you out."

"Thank you, Pietro, but I am a grown woman. I took the job."

"Yes." He motioned to the waiter and paid for a water and an espresso. "But we didn't count on Herr Köhler, did we?"

"No, nor the ins and outs of baby-making."

Pietro leaned forward and offered her once again his pocket square.

Sophie had managed to fix up a late Friday appointment the following week at the Osbourne Fertility Clinic with Bertram Conrad, the consultant recommended by the urologist. Both Sophie and Tucker felt impatient as they waited in the grey-green reception area. A clock struck four down the hall. Tucker fiddled with his phone, while Sophie noted the stacks of charts and endless stainless-steel equipment.

Finally, after being shown into a private office, they watched a charming, athletic man spritz his hands with antiseptic from the wall-mounted dispenser.

"Hello," he said while rubbing the insides of his fingers and the backs of his hands, "so, I am Bertram Conrad and you are the Mägi family. Let's see." He scanned the files in front of him. "Not an easy business, this. And you are…" he looked at Sophie, "forty-three?"

"Forty-two."

"Okay. Semen analysis…" Conrad pursed his lips. "Not brilliant… count, motility, morphology… but not unusual. Sadly, this is becoming the norm." He looked up. "Doesn't mean it's impossible, though."

Tucker put away his phone and paid attention. "So, we have a chance?"

"To a certain degree. Childlessness is a valid lifestyle choice – sometimes voluntarily, sometimes not. Most people come to grips eventually, process it and make peace with that very real possibility."

"I'm not ready to give up yet," Sophie interrupted.

"Mrs Mägi, I'm not suggesting that. I'm just looking at the facts. Based on Tucker's – may I? – very low sperm count, backward or no movement and some abnormally shaped sperm, I'd say you will have to use some sort of intervention. Even with normal counts, older patients nowadays use IVF or ICSI. IVF, in-vitro fertilisation, is a medical procedure whereby an egg is fertilised by sperm in a test tube or somewhere else outside the body. Since the first test-tube baby in 1978, IVF has continually been developed and improved. It's now the leading method for artificial reproduction."

Tucker asked respectfully, "Aren't you – the British – rocket scientists when it comes to this?"

"Hardly." Conrad smiled. "I think it's you Americans who took the science and ran with it. Spawned an industry, as they say."

Conrad further explained that ICSI was an acronym for

intracytoplasmic sperm injection, which he said simply meant injecting or forcing the sperm into the egg.

As the meeting carried on, Tucker had to make a prearranged call to Aytama and apologetically left the room.

"Should I continue," Conrad asked, "or wait for your husband to return?"

"Continue. I'll fill him in later."

"Very well." Here Conrad became serious and focused. "You must know the odds, and statistics vary, but generally, certainly with us, the success rate for any fertility treatment is fourteen per cent for women aged between forty and forty-two, dropping to five per cent for women aged between forty-three and forty-four, and two per cent for women aged forty-five and over."

"Slim then."

"But not zero."

"Not zero," Sophie echoed.

"Sophie, here's the protocol. I'm going to examine you and see where you are with your egg development and then we'll discuss your options. If it's good, and you have an egg of at least twenty-one millimetres, we try artificial insemination with your husband's sperm, which is almost a zero chance, but I want to cover the option. Then if you agree, we move to donor sperm and from there try IVF and if necessary ICSI. Some of these procedures, the latter two, can be considered aggressive or invasive to some women. Drugs are involved and there are side effects. I also must ask if you've considered adoption."

Tucker quietly slipped back in. He took Sophie's hand. "Sorry about the phone call."

"Not to worry. I think we have a plan," Conrad answered. "Speak to reception about your next appointment."

As Dr Conrad handed the file to the receptionist, he looked directly at Sophie. "While this isn't very medical, and I am not a fortune teller, I have a good feeling about you. I'm not sure how or when, but I believe sooner or later you will be a mother."

"Thank you, but it seems almost impossible." She held back her tears.

"Start mothering." He smiled. "Anything, everything. Really."

"Yes, I will."

Sophie caught up with Tucker on the street, where an unusually hot April sun beat down and Londoners sauntered by as if in Rome. Sophie smiled too, feeling a somewhat forgotten emotion.

Hope.

"Jesus," Tucker wailed, "let's eat. What a dick! Why not give him a cheque for dispensing thin air? I mean, what did we just pay for there… telling us what we already know?"

Sophie reached up and tousled his hair. "Tucker, I love you. Thank you for showing up today. I know that this is definitely not your thing."

"So, tell me," he softened, "what did we get?"

"Hope."

After Tucker left for Gatwick, Sophie took a long walk with Daisy, collecting Robin on the way to Battersea Park.

"The shards are found throughout the jungle between Panama and Colombia – age-old sites."

"You are a breath of fresh air, Robin. I'm in the mood to discuss anything but babies and Westcox Brown."

"Great because I'm in the mood to speak English. I have felt a bit isolated. I've got another dig, in the Galapagos – to ascertain where exactly Darwin had visited and what artifacts might be found to substantiate his writings from his time on the *Beagle*."

"That's amazing."

"Okay, Sophie, tell me. You *do* want to talk babies."

"No, I just wanted to know if you would come to the ICSI clinic, the Darley Clinic, with me. Once a week they give a tour of the lab and a presentation on fertility treatments, including a film about ICSI."

"No. I'd rather you tell me about Westcox Brown."

"I can't really. I've got a confidentiality agreement."

"You don't seem happy."

"I'm not sure what is going on there, and I am not sure I want to be a part of it."

"Don't you think it's odd, Sophie, that you met Köhler in Monaco and now you are working with him here in London, zipping back and forth to Oxford, jetting to Tallinn in his private plane…" Robin paused. "Did it ever occur to you that he might be in love with you?"

"No. I mean… yes. There was a moment, but it's all sorted now." Sophie stopped. "Robin, are you sure you don't want to go see this film on ICSI with me?"

"N-O, I don't want to see rusty canisters of stored sperm while folks mill around with tea and biscuits, then sit down to view Pierce the Egg."

"Okay, I get it."

Sophie blew her a kiss. Before she had a chance to unlock the door and disentangle Daisy from her leash, a text came in: *Come to the office. Important. AK.*

Yes, Sophie texted back. *On my way.*

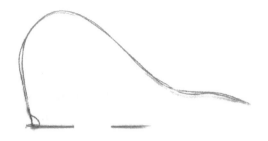

TWENTY-FOUR

Sophie walked into her office, not certain she wanted to be there any longer.

What's the urgency?

She didn't care that the market was falling at a precipitous rate. She missed Tucker already, didn't know where she might really be with *Project Bébé* and now that she understood the 'star' analyst game, she knew it wasn't her sport. She had wanted to advise leaders, sink her teeth into data and solve problems, not do in the small guy on Main Street, with his hard-earned cash.

Not be a Caterina.

Taking out her research, along with the *Financial Times* from her bag, she quietly slipped another book about babies into a side drawer of her desk to read when she had a minute. She knew she should be in a hurry, but she wasn't. Something about Alexander now frightened her. She drummed the cover of the book before closing the drawer.

Pietro popped his head into her office, asking if she wanted to join him and Marco for a movie; *Chocolat* was showing. Long before she said anything about anything, they were asking about everything. The moment she found herself depressed, wondering about decisions made or not made, especially about *Le Project Bébé*, they would ring up, asking her to join them for *Mousetrap* in the West End, a meal in the food halls at Harrods or whatever movie of the moment was on, like now. Sophie loved Pietro, and just as he understood her, she understood him, his tough situation with Marco. He would never be flying Marco to Buenos Aires to meet his strict Catholic family.

Start mothering, anything and everything.

Sophie recognised she loved Pietro like a son, and imagined he protected her the way a son might look after his mother. In doing the math, she realised that if she had had a child at twenty, he would now be the exact same age as Pietro.

Moving into the empty conference room, she hoisted her research onto the table and flipped open her laptop.

Alexander walked in, greeted her professionally and took the seat beside her. The scent of his fresh cologne sharpened her senses in some way. His exuberance flooded the room, and everyone, not just Sophie, was caught up on the wake. The whole building buzzed.

Who would make a killing?

Did her feelings for Alexander, like those for Pietro, count as mothering? Bertram Conrad's words rang continuously in her ears. She admitted she loved almost everything about Alexander: his organisation, his sophistication, his brilliance. She had fleetingly, like a kid in grade school crushing on another pupil, imagined what it might have been like to be Mrs Köhler.

"Penny for your thoughts," he whispered, as the rest of the team, including Caterina, filed in.

"Not for sale," she said.

Microsoft and the antitrust lawsuit led the agenda. Caterina, inadvertently touching her pregnant abdomen, again, led the discussion, as Sophie listened, twiddling her pen.

"Microsoft is guilty of monopolising, but what does this mean in the long run?"

"They will be broken up," Sophie answered. "The bull market is over."

"So where is the profit?" Caterina asked.

"Acquiring on the cheap," Pietro added.

"The law of the market will always prevail. Value is essential," Alexander said.

Sophie felt a long way from Rye, listening to the thrill in the room, taking in the view, and just for a minute succumbed to the small happiness of being part of a team, in the right place at the right time, doing exactly what she was meant to be doing. Everything felt buoyant and easy. She wanted to call Tucker, thank him for being generous, understanding even more than she had initially understood. She needed to be somewhere where she could work, use her talent, feel alive.

"Sorry," she called out to the group, startling them with her interruption. "I need to make a phone call."

Tucker took it at once, surprised to hear her voice. Before she could say anything, she burst into tears.

"Sophie, what's wrong?"

"Nothing. I just wanted to say I love you, and that I am grateful that we are who we are, you are who you are. I don't care if Caterina is a baby-making machine or if we ever have a child or not."

"Thank you, Soph, but you do want a child, and we will get there. And by the way, who gives a fuck about Caterina?"

"Not me," Sophie said.

Snapping her phone closed, Sophie took a breath, and swivelled away from her tiny view of the City. Alexander stood in the doorway.

"Everything okay?" he asked.

"Yes."

"Lunch? Dinner?"

"Lunch? Impossible. May I let you know later about dinner? I'm trying to ascertain which of the 'stars' have long-term, fundamental value."

Taking her files from her briefcase, along with the fertility folder, which always seemed to be tucked in, she paused for a minute, studying her chart. She was ovulating again. How could she have missed it? The next eight days would be critical. What was she doing here in London with Alexander, and not in Tallinn with Tucker?

Bad luck.

She turned to her slice of famous London skyline, now suffused with a grey-blue light, almost white.

A *silver lining.*

She closed her eyes and heard Bertram Conrad's words: "Not very medical of me, but I think you will be a mother."

Sophie worked nonstop, having lunch at her desk, twisting her pearls as she worked almost to breaking point. The big questions had for the most part now been answered; the team knew mostly which companies they would watch bottom out and then purchase. They had a plan through the end of the year, when the dot.com bubble they forecast should be completely deflated.

At about eight o'clock, Alexander startled her, reminding her about dinner.

"I'd completely forgotten," she admitted, closing her laptop, her desktop and open files.

"You need to eat. How about the Connaught?"

She had wanted to say 'no'. She had wanted to bury herself in cleaning up assumptions, and cleaning up the narrative. With Tucker miles away and *Project Bébé* beginning to feel like a pipe dream, maybe riding the dot.com bubble with Alexander and Westcox Brown might be her only success. Looking up again at that shiny City lining still glimmering, Sophie suddenly saw the dot.com speculation, the work she was doing, was like a fun-house with a never-ending row of mirrors, repeating itself over and over, and over again, inflating, deflating, re-inflating and replicating again.

Never-ending.

Hadn't she recently felt 'right place, right time'? But Tucker's voice had thrown everything out of balance, into disarray. She recalled for an instant the smooth glide of the banister under her hand as she walked up the polished stairs at Estonian House in midtown Manhattan on that bright May day: the sight of an onion-domed church, fields of wheat and a hewn log cabin.

Her choice.

Now invested in Westcox's success, Alexander's and her own, she questioned everything she had thought before, namely *Project Bébé.* What did she want? A baby? Investment banking? City of London? Had her MBA taken her where she had wanted to go? Industry adviser?

No.

Alexander Köhler could do what he wanted, when he wanted, how he wanted. He didn't need to work. He toiled for fun. He'd been a billionaire since birth, born with bottomless pockets, could turn on a dime, a whim, but she couldn't. She had a life, a career and a husband, and to work those levers carefully, cleverly, lovingly, fairly all the time, just to keep things in balance – to make a living and to have a life – made it seem all the more challenging, not to mention having a baby.

Even Caterina could play out her dream. She enjoyed the rise and fall of the market because she knew she made the market. The dot.com debacle would only stoke her love affair with the market, all the while maintaining her progression of babies and her Sunday lunches *con la famiglia.*

That's it.

Sophie snapped the last file shut and stood up, taking her jacket from behind the office door.

Ordering a San Pellegrino with lime at the Connaught, Sophie calculated. No matter the size of the paycheque, the cost might just be too high, no matter the use of talent, as Tucker would argue. Ovulating almost two thousand miles away from the man she loved didn't work, and the sad fact was that at her age, despite menstruation, ovulation didn't automatically happen every month.

Like clockwork.

She needed, wanted, to be with Tucker, and she didn't want to play the 'analyst' way that Caterina did, and there was something else she couldn't quite put her finger on.

"*Ciao, bella*," Alexander greeted her, seating himself beside her before she could finish her thought. "I have brought good news." He threw an arm around her shoulder and over the back of the banquette.

She poured his water, adding ice and lemon, rather than lime. "What's happened?"

Sophie smiled at this man, with whom she had now shared tables at most of the top restaurants in London. They had sat side by side at the Royal Opera House, entertaining Japanese guests, enjoying *La Traviata* and *Don Giovanni*. Pietro, and sometimes even Marco, had joined them, but tonight as friends they were on their own, had made no real plans.

Sophie listened to Alexander recite the events of his day. The truth was she liked paying attention to what he said. He knew the markets inside out. He wasn't a chancer, a speculator. He handled the markets like a Rubik's cube, appreciated their psychology, the driver, the euphoria one minute and panic the next. In his presence, she saw things as he did.

Alexander's hand folded over hers as it had in the car returning from the Cotswolds, and the rush of Monaco came back, the mistimed kiss and his apology. Without a hint of seduction in the air, they ate, talking through the forecast of events from now until December. After so much time spent together, his touch felt like that of a child taking a mother's hand or perhaps, yes, even a father placing a gentle one over his daughter's.

Mother anything, everything.

They left the restaurant, with Alexander motioning the driver off, suggesting they walk, if Sophie felt up to it.

"Yes," she said.

"Good," he answered, putting a protective arm around her as they took in the warm London air and the sound of night traffic.

"So why don't you have a wife?" Sophie asked unexpectedly.

"I do." He paused. "It's this." He waved at nothing in particular. "My work. Westcox Brown. The market. I hope this doesn't frighten you, but I could have married someone like you. You are perfect."

"If only that were true," she said.

"I'm thinking about writing a book."

"Brilliant. What on?"

"On speculation, the markets, investor behaviour. Maybe you could help."

Alexander walked Sophie to her door, while a light rain started to fall.

"Alexander, meeting you, working with you, has been a privilege. I have no idea what you should do next, and you don't need my opinion or my help, really. You are always ten moves ahead of the next person. But I do have another question. How is it that you have access to practically anything, anywhere, at any time?"

He closed his eyes.

"Sophie, my family is wealthy, always has been, dating back centuries. Köhlers have given so much to so many for so long, and that's how doors open. That obligation is now mine. While the markets are about making money, they are not just about gain, but the game – a way of life even. Not for everyone. I aim to contribute as much as to gain. I've been looked after by a lot of people, organisations, even before my parents died."

"You're an orphan?"

"At my age?" He laughed.

"How old were you when it happened?"

"Ten."

"I'm sorry."

"Yes, it was crazy, going through all that so young," he admitted.

"I am sure," Sophie said, and kissed him goodnight on the cheek. "See you Monday."

"See you Monday," he said, then, turning back, he added, "I almost forgot, the news. You and Caterina are coming with me to New York. Or maybe I should say, I'm coming with you two."

Sleeping to almost eleven the following day, Sophie ate breakfast and took Daisy for a long walk. She found it difficult to take in Alexander's history.

An orphan.

"Sophie, what's up?" Tucker shouted into the phone.

"Ready for Conrad move *Numero Uno*?" Sophie asked.

"Sure, I'm ready."

"Yes. Let's go. AI… artificial insemination."

Sophie studied her multicoloured charts, still ovulating, still casebook. She wondered if they should move straight to ICSI, but while Conrad had said they should move quickly, he had also said that they should move step by step; and artificial insemination, with her eggs looking so good, using Tucker's sperm, would be the first, least invasive step.

TWENTY-FIVE

"Perfect. Twenty-five millimetres. A better than perfect egg," Bertram Conrad said. "Let's get started."

Tucker handed his sperm sample to the assistant, as he was handed paper slippers and a paper hat, as well as a green surgical gown.

"Get ready." The assistant smiled. "Your wife is being prepped now. What sort of music do you want?"

"Music?" Tucker asked, as they walked along the corridor.

"Yes, some people bring their own."

"I didn't."

"Well, I have Mozart, or the theme tune for *Star Wars*." A second assistant flicked through a stack of CDs. "Neil Sedaka's Greatest Hits—"

"Neil Sedaka? No thanks, let's go for *Star Wars*."

Tucker loomed over Sophie in his disposable green gown and cap.

"Surgery, anyone?" he offered. "I got a porno magazine, and because another guy was using the ejaculation room – I mean, sample room – they shoved me in the loo. Good thing that wasn't full, or they'd have put me in the broom closet."

Laughing, Sophie hardly felt anything as the catheter and the washed sperm threaded their way to her uterus through her cervix. It was all over just beyond the *Star Wars* fanfare.

"Good chance of success here," Bertram said as he snapped off his gloves, and shook Tucker's hand.

While Tucker disrobed, Sophie stayed prone for another hour in another room.

"See you in an hour and a half at Pizza on the Park," Tucker said, as he kissed her goodbye. "Feeling lucky?"

Over an American Hot pizza with pepperoni and a house red for Tucker and San Pellegrino for Sophie they compared their experiences.

"Well done us," they joked like teenagers. Then, arm in arm, they strolled through Hyde Park, playing 'what if' games. 'What if' they actually had a baby? Boy or girl? Twins – it could happen with IUI, intrauterine insemination, or AI, artificial insemination. First names? Family names? None of his – too Estonian, too hard to spell, never mind pronouncing. Should they live in London? Tallinn? Return to the USA?

Seduced by children, of all ages, in sports gear, with mums, with dads, in strollers, prams, their questions kept coming. They rode a Victorian carousel, and then wandered down Walton Street, where Sophie popped into the same curio shop where she had bought her slender rocking horse.

"What'd you buy?"

"A surprise." She smiled.

At home, Daisy whined, so Tucker took her out before they all piled into bed, watching an old favourite, *ET*. Before lights out, Sophie unwrapped her package, placing the carefully embroidered sign over the brass doorknob.

"'BABY SLEEPING.'" Tucker read it aloud. "You bet. That would be me. I'm bushed."

Cuddling together, they both studied the new talisman,

both regretting they would be travelling on Monday, in opposite directions – she to New York City and he back to Estonia while Daisy went to a boarding kennel that picked up from the local vet. Unusually, the spaniel rested her head over Sophie's flat stomach and sighed.

"Tucker," Sophie said, just before falling asleep. "I am going to quit Westcox Brown. I am coming home."

"To Tallinn?"

"Yes. To Tallinn."

On the ordinary flight to New York, Sophie reread her files on the bubble, the bust and the dot.coms with remaining value. She, Caterina and Alexander would be presenting to Westcox Brown's New York-based CMT team, including three senior partners.

BABY SLEEPING.

She had lost her battle at the airport in WHSmith, broke down and bought *Mother & Baby* magazine, poring over it more intently now than any of the files for the New York team. She said no to coffee, to alcohol and the soft, white dessert cheese offered by the air steward.

Caterina met Sophie at JFK, whisking her off to the Conrad New York Downtown Hotel, not far from Westcox Brown in Lower Manhattan, where they ate a late lunch, ostensibly to catch up on business and review the next day's presentation.

Sophie asked her question as soon as the oversized menus were placed in their hands.

"What can pregnant women eat?"

"Whatever you like," Caterina said like an old pro. "It doesn't really make any difference. I ate whatever I wanted, even shellfish – marinated shrimp with caviar and scallions, octopus and potato salad, fried eel, crab salad, spaghetti with shrimp, macaroni with clams and artichokes, shellfish with squid ink pasta, pan-fried squid with white beans. *And* soft white cheese."

"No." Sophie laughed.

"Yes," Caterina said, "all of it. Okay, maybe I was careful with baby number one, Bella, but by pregnancy number four, forget it. I believe in germs. Think about it. What I do for a living, I am constantly travelling, eating out, and who knows what goes on in half of these kitchens, and let's not even talk about stale air in aeroplanes or hotels. What could be worse than that?"

Caterina lifted her glass. "We are toasting."

"What are we toasting?"

"You," Caterina said, leaning back in her seat, "me, Alexander, Pietro, the tech bubble, fundamentals – and the flaming fact that I am carrying twins."

"No."

"*Sì.*"

"I don't know what to say."

"For today, Sophie, say I'm sorry. Because I am really sorry that I'm a f'ing bloody baby-making machine."

The two women faced off.

"And by the way," Caterina said, beginning to slur her words, "be careful. People are talking. You can't be blind. Köhler is in love with you."

"Don't be ridiculous, Caterina. We are colleagues, that's it."

As lunchtime turned into evening, Caterina refused to discuss the presentation and Sophie let her grumble and complain before finally excusing herself.

"You know you shouldn't bemoan not having kids," Caterina said, leaving the table. "It's not all it's cracked up to be."

Sophie nodded without saying anything, then paid the bill and finally made her way to her room. It never made sense to her where lightning, or life, for that matter, struck – science or not, Caterina was a lightning rod.

Twins?

The women had agreed to meet in the morning. Sophie didn't take anything Caterina had said seriously but did momentarily wonder about her comments concerning Alexander and her overt knowledge that Sophie wanted a baby. Was it written on her face?

Sophie waited, working away in her hotel room on the presentation all morning, expecting Caterina to telephone, to at least verbally go over their game plan, to have breakfast, maybe. While not really necessary, Westcox Brown New York always checked up on its European partners, and Sophie in particular wanted to make a good show, especially as she was the only American on the London-based team.

Caterina telephoned minutes before Sophie had intended to walk out of the hotel. "I'm not feeling well, Sophie. Let's meet for dinner. You'll be fine. I am sorry. I just can't make it this morning. I am sure you understand."

Before Sophie could respond, Caterina hung up. On the short walk to the Westcox building, Sophie weighed up whether or not she could make a quick trip to Westchester County to see the old haunts. She even considered calling in at Estonian House to see the old gentleman who had stood behind the high, towering, glass wall.

"What's going on with Caterina?" Alexander shouted into the phone. "She's a no-show. I'm catching a cab now from JFK."

"Don't know either," Sophie shouted back.

Twins.

"What?"

"Don't worry," Sophie said. "I have this."

Alexander made his way into the conference room as she finished the presentation, and the two New York partners jockeyed for position.

"How long are you staying?"

"Lunch?"

Alexander intervened, and just as he was accepting the invitation, Sophie interrupted.

"Sorry, gentlemen. I can't join you. I have a plane to catch."

Smaller than a grain of rice, she dreamt of her baby, before actually falling asleep, as Concorde made its short three-hour flight towards London. She couldn't get home soon enough.

"Miscarriage," she heard the ER attendant say. "Nothing major. Get some rest."

Nothing major.

Did the transatlantic flight cause the miscarriage? Stress? She had been pregnant. Maybe it was work, or the clear understanding, deep down, that despite the wide berth they had now given her thanks to Alexander at Westcox Brown, she didn't want to be the kind of analyst they really expected, or maybe it was the shock of Caterina's disappearance and her comments about Alexander's intentions and kids not being all they're cracked up to be; maybe it was that the risk was not worth the reward, or maybe the early miscarriage was caused by the clear, concise and immediate decision she had made to leave Westcox Brown.

She would see Anne later, take a few minutes to curl up and cry. She had known when the tiny grain of rice had let go, and the miscarriage had ensued. She went like a homing pigeon to the International Women's Club Fertility Group. Having already gone twice, she wanted to talk about miscarriage, loss, hope and Conrad Move Number Two: donor sperm.

"Hang with them," Robin had said. "They know. I don't. I'm temporarily setting up shop in Santo Domingo. I've been awarded a multiple-site dig."

The group met in a Knightsbridge townhouse on Cadogan Square owned by the chair, who had started the group five years earlier, when she had had a third failed cycle of IVF. Most of the smartly dressed women were young, in their late twenties, and traumatised, dealing with issues unrelated to age.

The chair's five-year-old son, apparently conceived naturally, sat on the stairwell overlooking the living room. Ten women sipped tea, ate healthy snacks and discussed treatments Sophie had never heard of. Feeling like an interloper, she didn't want to say that her ovulation was casebook perfect, but that she was forty-two.

"Your issue is age," the chair said without pausing and without malice. They talked over and around Sophie.

Age.

"I'm game," one woman said. "I don't care if it takes twelve cycles."

"I'm flying to Belgium tomorrow."

Everyone smiled frankly.

"Stem cell innovation. Mitochondria can be added to a poor-quality egg. It could possibly increase the odds."

Sophie nodded along with the others, and then quietly slipped away, but not before acknowledging the little boy, who seemed to her forlorn, abandoned, as if his mother were very far away.

Outside, walking towards the King's Road, Sophie thought of Tucker in his paper hat in the insemination room.

Fuck it.

Sophie laughed aloud just as a woman touched her arm. Sophie recognised her from the fertility group.

"Hi," she said, "forgive me, but I just wanted to catch up with you and ask if you wanted to speak. We have a couple who monopolise the group, and not everyone gets a chance."

"Honestly, I'm good," Sophie told her. Then, detecting the other woman's accent, asked, "Where are you from?"

"Austria."

"So, how's your fertility?" Sophie smiled.

"Been there, done that. I just took a friend today who is flagging a bit. Will have to do ICSI. Her husband's sperm is poor."

"I might too, but where do you draw the line? When do you just stop?"

"Some don't. I did ICSI twice. I have a little boy now, just a few weeks old. It's tough. I'm not going to do it again. I still don't feel

188

well. The drugs are so strong. There are side effects no one really wants to talk about. If I were on my own, I would adopt."

"So why didn't you?"

"My husband wanted his 'own' child."

The slight woman in the navy pea coat said she had to run, but before leaving she told Sophie, "Good luck, but don't fool yourself. There are repercussions from any treatment – side effects for you and your newborn, too."

Before Sophie had a chance to say anything else, the slight Austrian woman waved goodbye and disappeared into a crowd of shoppers.

Side effects? For me and my newborn.

Sophie imagined Robin holding her phone, leaning over a railing, perhaps surrounding a terrace, overlooking a beach near Ensanche Piantini in the Dominican Republic.

"Okay, talk to me," Robin said.

"Another fail. Who knows why? Insemination doesn't always work."

"I'm sorry, Sophie."

"Thanks, but there's no need."

"It may be too early for this, but I have a cousin who adopted two children from Ukraine. She heads up one of the top paediatric pulmonary practices in California. Now why would she adopt when she is a doctor by training and has probably one of the top assisted conception departments in the world within spitting distance? Maybe have a chat with her?"

"Okay. Text me the number. I'm not quite ready yet, but almost. Can't hurt to talk. I'm supposed to go watch a film on ICSI at a different fertility clinic. They serve champagne, along with the tour."

"Have you thought about when you might call it quits?"

"I don't know, but I have thought if I am not pregnant by Christmas, or with a baby in my arms, maybe I should divorce, just let Tucker go."

"What?"

"He deserves a family."

"Well, what is a family, Sophie?"

"Children."

"Not for everyone."

Meeting Anne at Foliage in the Mandarin Oriental Hotel was a welcome relief from Westcox Brown, fertility clubs and even the daily weighing up of what to do about Tucker and Tallinn.

Haven't I already decided to quit Westcox Brown, return to Tallinn? Haven't I talked it over with Pietro and Marco so many times?

Sophie admitted she loved turning everything over to her mother, even for a few minutes, which seemed to settle, at least for a while, the storm raging in her head. It had always given her a sense of balance, a chance to think, slow down. Sophie admired her mother as she ordered her favourite fried zucchini and *pasta primavera*, with *mocha granita* for dessert. She always seemed to have it together.

Once they settled in and the maître d' stopped fawning, Anne turned softly but firmly towards her daughter.

"What's going on with you and Alexander?"

"Alexander?"

"Listen, my love. It's rarefied. Everything you share with me about him is just a bit exclusive, and has always been, since you first met him in Monaco. Do you recall? I think you are forgetting yourself and underestimating the power you might have over him, or even what he may really want from you, other than your analytical skills."

"He's a colleague, Mom."

"You don't think he may have engineered your coming to Westcox Brown?"

"No. I don't. The offer came through Pietro."

Mother and daughter ate in silence, listening to the soft sounds of refined dining.

"Mom, I know you have my best interests at heart. You always do. You might be right. I am worried, and I do plan to resign. I miss Tucker and making a baby long-distance at my age is impossible, if not ridiculous – no matter what Alexander may or may not be up to. I truly believe, Mom, that despite a few moments, Alexander is just a friend, a colleague. Nothing more."

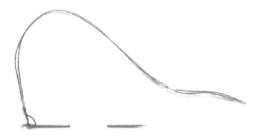

TWENTY-SIX

Monday morning, Sophie called Alexander's office to schedule an appointment. She needed to, wanted to, get things back on a professional basis. If even Anne found their relationship suspect, it probably was questionable. Maybe Caterina had been right. Maybe this was, for Alexander, love. She wanted to thank him and she wanted to hand in her resignation. She wanted to go home, wherever Tucker was – to Tallinn.

"Whenever it is convenient for Mr Köhler," she said.

"Tricky schedule, but we know he always makes you a priority."

"Thank you, but that won't be necessary. Just an open slot in the diary."

"That won't be until late Wednesday, 4pm, or Friday, late."

"Fine."

No sooner had Sophie snapped her phone closed, than Alexander suddenly and unexpectedly stood towering over her at the entrance to Westcox Brown. Any passerby might have thought that they had arrived together, a couple.

"Morning." He grinned.

"Morning," she said, "I just called your office. I need to speak with you."

"Why didn't you just call me?"

"I would like to speak with you—"

"Dinner tonight then," he called back as he raced into the building. "The usual."

Harry's Bar was all but empty when Sophie arrived. As was typical, she arrived early, and had time to reflect. In many ways, she didn't want to say goodbye to Alexander. He had time for her, something Tucker often didn't. She was seduced by his genius and the last many months had been the pinnacle of many things she had once only dreamt of, but now her dreams were changing. Isn't that what Pietro and Marco said, 'dreams change'?

As soon as he bolted in through the door and across the dining room, Sophie melted. She felt again that he had become a brother, a father. She trusted him, and for the first minutes at the restaurant, she just let him take over, as usual, even once again ordering for her.

"I bought the restaurant for the evening." He laughed and quickly kissed her on either cheek. "So, talk."

Rarefied.

She wasn't ready to open up just yet so they talked about any number of things, until, over a pot of fresh mint tea at the end of the meal, and putting a hand over his, she found herself saying at last, "Alexander, I'm quitting. I'm moving back to Tallinn."

"Don't."

"This life is not for me. I loved business school, and I am grateful for the opportunity you've given me. What a ride it's been, but this is not for me. There's more to life than following the market. It's all one large casino, really, which I love, but I want something different. I care about my Tucker, and while I am creative here, I want something else, to make a difference, a contribution, an impact. Something more tangible. I want to be with my husband."

"I love you, Sophie."

"Alexander, if this were a different time, place—"

"Look at this," Alexander said, interrupting her, pulling a carefully printed document from the Darley Fertility Clinic out of his attaché case. He slid the report in front of her.

Sophie sat horrified, ready to smack him. Alexander's scores read perfectly down the page from motility to quantity. Speechless, then alarmed, she regained her composure. "This is none of your business. How did you know any of this?"

"Who doesn't know, Sophie?"

"I'm quitting, Alexander, consider this my resignation dinner. You'll have my letter on your desk tomorrow morning."

As she stood up, he pulled her back, into an embrace.

"Stop," Sophie said loudly, pushing him away, and the maître d' came forward at once.

"A taxi, madam?" he asked.

"Yes." She pulled on her jacket, looking back at Alexander for one second, with his folder opened, details of his perfect sperm count spelled out before him along with his perfect textbook sadness.

In the cab, Sophie turned what might have been tears into a precise analysis. Robin had been right. Tucker, too. Even her mother, and Caterina. She and Alexander could never be just friends. Leaning her head on the headrest and closing her eyes, she wanted only one thing now: to get home, first to her flat on Eaton Square, and then to Tallinn.

She texted Tucker: *I love you. Be home soon.*

At the apartment, pulling out her laptop, she wrote a simple resignation letter addressed to Alexander. Then she found her fertility chart, reminding her of a lottery ticket, thick with columns of red, yellow, green – period started, day one, two, three, four; light spotting, day five; circle day six, dry; day seven, dry; circle day eight, slight thick mucus; day nine to sixteen, baby, baby, baby,

baby, baby, baby, baby, baby, dry days; day seventeen no mucus; right on out to day twenty-one.

"Hi," she said quietly to the cover of her *Mother & Baby* magazine, "I'm not giving up on you. I will find you. Soon." And in the morning, after posting her resignation letter, Sophie called Bertram Conrad.

TWENTY-SEVEN

"Bertram, I don't have it in me," she said over the phone. "I missed the boat or maybe I am just not cut out for children. This isn't anything I planned, or didn't plan. It just didn't or won't happen. Besides, I am leaving London."

"Sophie, if I may?" Bertram entreated. "It's not my role to cheerlead, or mislead. Let's see where you are. If you've got a proper-sized egg, we can try artificial insemination with donor sperm as planned, or not. Your choice, always. You can still travel."

"I think I've had enough."

"If I may, you don't sound yourself. May I suggest we follow the protocol? Come in. We will remain ready all day. If it's a green light, we go."

Sophie took her tea in bed, while Pietro and Marco took Daisy for a long walk, reminding her they were thinking about going to the opera or the cinema that night and that it would do her good. She weighed Conrad's suggestion.

Follow the protocol.

At that moment all she wanted was a bottomless cup of tea and to sit cross-legged, leaning against the headboard, sipping for

196

eternity. Alexander, Westcox Brown and London were over. As she sipped the dark Harrods special blend from the tall mug Tucker had brought from Tallinn, she studied the design of medieval buildings around it.

She thought of Westcox Brown's sleek building and of Alexander, who had texted. She studied the pastel Hanseatic League buildings surrounding her square – Raekoja Plats. Mesmerised by the tiny world warming her palm, the townhouses seemed to wink at her.

Don't give up.

"Okay," Sophie told the clinic registrar, "I'll be in this afternoon, today, prepared for anything."

"That's wonderful," the secretary said. "I've pencilled you in."

"Thanks," Sophie said, feeling that Bertram and his staff were becoming family, something the fertility articles warned against. She wondered if she should call Tucker and tell him. Coupled with his preoccupation with another site and his inability to retain the alphabet – LH, FSH, IUI, ICSI, IVF – Sophie chose not to call him right away.

The sonogram showed a perfect, twenty-one-millimetre egg.

Casebook.

Sophie signed forms, and after agreeing to the blue-eyed, blond-haired mystery donor, turned herself over to the clinic staff. *Where No Man Has Gone Before* rumbled in the background, as Sophie laughed, listening to the intergalactic space opera once again.

In the same post-IUI room, less than thirty minutes later, the nurse suggested Sophie keep her feet up and take a nap, which she did until her phone vibrated.

"Robin," Sophie almost shrieked.

"That would be me," Robin said.

"Where are you?"

"Here."

"London?"

"Yes."

"Come and get me. Please."

"Okay. Where are you?"

"Osbourne Fertility Clinic. Park Crescent."

After buying a few delicacies from Harrods, they walked to Hyde Park and rented two canvas sun loungers. They relaxed in companionable silence for a while, until Robin finally spoke. Instead of chatting about Santo Domingo, her most recent dig and another rare find, she spoke about something else entirely.

"Brace yourself," she warned.

"Okay," Sophie answered, shaking the last bit of icing sugar from her fingers, "I'm steady."

"I'm expecting."

Sophie jumped up. "As in 'having a baby'?"

"As in 'having a baby'. Long, breezy nights in Santo Domingo, I guess."

"I am so happy for you."

"Not so fast," Robin added. "My GP has read me the riot act: the risk – older mom, gran, nan thing – is defects."

"Down's?"

"Yes."

They both knew it meant blood tests, scans, a CVS – a chorionic villus sampling – and amniocentesis, sampling cells from the foetus. The test would confirm anomalies but also carried a risk of miscarriage. Sitting until past dusk, they only relinquished their loungers when the chair warden came to collect them. They fed the geese, hugged and each went their own way, Robin to meet Eli, and Sophie to meet Marco and Pietro, who had bought last-minute tickets for Rossini's *La Cenerentola* at the Opera House.

2WW, Sophie texted Tucker that night, even though he already knew she opted with his agreement for the Conrad next option: donor sperm.

Two-week wait.

Over the phone they did not discuss 'what ifs'; instead they put their heads together and counted all the benefits of going childless.

"Having you all to myself," Tucker started.

"Being the *only* child." Sophie chuckled.

"Centre of the universe."

"Enjoy other people's kids."

"Focus only on you."

"Focus only on *you*," she retorted.

"Do what I want, when I want."

"Spur of the moment."

"No screaming babies, teenagers. Yikes."

"One up on all the half-wits who didn't have a clue what they were doing, and now regret having a kid."

"Be richer. Less stressed."

"No bedtime reading, cajoling, discussions of vaccines, disease, schools, diapers, toilet training, breast pumps."

"Better job opportunities. St-Jean-Cap-Ferrat, instead of Disneyland Paris."

"In the end leaving all our money to Médecins Sans Frontières, rather than kids who stalk us for their inheritance."

"Tell me again. Why do we want a kid?"

"For the sheer joy of it."

"Okay." They both laughed.

Over the next two weeks, Sophie spent time seeing everything she'd missed in London when buried under the mountain of work at Westcox Brown. She caught every show, loving life as a tourist. She had no idea if Alexander had attempted to contact her because she'd blocked his phone and his email address. The single, simple bouquet of lily of the valley he'd sent, she accepted, and then without remorse tossed away the minute they yellowed. It was over. She acknowledged his apology and made hers for whatever role she had mistakenly played.

Sophie packed, read baby magazines and scoured the Internet for business ideas, looking half-heartedly for jobs in Tallinn. Tucker had said he had ideas, but they could wait.

Start her own business?

"I'm so happy you are still in London," Sophie practically shouted into the phone as Robin picked up.

"Sophie, it's seven in the morning. What is it?"

"End of 2WW. I haven't started my period. I can't do the test alone. I don't want it to be negative."

"You can."

"No. I can't. Please? Come over."

"Okay. Two hours. Let me wake up. You know we're leaving for Santo Domingo tonight?"

"Thank you, Robin. You are a true friend."

"Okay, but you know what this means, don't you?"

"I owe you lunch?"

"No. You have now gone past the 'it doesn't really matter one way or the other' stage."

"Okay. I agree, but just get here, ASAP. It's not the test; it's the results."

"I get it. See you shortly. Take Daisy for a walk. Oh, and breathe."

The value carton, three-pack test kit sat on the bathroom vanity. With Daisy on the leash, knowing the way to Battersea, Sophie went on autopilot, alternately talking herself into and out of one result and then the other.

Stay calm.

Of course, she told herself, *I hope, but I get it – the odds are zero.* Did she care that Robin's pregnancy was now definitely confirmed by ultrasound? If it could happen naturally for Robin, couldn't it happen for her, even with, or *especially* with, a blue-eyed, blond-haired, tall mystery donor? Daisy pulled against the leash, finally turning Sophie back towards the garden flat. Even the Japanese pagoda or strutting peacocks in Battersea could not distract either one of them from the looming pregnancy test.

Robin showed up right on time with two coffees and two croissants.

"Caffeine?" Sophie screeched. "You can't drink caffeine. It has a negative effect on—"

"I'm pregnant already."

"But the embryo?"

"You are in too deep, Sophie. If this baby wants to hang with me, secure her ticket to ride through the pollution in Santo Domingo, the best soft, white cheese around and Eli's Havana cigar smoking, then a latte is nothing. I'm prepared for anything, including miscarriage, which I am told is a very real possibility, along with birth defects, and yes, I am going to have an amniocentesis. And if that is not conclusive, we will opt for the CVS."

"You're right."

"Unwrap the stick," Robin said, taking a sip of her coffee.

Disappearing into the bathroom with the three-pack set, Sophie froze. Not really wanting to know the results if negative, she regretted persuading Robin to come over, to help her process the results – good or bad, positive or negative. With the entire world seeming deathly still, Sophie listened carefully, and to her relief she heard the distinct, subterranean rumble of an underground train passing by.

"Inconclusive," she called out to Robin.

"Okay, try again. They're supposed to be foolproof. Ninety-nine per cent accuracy."

Robin waited by the bathroom door.

"Positive," Sophie whispered, her stomach swooping and her knees buckling. "I'm going to take one more test just to make sure."

Speechless, they hugged, and barely made it out the door to the Chelsea open-air market. They grinned, thunderstruck. Finally, after ordering an omelette, Robin said, "Go ahead, say it out loud."

"I'm a mom!"

"Good. Now for a strong cup of coffee…" Robin joked. "Just kidding."

"We're both pregnant."

"Don't you want to call Tuck?"

"I want to sit with this for a minute. He's on his way in from Gatwick now."

"Congratulations, Sophie."

"Thank you."

"Be courageous. It's not unreal. I can't believe you had to take three tests!"

"Unreal. Think about it… Fifty per cent chance of miscarriage, fifty per cent chance of abnormalities and equally a fifty per cent chance of going full term, with a fifty per cent chance of a healthy baby. I don't want to know any more, any more statistics."

"Now let's get really real. Can't sit around wrapped in cotton wool, incubating."

"I know, but right now, this instant, I want to be really still, enjoy this moment, being pregnant. I am thrilled, Robin, and if nothing else, I'm happy, really happy."

"Fair enough. Let's go find Eli and grab my bags, if you are catching a lift with us to Gatwick."

At Gatwick, Robin and Eli caught their flight back to Santo Domingo, while Sophie surprised Tucker with the news that she would meet him off the plane. Excited by the possibility, even if early days, Sophie wanted to celebrate with her husband, who she knew would whoop, and twirl her around, and say, "I knew it!"

Sophie bought the new issue of *Mother & Baby* and a second copy of *What to Expect When You're Expecting* for Tucker, keeping it hidden in the WHSmith bag. Lingering in arrivals, Sophie bought an oversized, illuminated Swatch watch, which she assumed she'd need, fast-forwarding to getting up in the night to feed a little one.

Without fanfare, Tucker emerged, bag thrown over his shoulder, head down, determined. All the ways Sophie had imagined springing the news evaporated into thin air. Detecting he was not himself, thinner, stressed and preoccupied, Sophie hesitated. Despite living in different countries, running a marriage via phone, Internet and fax, she knew Tucker as well as she knew herself.

"Hi," she said, swinging the bookstore bag behind her.

"Hi," he answered, looking forward. "Want to take a cab or Gatwick Express?"

"I don't mind."

"Let's take a taxi," he said, "I'm beat. Good to be back in civilisation."

Sophie gave the driver directions, as Tucker tossed his single bag onto the floor of the cab.

"I'm exhausted," he said. "You know," he added with his head thrown back against the leather headrest, "I think I may have bitten off more than I can chew."

Sliding the plastic bookstore bag beside her leg to the floor, Sophie listened. When they arrived at Eaton Square, Tucker lumbered inside, his shoulders sagging and his head down.

"I'm not hungry. I just want to sleep. I'll take the sofa." He kissed her on the cheek. "In the morning, when you have time, we need to speak."

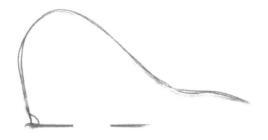

TWENTY-EIGHT

Tucker awoke, looking drawn and tired, as if he hadn't slept much. Sophie handed him a glass of orange juice and they shared two pieces of French toast. They had, as they often did, dressed unintentionally identically in jeans, white shirts and sneakers.

"What are we," he asked, "twins?"

"I don't think so." Sophie laughed.

Tucker readied Daisy for a walk. Afterwards, they made their way to Exhibition Road, past the Victoria and Albert Museum, and into Hyde Park, sitting for a while at the base of the Albert Memorial in Kensington Gardens.

Lacing and unlacing his sneakers, Tucker got to the point. "I want to annul our marriage."

Birds twittered. Children screamed. Sophie said nothing, too shocked to speak.

"Don't you agree?" He paused. "You are talking about returning to Tallinn, but haven't we actually been apart for too long?"

Sophie sat listening, as if she could hear something in the far distance, perhaps a bus in Knightsbridge.

"You deserve to be with someone who can give you a child. I want you to have that chance."

Alexander, with his neatly printed copy of his perfectly motile sperm, came to mind, but Sophie remained completely still, with her hands folded one over the other, amused despite herself, in some bizarre way, that they were both wearing sunglasses, a rare event in London.

A late June sun backlit Hyde Park, turning it from a rich green to a vivid emerald. Wisteria scented the air. Rain and sun shone in the same instant, creating a rainbow, along with a thirty-second volley of bright, white hail.

"What do you think, Sophie? Divorce?"

An ice-cream van came by, and Tucker halted it long enough to buy two cones, then sat back down, as if he couldn't figure out what else to do.

"I can't think right now. I don't know what to do. Maybe smack you. What's wrong with you?" she said.

Sophie threw her cone into the bin, then walked with Tucker through the park, past the swans and Kensington Palace to the Diana, Princess of Wales, Memorial Park, where they sat once again, hip to hip and shoulder to shoulder.

She fumed and yet felt clueless as to what to do. She thought of her discussion with Robin about divorce, her letting Tucker go by Christmas if there were no baby, but here he was offering her a baby, even if it meant letting their marriage go.

Tucker held out his hand to her as they boarded the great wooden pirate play ship, clambering up the ropes, sitting high atop in the crow's nest.

"I have news for you," Sophie said.

"You can have everything, the house—"

"I'm pregnant."

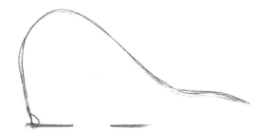

TWENTY-NINE

"Guess we don't need these then?" Tucker said, taking a sheaf of papers out of his canvas satchel, while packing for his trip back to Tallinn.

"What are they?"

"These are adoption papers, not the divorce paperwork." He paused. "Sophie, I am sorry about being confused and suggesting you walk away. It is just so different than I imagined, or you did even. I thought we'd just get pregnant. Like in the movies. I am sorry. I just love you and want to make you happy."

"You do."

"We've got the green light for adoption, if we pass a couple of psychological exams, and make it through a family investigation."

"That's amazing. You did this, Tuck?"

He stopped packing. "I did."

"Thank you."

"It doesn't mean we're going to get a kid. Estonia's a small country. If a child comes up for adoption, someone in the family usually takes him."

"Or her."

"Slim pickings." Tucker whistled. "Virtually none, but that doesn't matter now. Does it?"

Sophie sat on the sofa in Tucker's oversized shirt and loose jeans. Taking a bite from her onion bagel, followed by a swish of fresh apple juice, she nearly choked.

"Of course it matters. This is great news, a pregnancy plus an adoption! When it rains, it pours! Why didn't you tell me straightaway?"

"Cold feet," he said as he zipped his bag. "Do you know how serious it is to adopt a kid?"

"Tucker, where have you been for the last year?"

"Well, the light bulb came on when I got the go-ahead."

"Good," Sophie said, "let's sign and sort it. Don't throw those papers out. Only I can't travel. I mean, I refuse to for a while."

"Are you sure? What happened to 'I'm finished with Westcox and I'm moving home to Tallinn'?"

"I am finished with Westcox Brown, and I am moving to Tallinn, but why, at this minute, chance it? After all the flying between Tallinn, London, New York, and no pregnancy being successful, I'm going to stay put. Remember, we don't tell a soul for twelve weeks."

"Three months? I think you can share it with Pietro and Marco? Your mom?"

"Maybe. The rules, though... should I miscarry. Odds are fifty/fifty," Sophie recited, pulling Daisy onto her lap.

"I'll take those odds."

"Me too." She smiled. "And, by the way, I think you will make a great dad."

"What colour eyes do you reckon the baby will have?" he asked.

"Same as yours."

"Good. Sign here, Mom. Gotta go. Flight is in two hours and I'm already late."

"You'll make it." She signed her name to the adoption papers. "You always do."

Sophie made notes, discarded her collection of temperature charts and worked out that by August 15th she should be able to travel. She fleetingly thought about Robin, who hadn't called or texted, but brushed the thought off, assuming her friend was busy with clients, her dig and, of course, her own pregnancy.

The next day, as she walked, Sophie thought about Anne, about motherhood. Anne certainly hadn't exemplified a stay-at-home mother. Westcox was over, and she had no interest in that treadmill anymore, with Westcox or any other bank. A good life for some, but along with the baby, Sophie wanted something else. With the luxury of time, she strolled to Starbucks on the King's Road. Scribbling, jotting down ideas, she literally knocked over her rooibos tea when she wrote with a flourish: 'I want my own business.'

Estonia had opportunities. No more Ascent Magazines or Westcox. She would be her own boss, make a contribution. Could the stakes be higher? As she tucked into a granola bar she caught sight of *The Times*, folded into the bottom rung of a magazine wall rack: 'STAR WESTCOX ANALYST SIGNALS POTENTIAL CREDIT CRISIS'.

Caterina wore her upscale Dior suit with her neat black heels. Smiling demurely, elegantly even, in front of a professional, blue backdrop, with one hand, as always, resting on her ballooned abdomen. Sophie scanned the article. Experts touted Caterina's past experience with routing out the tech debacle. Amused, Sophie read on. No mention of Alexander, Pietro or even herself for that matter, despite her recent research being quoted in its entirety. There was just Caterina, smiling broadly.

"To the Cat," Sophie toasted with her small, half glass of water, giving way to a waiting mum with a giggling toddler in a plaid stroller. She paid her bill, and put Caterina back in the rack, all the while thinking about what she had written: 'my own business'. She knew it would be in Estonia, but she just wasn't sure what just yet.

For some reason she thought of the embroidery she'd once seen on the hem of a dress. It seemed almost lost in time. As she made her way through St Luke's Gardens, she marvelled at the lightness she felt, the feel of her feet in her sneakers and the softness of her jeans. Dior? She could take it or leave it, and as for Caterina, with her witchy smile and hand atop her straining belly, Sophie simply laughed aloud.

I am pregnant, too.

From a table on the narrow, outside terrace at Harry's Bar, Sophie waved to Anne. While not keen on the traffic, pollution and noise, she did crave the brilliant weather, dining alfresco and sharing her secret with her mother, despite the informal self-imposed news ban. Sunshine in London always seemed momentous, when British gentlemen disrobed, loosening their ties, throwing their bespoke jackets over the backs of chairs, only to have them collected by a swift-moving maître d'.

Sophie pulled her chair close to her mother's and gave her a kiss on the cheek.

"So, I'm going to be a grandmother?" Anne asked.

"Fingers crossed."

Anne poured her daughter a glass of white wine. "Congratulations!" she said, raising her glass.

"Just water," Sophie demurred. "I don't want to take any chances."

"Seems you are taking a pretty big one," Anne teased. "By the way, did you see *The Times*? Lead article? Anything to do with you?"

Sophie laughed, and before she had a chance to say anything her mother said, "I am proud of you, and now, a baby."

"I am prepared for anything."

"What about work? Still need money?"

"Still need money."

"But more than money, Sophie, we are workhorses, milkmaids, sort of." She chortled. "What's next?"

"A business. It sort of came to me all at once."

Not surprised, Anne ordered pasta with wild asparagus for both of them, as Sophie explained the new idea.

"The Estonian island of Muhu has, maybe, the strongest tradition of embroidery – poppy fields, bleeding hearts, cornflowers, roses. It's an art form, and I think it deserves designer recognition. I can support women who are looking to become part of the new economy. I've made a bit of capital so maybe I can supply loans – with easy terms. Maybe I design, produce and sell."

"So how risky is it?" Anne asked.

"Not at all. The product is there, even designers. Have you seen Ivo Nikkolo's work?"

"No," Anne said, putting her hand over her daughter's, "I didn't mean that. The pregnancy. How risky is it?"

"I'm ready for anything," she told her mother.

"Strawberries?" the waiter asked, motioning for the pastry trolley. "Fresh or a traditional *Sbrisolona* strawberry tart." He waved his hand over the cart.

"Vanilla *zabaglione* with raspberries," the two women said in unison, against a background of dishes being served.

"Lovely," he approved. "Espresso?"

"Double," Anne answered, "with lemon."

"Certainly, Signora. Miss? Espresso?"

"No," Sophie almost shouted once again at the mention of caffeine.

"Certainly, Signora," the maître d' said, pirouetting away.

"You didn't have to part his hair, darling."

"Sorry. I almost said 'yes'. Caffeine is absolutely the worst."

"Relax, Sophie. I know in your mind's eye that this is 'it', but stress will not help." Her mother paused, considering Sophie's plan. "I like your idea. I can see the models, the runway, the red linen with a design of leaves, birds, all in forceful colours – pink, violet, green. Exceptional."

As she drank her mint tea, Sophie wished she was still young enough to curl up in her mother's lap, the way she had as a little girl, breathing in her flowery cologne. Instead, once again, happy just to sit with Anne, she absorbed all the love and the confidence her mother passed on.

"Just remember, Sophie," Anne said as she put down her demitasse, pressed a napkin to her lips, "I, like every other mother I know, didn't have a manual. There's a lot of winging it."

Sophie nodded. "I know."

They sat in silence for a minute before she carried on. "I miss Estonia, my house in Kadriorg. There is so much to love about Estonia, or, as Tucker calls it, 'the little country behind the back of God'. It's a jewel, a patchwork of the most sublime nature you will ever see, with some of the most horrid and romantic periods in history."

"Like London, holding on to the forties and their Finest Hour?"

"Maybe. Tallinn holds on to its medieval-ness, its chivalry. It's a castle town with slender blondes spilling their locks down to the backs of their knees, and young men showing up with single, long-stemmed roses."

"Perfect."

"It's the children I adore. I don't know why; they capture my heart – everywhere. It's impossible to overlook them. Something different, something special. I can't put my finger on it. I just love them."

"Yes," Anne acknowledged as she paid their bill, and they walked down South Audley Street, both raising their arms in the same instant to hail the same black cab. Anne kissed her daughter goodbye and opened the door of the waiting taxi for her.

"You go first," she said. "Broody daughters first."

"Brooding," Sophie corrected her mother, and then watched Anne as the cab pulled away. She considered her mother until she became a single, graceful speck of elegance, blowing her daughter a kiss, the same one she'd been sending her way for what seemed like a million years.

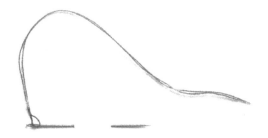

THIRTY

Sleepy, but awake, Sophie picked up her vibrating cell phone. "Robin?"

"No. It's Eli."

"What's going on? What time is it?"

"7am your time. 2am ours," he said, allowing Sophie to come fully awake.

"Where's Robin?"

"She's miscarried, Sophie. She's in hospital. Happened around midnight. She knew it was coming. She's not speaking to anyone. Will you call her?" He spoke bluntly, holding himself back, giving away nothing but the facts.

"Yes. Of course. I'm sorry. I'm really sorry."

"Nothing to say, really. Thank you, Sophie. I never expected it to go to full term, to be honest."

"No?"

"What are the odds? We're both well over forty. I'm a grandfather, for God's sake."

Sophie let him open up, ramble on, assuming he was completely unaware she was pregnant, that her terror was miscarriage. Getting pregnant at over forty was achievable; staying pregnant – that was the challenge.

"When should I call her?"

"Noon. She's sedated now. I'm worried. She's not talking, despite having played it light since the beginning, but especially in the last few weeks – didn't mind flying, didn't mind going on the dig, didn't mind sleeping outdoors, onsite, didn't mind mosquito repellent."

"Eli, it's okay. I'll call her. She'll survive this. For now, let's let her sleep. Tell her I phoned, and I will call noon your time."

Sitting up, wide awake now with the lights on, Sophie looked at the voluptuous, pre-Colombian squat-butted fertility goddess Robin had given her. Holding still, she crushed a desire to rail just as Daisy jumped on the bed.

"Daisy," she spoke softly, "I'm not giving up."

An icy coolness descended on the room. Had Robin been fooling herself? Was Sophie misleading herself? Was it all too good to be true?

Sophie studied the rocking horse she'd bought on Walton Street what now seemed liked a lifetime ago, then felt the bottom drop out of everything as she suffered Robin's pain and started sobbing. With the bedside lamp casting a shadow behind the horse's slender neck, the animal seemed to rock, dipping ever so gently forward. She pulled the covers up and held Daisy close.

Sophie watched the time, read, tried to sleep, checked her new watch again, fiddling with the wristband. Finally, at noon, she called Robin, but no one answered. After trying once more, with no result, she texted: *Trying to reach you.*

On the third try Robin answered.

"I can't speak, Sophie."

"I know."

"But I can listen."

"Okay, Robin. I'm here. I'm shaken, too. We're in this together. You will survive this. You are the most amazing woman I know.

Just think, Robin, you've done it twice, and you've always said: what happens, happens. Right? You've been a mom, Robin! I'm not going to lie and say you can do it again, even if you can. I know the odds and you know them, too. But always remember, you have been a mom, even if for just a little while. A mom, Robin. You have been a mother."

"But I really wanted this baby."

"I know," Sophie answered, "I wanted it for you, too. I wish I were there. You would be such a brilliant mom. You are so good, so kind, so nurturing. Ask anyone. Ask Eli. Let him hug you, and do me a favour? Hug him for me."

"Why did we wait so long?"

"I don't know. Busy, I guess."

"Enough, Soph. Comforting is not your strong suit. How are you?"

"Terrified," she said. "Every cramp, every spot, every everything I'm ready to go to ER, but Robin... I keep having these weird sightings of – you know, *the* baby."

"Keep her close, Sophie. It might come true."

"I do. I know. I hope. Get some sleep, Robin. I will call you again in a few hours, and may I make one suggestion?"

"Yes, always."

"Go out there and mother. That's what I was told to do. You know you don't need a baby to do that."

"Yes," Robin said. "I understand."

"Whatever happens, happens. I love you."

Sophie clicked off the phone, unsettled, telling herself to stay off Dr Google, but she couldn't help herself. A miscarriage was what she most feared. Typing 'Signs of Miscarriage' into the search box, reams of information spilled out: vaginal bleeding, light or heavy, constant or irregular; bleeding with pain; cramps; bellyache; backache; pain before or with bleeding; blood clots; difficult to determine; doesn't happen in an instant, but over the course of time; different for different women.

Sophie pulled herself away from the laptop, forcing herself to take Daisy outside. She would just put her faith in life and invest herself in 'whatever happens, happens'. She felt she was taking the best care of herself, but could not deny the fact that every wince, spasm or flutter made her catch her breath, and found on occasion she had to sit down and remind herself to breathe.

Sophie's phone buzzed as she made her way over the Prince Albert Bridge into Battersea.

"Any new news?" Tucker asked.

"Hi. No. All good." She intentionally did not mention Robin.

"When can you travel?"

"Technically, now, but I'm still being careful."

"Okay." He paused. "This adoption thing… maybe this isn't the time, but if we don't complete the interviews and investigation, we are going to the back of the line. Think about it. It would be good if you could come to Tallinn. With my Estonian passport, we are counted as a domestic adoption, which is a good thing. Luckily we've got a bit of time on our side, as the cutoff age is forty-five. But we need to get a move on. The odds are low."

Just as Tucker emphasised 'low', Sophie felt a slight cramp, deep and centred in the middle of her back.

"I'll give Conrad a call for his advice on flying."

"Good idea."

She paused, and then blurted out, "I'm just worried about cabin pressure."

"I know, but without the interviews, Soph, the possibility of adopting is zero."

THIRTY-ONE

The following morning, Bertram Conrad told Sophie to dress and to meet him in his consulting room.

"Nothing out of order with you or the baby. Perfectly normal for six weeks. As regards flying, just stay hydrated, drink lots of water and get up and stretch. There's no danger. The flight to Estonia, what… three hours?"

"Yes."

"Take a warm bath, get a massage. Your back pain appears to be nothing significant, just the biomechanics of early pregnancy, hormones – progesterone surge, slowly loosening things up or," Bertram paused, "stress."

"Okay." Sophie nodded.

"You can take paracetamol, but only if really necessary. There's a risk of miscarriage with other painkillers. Just try to rest, use cold compresses for back twinges. Take your mind off things."

Leaving Conrad's office, Sophie strolled towards Hyde Park, taking her time, popping into a few children's shops. July already drenched London in a lemony light and sticky heat. Taking herself to lunch at the Chelsea Market, Sophie chose the exact table where she and Robin, only months before, had discussed whether or not they could or would carry a baby full-term.

As she picked at her garden salad and sipped an iced mint tea, Robin phoned.

"Thanks for getting me out of the doldrums. Eli was useless. I did hug him. Looking after him is getting me over it. I think he may have wanted this baby as much as I did."

"Good," Sophie said.

The two women fell silent. Then Sophie broke the quiet, telling Robin exactly where she was sitting, what she was thinking, as well as her visit to Bertram Conrad.

"Funny journey, eh?"

"Funny journey," Sophie answered. "And guess what? Tucker's picked up his pace on a possible adoption in Tallinn. I have to get myself there."

"Well, some wives do live with their husbands." Robin laughed.

"But just for today, Robin, the sun is seriously shining – especially for London. I could be in Monaco! The South of France. Florida. California."

"Wait five minutes," Robin chided.

"Very funny. No, seriously, I feel happy. Not that I wasn't when I was in Monaco or at Westcox Brown in some moments, but just for today I've got a baby on the way."

On her Finnair flight to Tallinn, Sophie folded her hands over her seatbelt.

"Hang on," she told her little one, "hold tight."

Walking the length of the cabin, and in the toilet, Sophie stretched, folding one leg up to her chest, then the other, then pulling each heel up behind herself. She crooked one arm back and behind, and then the other. Stretch, Conrad had said. She asked the steward for a mint tea, *anything without caffeine*, and a second bottle of water, which she read came from a spring in the north. Lapland. She studied the smooth glass bottle that suggested a pristine glacier, water filtering through age-old rock.

Arrived in Tallinn at last, Sophie belted her cashmere coat

before leaving arrivals, but she needn't have bothered. The temperature, close to eighteen degrees Celsius, felt practically Mediterranean for Estonia. Tucker stood waiting for her, with his now traditional single rose.

"Expecting snow?" he teased her.

"Well, I wasn't expecting weather like this," she countered, slipping out of the coat and handing it to him while taking the rose. "Thank you, Tuck."

"Are you excited?"

"About what?"

"Adoption interviews. I think it is good to cover all the bases. We never know, do we?"

"No, we don't…"

"Also, they asked if we'd be interested in an older child."

"How old?"

"Twelve."

"I'm not against it, Tuck, but let's try for as close to newborn as possible."

"Okay."

"By the way, we can visit the home, and they do have a couple of twelve-year-olds."

Tucker took Sophie to what by now he called his favourite restaurant, a Mexican café within walking distance of their home. There, he gushed over all the latest possibilities for Estonia – joining the EU being just one. Even in bed, Tucker reeled off one project after the next – their status, success and value – until he realised Sophie had fallen fast asleep, snuggled up close, snoring in tiny, almost inaudible breaths.

"Welcome home," he whispered, before turning out the light.

Navigating the sky-blue door to the psychotherapist's office proved to be a test on its own. Like a lot of doors in Tallinn's Old Town, a door might be a standard door, a portal into a building constructed into the side of a hill or an entrance leading down through decades of earth and rock, heading to an ultramodern office, busy restaurant or quiet home. This door, cut from thick, ancient timber, felt smooth to the touch, worn down by at least a century of palms pushing firmly forwards.

Descending the steep narrow spiral stairs, Sophie held on to the cool wrought-iron banister. With the railing wrapping around the stone walls, the building appeared to have once been the subterranean base of a castle turret.

To herself, Sophie counted the days and weeks she was pregnant now: two months and three days. In another month, she could trumpet her secret to the world.

Curiously, the waiting room appeared to be an ice castle. Valhalla? Tallinn never failed to surprise. Painted with a sort of opalescent glaze, like ice at twilight after newly fallen snow, the walls matched the soft, white leather barrel chairs.

Taking his time, ducking his head in and out of his mini Promised Land, the therapist finally strode towards Sophie and Tucker from a corner door.

"So," he said, "you are adopting a child?"

"Yes," Tucker answered, as they both rose from their comfortable chairs, metres beneath the earth.

In his tweed jacket and freshly starched shirt, the raven-haired therapist motioned them in and to sit. Ignoring Sophie, he studied Tucker, as he asked perfunctory questions and scribbled notes. Most of the answers he already had, buried in the folder in front of him, but after satisfying himself with the more mundane questions, he made a final enquiry.

"Tooker, do you have feelings of grandiosity?"

"What?" Tucker queried.

"Grandiosity. Unrealistic sense of superiority? *Grandioznost. Suurejoonelisus*." The therapist turned to Sophie.

"I'm sorry," she said, "I don't speak Russian or Estonian, at least not more than a few words."

"Do you have delusions, illusions, of grandeur?" the therapist asked Tucker again.

"Do you mean do I think more of myself than what is on the page?"

The therapist nodded, now scratching his upper lip with the steeple of two folded, pointed, index fingers.

"No. I don't have delusions of grandeur."

"*Khorosho*. Good. Mrs Tooker, do you agree?"

"I agree."

"*Hea*," he said, "good."

After a few more obligatory questions, the therapist pulled out a large rubber stamp from another century, ran it back and forth on a pad of red ink, and stamped the three-inch high paperwork. With a noncommittal smile, he said, "Goodbye."

In the startling, almost blinding sunlight outside, Sophie asked Tucker what that all meant.

"Did we pass?"

"Of course. He's just looking for the brown envelope and a bottle of Smirnoff."

"I don't think so."

"You don't understand how it works."

"This isn't business, Tucker. It's an adoption."

"Same difference."

"Same difference?"

"Okay. Whatever. It's a done deal. No delusions of grandeur. Ice King on side. Lunch?"

"Yes."

"I am feeling deluded, have visions of grandeur: beets, cabbage, pork, roasted potatoes. All of it at once."

"I'll settle for Witches' Casserole, if that is okay."

"Your wish is my command."

The children's home came up abruptly as they made their way off the main road and onto a leafy side street. The building, antiquated, like many of the buildings in Tallinn, streaked with rust and moss, teetered undecidedly between a Bauhaus hotel or a Soviet asylum.

Taking Tucker's hand, Sophie momentarily couldn't decide whether to run in or run away. At the front door, a young woman in a bright shirt-top apron smiled, motioning them in.

Sophie noticed the tight embroidery at the V-neck, front and back, as they followed the woman down the hall and into the director's office, who then signalled that they should sit, as she signed off the phone.

"Welcome," the director said. "You do us a great honour, Mr Mägi. Mrs Mägi."

"Thank you," Sophie said, "I think you do us the honour."

"Most of our children are with us," she said, as she uncapped her pen and opened a folder, "while one parent or the other sorts themselves out, perhaps both – drugs, alcohol, income reversal. A real orphan is a real rarity. Come, let me show you our home."

The white-haired manager observed Sophie and Tucker with the attentiveness of a private investigator, as they walked up one clean hall and down another. The smell of lunch wafted through the corridors, and Sophie recalled the black bread and soup she'd first tasted in midtown Manhattan one clear spring day. A piano lesson from a floor above sounded one note painstakingly at a time, followed by a gush of praise and clapping hands. A gym class came from below, accompanied by the sound of a taut drum and a tambourine, echoing from walls that Sophie imagined to be an auditorium.

"Üks, kaks, kolm, neli. One, two, three, four," a soprano voice rang out.

Plaid prams and green pushchairs lined a corridor leading to a back garden. Out in the crisp sunshine infants napped. Sophie ached to scoop up each and every one. A striking, young father seated on a wooden bench chatted with his flaxen-haired son. On his father's knee, the child leaned in, negotiating a secret.

"It's virtually impossible to adopt," the director warned Sophie and Tucker as they made their way back to her office. "It is nearly unworkable." She paused, looking them over. "Orphans in Estonia are not true orphans. There is always someone within the family who will take the child. Estonia is, after all, a small country or really one large family, as you, Mr Mägi, I am sure are aware. I am accountable for the welfare of these children, each and every one, and as I am sure you realise, I take my job very seriously."

Owl-like, the director peered over her half-moon spectacles, taking everything in, every detail, down to the rhythm of every uneven breath. Unlike the Ice King, she appeared less than interested in Tucker, totally focused on Sophie.

"Mrs Mägi, why do you think you will make a good mother?" she asked. "Why are you here?"

Tucker turned to Sophie, who studied the older woman and her office with an equal gravity, taking in the small, stuffed animals, the numerous baby photos and any number of pastel-illustrated toddler books.

"Because I believe I am one already."

"So why have you waited so late?" The woman folded her glasses neatly, placing them on top of the now closed Mägi folder.

"I didn't realise it was late."

Tucker twitched, crossing one knee over the other, holding tightly to the phone in his front pocket.

"You are still three years within the limit to apply for a child, but I judge carefully, Mrs Mägi, especially as you both are considered older parents. At present there is no child up for adoption, unless, of course, you want an older child, or a child who is physically or mentally challenged, or a whole family. By the time a child becomes available, unless we have some miracle, you will be, I am afraid to say, even older."

The room stilled, and all three fell silent.

"I'm going to ask you a favour, Mrs Mägi. I want you to take a twelve-year-old out to lunch. I want you to see how it feels, being with an older child, mothering an older child, a child that might have been yours."

Sophie nodded.

"Good." The boss clapped her hands together once, loudly and with emphasis. "Please call me Krissu. You, Mrs Mägi, have passed. You will be a mother. I don't know how, when, where or if I can help with that, but I approve. I turn people down all the time, but you pass because, unlike most, you said exactly what I need to hear. You said, 'I am a mother.' Not everyone can or will say that."

Krissu no longer circled Sophie or Tucker warily but instead, with a sort of easiness more reminiscent of family as she walked them to the door. Holding out a hand, she shook theirs.

"You, Mr Mägi, needn't worry. You will make a good father."

"Cool," Tucker said, opening the front door for Sophie. "I think we are in."

"In what?"

"The Club. The Family. Don't you get it, Soph? We're in the family. Estonia is one big family, and we're part of it."

With the call for a home interview having come up immediately and with no notice, Sophie prepared the Kadriorg house.

"Tucker," she said at breakfast, with not much subtlety, "the living room is a bit much."

"Delusionary, you think?" he teased.

"Well, no, yes… grandiose maybe, unless of course you are going for that Hanseatic long-lost baron look – scratched mahogany, worn tapestries and dog-faced portrait of long-dead dowager."

"I see. Not the place for a bouncing baby?"

"Not the place."

"I guess it is a bit of a storeroom. Do what you like."

In the kitchen, Tucker had got it right. Like some fairy tale imagined years ago, the room, painted in optimistic colours and framed with antique Scandinavian cabinetry, welcomed cooking, talking and sitting, inviting in the typically suffused morning light. Upstairs the rooms, all well lit by small windows and skylights, were not unlike the hand of a master embroiderer, with one focal point threading its way unexpectedly to the next. Eccentric, bold, happy animals danced across bedspreads and bathroom towels. Estonian folk tales came alive on a wall mural, as well as in framed prints of the Child Who Came from an Egg, the Grateful Prince and the Headless Dwarfs.

As she put the house in order, her mind turned to the idea of her business venture. At the kitchen table, she pieced together a plan, making notes on different districts, the islands, their typical designs, the financials and the sustainability of an embroidery business. She telephoned Laura Laar, who knew all about Estonian embroidery.

"Okay," Tucker said that night, "one more interrogation and we're done with the Adopt Squad."

"It's just a visit."

"I know. Just kidding."

She slipped her arm through his as they took a quick stroll through Kadriorg Park, enjoying the firs, the palace renovations and the still-hissing Soviet gas lamps.

"Beautiful night," Tucker said, as they turned back towards home. "I think, Sophie, we may have got it right this time."

"I think we have."

"Two babies on the way?"

"It appears that way."

The following morning a red-headed woman shared tea and ginger snaps with Sophie at her kitchen table. As usual, the social worker commented on Sophie's age.

"Over forty?"

"Yes."

"Do you like to cook?"

"Yes."

Upstairs she counted bedrooms and bathrooms, and made more notes.

"Perfect." She mimed for Sophie in her broken English. "Happy upstairs, happy kitchen. Too dark downstairs… But here," she threw her arms open wide, "you are ready for a child."

Outside, on the deck, overlooking the evergreens, the duck pond, the gazebo, the Summer Palace and Peter the Great's hunting lodge, the woman stood in awe of her own city park.

"*Ilus.* Beautiful." She nodded. "I will work fast. What child would you like?"

"Healthy."

"A boy?"

"We don't mind."

"Blond?"

"No preference."

"I speak with Krissu and we work. Congratulations."

"For what?"

"Moving up."

"To what?"

"Top of the list. Don't worry. It could still take a long time, but you are different. You are a breadbasket, with arms open."

"My arms are open," Sophie said, taking a minute, deciding whether she should speak or not. "I have a vision. A baby I see. Often, she's blonde, a little girl, smiling, waiting for me."

"Yes, you do." The social worker took the comment in her stride. "I see her, too."

The two women walked out through the garden with its apple trees, white roses and pink-painted window boxes, bursting with red geraniums. Embracing her at the wooden gate leading to the park, Sophie said, "*Head aega.*"

"Goodbye." The redhead stepped back, laughing happily. "*Head aega.*"

THIRTY-TWO

Charmed, spellbound even, Sophie stood rooted to the spot in her garden, as if a character from a fairy tale had just promised her the moon. Looking up at her pastel-painted home, from the turn of the century, Sophie reran the interview, pondering what seemed like magic, or at least some sort of ESP.

"Telepathic," she told Tucker, "or maybe just pregnancy hormones."

"No," he said, "that's Estonia. Sometimes it's just magic." He paused. "Or it's just the way you learn to communicate after fifty years of Soviet brutality."

"It was talking without talking, otherworldly, a paranormal tête-à-tête."

Tucker laughed aloud. "You are in, Sophie; you are so in."

Later that night, as she contemplated the nursery, with Tucker's arm draped over her shoulders, he asked if she'd like to hop on the ferry to Helsinki, shop for nursery things.

"We can't have Mrs Dog-Face looming over the crib."

"Certainly not."

"Sunday?"

"I don't think we need to go all the way to Helsinki, though. There's plenty in Tallinn. I saw a few things in Old Town."

"Okay."

"By the way, I forgot to mention it before, but I'm meeting with Laura Laar tomorrow. Apparently she knows everything there is to know about embroidery, Estonia, inside out."

"Great. Her husband is a good guy. My best worker, my right-hand man. They're a good couple. And by the way, it's a great business idea, if you need my opinion."

"Thank you."

While not wanting to leave her comfy home, apple trees, wild roses and picket fence, Sophie wanted to meet Laura Laar, whose grandmother she'd heard ran a well-respected embroidery workshop in a thatch-roofed country long house somewhere outside of Tallinn. Meeting at the Hotel Olympia, Sophie was keen to test her idea.

"Thank you for coming," she said, standing up as Laura walked in.

Quintessentially Estonian, Laura might have graced the cover of *Vogue*. At six foot, with glossy hair braided down her back and impeccably dressed, she turned heads, even in a country where her kind of beauty was commonplace. She wore a Soviet-era, starched white blouse over Gucci jeans, most probably bought in Finland, possibly in Stockmann's.

Laura took Sophie's hand. "Hello."

After a moment of quiet reserve, the hangover from fifty years of Soviet occupation, when the wrong look, gesture or even thought might send you and your entire family packing for Siberia, the women started chatting.

"I'm pleased to meet you," Laura said in flawless English with what appeared to be the smallest curtsey.

"How is it," Sophie marvelled aloud, "that everyone here speaks English so well?"

"Television." Laura smiled back. "Once we got the signal, we picked up Finnish television with programmes in every language."

"How many languages do you speak?"

"Five. Estonian, firstly. I am Estonian and while we couldn't study or speak it legally, we spoke it with family, carefully. Our parents taught us, even if we were educated as Soviets, taken away from our parents at birth and raised communally. Terrible. Obviously I speak Russian; Finnish from television, English from Finnish television. My grandparents spoke German. Remember, we are Baltic German. Is that five? In my case, I studied French also in school. I thought it romantic, dreamt of Paris, one day going there, seeing the Eiffel Tower. I think that is six?"

"You can go to Paris now."

"No. It's too expensive. My husband and I are refurbishing our old apartment. We have two children. Maybe when they are older. And we are now middle-aged."

"Middle-aged? What do you mean?" Sophie asked incredulously.

"I look young, but I am twenty-seven."

"Twenty-seven? If you are middle-aged, then what am I? Dead?"

Laura laughed and stirred a sugar cube into her black tea.

The two women ordered apple tart and Estonian ice cream. Laura described the transition she'd gone through from lining up for bread and cheese, most days finding nothing in the shops, which is why every family had a vegetable patch and animals. She had laughed in disbelief at Finnish television commercials, showing women waltzing down shop aisles with shelves groaning with food. She had once believed, and the Soviet machine said, it was all propaganda, make believe.

"Now when I go to the supermarkets," she added, "springing up everywhere – the ones our husbands are building – I sometimes feel nauseous, confused, sick to my stomach. I don't recognise cheese anymore, the way it's packaged, so shiny, so many kinds, colours."

Sophie ordered a second pot of tea, which arrived with ginger snaps and edible flowers, allowing Laura to carry on.

"When we finally made a trip to Helsinki on the ferry, the eight-hour one, because the hydrofoil didn't exist then – never mind the helicopter – we felt like two little kids from a lost land, hand in hand; even our clothes were out of step. The transition has been so fast. Did you know that before the Russian occupation our living standard was equal to Helsinki's, and theirs was the highest in the world?" She smiled. "We will get there again."

"You will."

"Now, tell me about your embroidery idea."

"I brought a few things, mostly from the island of Muhu. The embroidery is impeccable. I envision these being used by Dolce and Gabbana, Valentino, Christian Dior."

"Yes. I see that, too."

Still amazed that Laura would call herself middle-aged, Sophie tried to grasp that fact. Perhaps she was correct. If life expectancy was sixty here, as she had read, then twenty-seven would be nearly halfway there.

Both women looked out the plate-glass window of the renovated Olympia Hotel at the wooden Orthodox church below and the Soviet star on the building next door.

"Independence is only nine years old," Laura said, "and here we sit discussing travel, an embroidery business and profit. Do you know how alien this would have been unless you were one of our young economics students from Tartu University who were just ready to jump, waiting for the Soviet Union to crumble, so they could start a bank? Of course, there was the stealing and exchanging of metals before that. Notice all the missing copper pipes?" She chuckled.

"Investment loves a vacuum."

Looking at the traffic below, the combination of old cars and new, they watched an elderly woman in a traditional Russian scarf of spring flowers against a black background edged in red navigate the intersection.

"Laura, why didn't you – or your family – ever leave?"

"You couldn't," Laura said as she placed her hands over the designs spread out over the table. "My husband and I sat many times in the harbour when we were kids, looking out towards Helsinki, wondering if we could just sail there in a small boat, but it was virtually impossible. Some tried. It was wonderful target practice for the Soviets. Many disappeared. The price was just too high."

"But your parents? Grandparents? When there was still time, before the Russians closed in."

"Parents, no. They dreamt of it, but my grandparents did try. Many came to get on the last boats sent from Sweden, but there wasn't enough room or time. So many couldn't board and just watched that last great white ship sail away. My grandparents had a small, sturdy boat that might have made it to Helsinki. They were prepared. The Soviets were on their way. They still had time, but on that night a storm started up, and the swell wasn't right, and my grandmother was pregnant with my mother, and had a sick little one in her arms. She and my grandfather knew that it was either the trip or the life of their firstborn, and maybe their second unborn. But that is her story, and maybe she will tell you herself one day."

Laura trailed off, and then pulled out her portfolio with samples of embroidery from different parts of the country. She looked up, as Sophie studied her.

"Are you thinking about my age again?" Laura chuckled.

"I am," Sophie said, "I am trying to make head or tail of you calling yourself middle-aged."

"Think of it like this. My mother is forty-five."

"What?" Sophie spluttered. "How can your mother be forty-five? I am forty-two, almost forty-three, and I'm pregnant for the first time. You say forty-five like she's off in the mist somewhere."

"You can't be forty-two and pregnant?" Laura gawped, covering her mouth.

"I can and I am," Sophie said.

"Think about it. My mother had me at eighteen, and I had my children at twenty and twenty-one. That wasn't young here. If you wanted your own flat in Soviet times you had to marry, and then of course there were other perks when the children came along. They were simple things, but that was the life. Maybe if I had other choices, or my mother did, I would have taken more time, but I took the life laid out for me, and she took the life laid out before her. It was a poor life in some ways, but not in others. Can you visualise a Christmas when one shared orange was a miracle? Just to smell it was a dream come true. Now, as I told you, I get dizzy in an aisle of oranges from Israel, tangerines from Turkey and dates from who knows where. My life is not unusual to me. To me, you having a baby at forty-two is odd. Didn't you consider it earlier; didn't your mother push you? Wasn't there some benefit?"

"No, no and no."

"I'm sorry," Laura said. "In Soviet times the choices were simple and the road very narrow. Perhaps it made us old before our time? The shelves were bare, but never mind all that. I am happy for you. You are pregnant."

"Or I might adopt."

"I can't even think of a life without children. They are the…" Laura paused, looking for the right English words, "the poetry of life."

Sophie and Tucker spent the weekend roving through Tallinn's antique shops and some of the more modern stores, further outside the city. There they found a delicately carved crib, a high-backed rocking chair, a child's wardrobe and a changing table.

"Sprinkled with pixie dust," Tucker said as he admired them from the nursery's doorway, with a mug of coffee in hand. "You never know with these Estonians."

"Really perfect," Sophie agreed, trying out the rocking chair, admiring the small cupboard full of soaps, the baby bath, the small one-piece pyjamas and a traditionally knitted cardigan with a hood.

"I like the sunflowers and the swallows," Tucker said as he now sat cross-legged on the floor beneath them. "I have a little something to add as well." He smiled, pulling out a heart-shaped leather box. Inside, nestled in tiny spirals, was an infant's necklace of small amber beads.

"It's beautiful," Sophie said, as she placed it neatly beside the small white brush and comb. "Did you know that amber is a healer, or so they say – it cleanses the body and the mind."

"I hear it brings success, happiness and power – or at least freedom from the common cold."

"Let's take it all," Sophie said, as Tucker drew close, resting his head against her leg, while she reached up to flip off the overhead light, leaving only the night-light, a small replica of a townhouse on the Town Hall Square, glowing, flickering from the light inside.

At breakfast, Sophie showed Tucker the designs being sent to Milan and Paris, even London. She handed him a sheaf of papers and asked him to go over the numbers and to give her an opinion.

"Don't rewrite it," she told him, "just review it. I don't want to be too optimistic."

"I'm sure you're not," he said. "This business is a no-brainer."

"I forgot to mention I had a call from someone at the Kumu Art Museum and they think they have a piece I might like. From their private collection. They are looking to raise funds to renovate."

"Word must be out."

"What does that mean?"

"That my wife is looking for baby things?"

"Don't be daft. I'm just looking for a painting for now, and for the manor one day."

As Sophie made her way up to see the painting on offer at the Kumu Art Museum, now housed in the Knighthood Hall just opposite the Dome Church on Toompea Hill, towering over Old Town, she hummed, spoke to her 'little one'.

"All good," her new Estonian obstetrician had said. "Just remain careful and cautious. Keep an eye on your blood pressure."

Just as Sophie started to amble up the hill to Old Town, two young skateboarders sailed past, jumping sidewalks, looking for the flat spots between the crumbling sidewalks and the ancient cobblestones. The excruciating pain that abruptly detonated in her lower back took her by surprise. She felt as if a shard of glass had just severed her lower vertebrae.

Leaning on a tree, her cry so sharp, an older woman came running to help, steadying her with two sturdy arms, after dropping a mesh bag full of groceries.

"*Kuula mind…*" she said, but Sophie's eyes had already rolled to the back of her head, and she had passed out, supported by the arms of a stranger who knew exactly what was going on.

"I don't remember anything, except a piercing pain and an older woman catching me," Sophie told Tucker, who sat quietly. "We lost the baby, didn't we?"

Tucker nodded.

Sophie studied the pale grey, painted cinderblock walls, seeming even more severe against the delicate wildflowers on the cotton curtains. A light perfume of dusting powder scented the bedclothes and her gown. Recalling the detonating pain, almost turning around to see who hit her, expecting to see a ruffian of some sort, she saw the face of an older woman, looking her in the eye, willing her not to give up. She remembered the eyes and the voice. She recalled the fine, white woollen Haapsalu shawl, meant to be so fine it could be drawn through a woman's wedding ring, around the woman's shoulders. She remembered the mismatch against the modern cashmere jacket. Then all went black. She had no memory of the ambulance, or the race to the operating room. There had been a foggy cascade of foreign languages, someone going through her bag.

"*Kes ta on? Ameerika. Nurisünnitus. Ei ole eluohtlik.* Who is she? American. A miscarriage. Not life-threatening. *Kto ona? Amerikanskiy. Vykidysh. Ne ugrozhayet zhizni.*"

Tucker and Sophie held hands.

Sophie considered the pleated folds in the starched curtain separating her bed from the next when suddenly someone who might have been Laura's twin popped her head through and smiled.

"Feeling better?" she asked in perfect English.

"Yes," they answered in unison.

"We thought at first, 'Okay, internal bleeding. A hit and run,' but... I'm very sorry for your loss. It took us a little while to establish that you were pregnant. You know, a miscarriage is not so unusual."

Sophie and Tucker looked at the young medic, another slender, flaxen-haired blonde.

Sophie cried quietly.

"You should see Dr Härma. He has an amazing clinic. You must have seen 'his babies', Härma babies, all over town, the women pushing – really heaving – their triplets around in three-seater strollers. You see them everywhere. His fertility clinic is not far. People jokingly call him 'Artz Frankenstein'. Don't give up. Have you thought of donor eggs? You can do this right here in Tallinn."

Sophie slept fitfully for the next forty-eight hours with Tucker popping in and out, offering fresh juice and quiet support. Losing the baby was not unexpected, but it was not assumed, even if she knew, had read, many times over that a miscarriage was nature's way of dispelling embryos that would never have had a chance at survival anyway. Sophie sensed motherhood slipping away. It wasn't the science, the facts, the loss or even the regrets. It was the powerlessness. That was what she couldn't bear to contemplate.

When was enough, enough?

THIRTY-THREE

Try as she might, Sophie didn't understand, didn't want to recognise, the tears, the fears, her inability to let go. What had happened to *Project Bébé*. Alone, she cried, and with her pillow damp, admitted: the emptiness of her own body dragged everything else about her into her feeling of nothingness.

She counted the minutes until her mother arrived, and she commiserated with Robin by phone.

"Clearly, this body," Robin said, "my body – this old jalopy – was saying N-O, no."

"I guess you're right."

"I'm glad your mom is coming. And get back to work, eh? That's been my salvation. My joy even."

Sophie listened to Robin talk about her digs, Panama, the San Blas Indians. About trying to make a trip to Tallinn as soon as possible.

"Robin, you know what I wish?"

"Tell me."

"I wish at times like this that I had a father, a real one, not my mother's memories or a brilliant portrait. I feel he would give me a backbone. I am grateful for Mother, Tucker and, of course, you! But I've never said it out loud before. Every day of my life I have missed having a father – my father."

Anne flew directly from Patagonia, a flight of almost ten hours, and Sophie met her at the airport, with a single rose.

"I'm so relieved to see you," Anne said, embracing her daughter. "I'm so sorry. How are you? And Tucker?"

"I'm okay, Mom. He's good. I am so happy you are here. I could use lunch."

"Yes, my love, me, too. That's what I am here for – to do whatever you want."

"I wanted that baby."

"I know you did, Sophie, I did, too. Come on, let's get you home and sort something to eat."

Later, curled up together in the guest room, Anne asked about work.

"Work might be just the thing," she suggested.

"Robin said that as well."

"Whatever happened with those people who were working on the computer-to-computer video chat?"

"They're still on it."

"Are you still putting out feelers for work with a bank?"

"No." Sophie smiled for the first time since her mother had arrived. "I'm working on the embroidery company, remember? Selling to high-end fashion houses – I have interest from Milan. I'm testing Internet sales."

"Embroidery," Anne said, as she and Sophie moved to the kitchen for black bread, jam and raspberry tea. "Yes. That's right. I remember now." She paused for a minute and then asked, "How's Tucker taking this?"

"He's my rock. He's felt it bad, just like me, but it's clear I am his priority, and I am so grateful. I didn't think it would hit me so hard. I actually thought I was stronger."

"You are resilient. The loss of a life takes time. I am so happy you are back here in Tallinn."

"Me too."

The muted sound of traffic and a ferry horn leaving the port travelled through the house.

Sophie for a minute was caught off-guard by the presence of her mother, the beauty of her own home, the richness of her life despite the loss of a baby that she wanted more than anything in the world.

"Let me show you something," she said, drawing down her portfolio from a top shelf where she had left it the day before. "This is whitework. Traditionally it's white thread on white fabric, used for bridal and christening wear, and for ecclesiastical embroidery."

Anne ran her hand over the fine threads, with the other held over her mouth, practically holding her breath. "It's beautiful."

"You see, it's a sort of counted thread embroidery based on removing threads from the warp or weft from a piece of even weave fabric, usually linen."

"Who did this?"

"Who doesn't?"

Both women laughed.

"I found this in a workshop on St Catherine's Passage. We can go later."

Sophie served her mother a cinnamon coffee with a slice of kringle.

"You know, work doesn't just take your mind off things," Anne said. "It's a bit of a baby all on its own."

"Yes," Sophie agreed. "I am so glad that you are here. I am a bit tired, so many twists and turns since saying 'yes' to Tucker. Spinsterhood may not have been such a bad idea?"

"Maybe." Anne chuckled.

"Think about it. Uprooting from Rye, getting married, an MBA in Monaco, Westcox Brown and Alexander Köhler. Now Tallinn. Having, but not really having, a pregnancy."

"You've made all the right decisions, Sophie. You may just be old enough to be somebody's grandmother, but the fact is that you are not, and you certainly don't look like it."

"Thanks, Mom, but why didn't I ever think about age, basic biology?"

"I don't know. Life can be very busy, enjoyable, fulfilling?"

They did the dishes together and continued to talk.

"I heard about a local doctor," Sophie tested the waters, "who has a fertility clinic. Bit of a cowboy, but I thought why not?"

"Isn't that a bit dangerous?" Anne asked as she helped load the dishwasher.

"He seems to have a high success rate."

"Sophie, I'm behind you all the way, but at some point you will have to dig deeply and ask yourself what you really want and why."

"I want a child. I want to be a mother with every fibre of my being."

"Why?"

"Joy. How many times do I have to answer that question? It is simple. I can bring a child joy. Joy can enhance our lives, and because if everything in my life was taken away, stripped down, and I had to keep the most valuable experience in my forty-two years of life," she smiled, "it would be the love we share, Mom. That bond. I want to perpetuate that, Mom. Love."

Anne pulled her daughter into an embrace, as a late summer, late afternoon, light filtered through the kitchen windows, showering the Scandinavian cabinets with a sort of prism, creating a sea of small rainbows that bounced from wall to wall, unseen by either woman, and disappearing in almost the same instant.

"It is the most valuable thing, isn't it?" Sophie asked, pulling away. "When all is said and done, what carries on, Mom? Look at you and Father. He is with you constantly, and the love you have given me? Sounds silly, but it does," she paused, "make the world go round? I want to get on the merry-go-round, even if I'm a bit late."

"Perhaps I should have pushed you." Anne brushed her daughter's hair back from her face, her fatigue from the long flight from Patagonia and worry for Sophie now beginning to show. "But let's look ahead now. To Life, then?"

"To Life." Sophie laughed. "I have made an appointment to see a fertility specialist here – Dr Härma – and adoption might be a possibility."

Sophie watched Daisy in the garden, running the length of the picket fence, chasing a Jack Russell on the other side, then went straight to her laptop to find Dr Härma's website.

She paused only for a moment to observe the foot traffic through Kadriorg Park. The odd trill of laughter came from children in the playground, and she noticed older children, even teenagers, strolling, still holding their parents' hands.

The Härma website popped up immediately. It took a few seconds for Sophie to register the images. Two perfectly coiffed women displayed their most intimate parts from every position. Sophie recoiled and closed the lid, sat back for a minute, and then called the clinic.

"Oh, sorry, that's the porn site. For the sperm donors," Dr Härma's secretary explained, without missing a beat. "You should have the clinic website."

"Okay," Sophie answered, still surprised, wondering again if it wasn't time to draw the line.

"I can email it, or I can give it to you when you come in at five o'clock with Mr Mägi?"

Arriving right on time, Tucker waltzed Sophie around the kitchen. Since her arrival in Tallinn, he had challenged her for the directorship of *Project Bébé*, and on occasion, she turned it over to him. While her energy flagged, his flowed full tilt.

In Old Town, and again through heavy, carved doors, they found themselves in a spacious, modern fertility clinic. A young man in a mock Harvard varsity jacket flipped his long blond ponytail over his shoulder, and strode out as if, after visiting the Härma pornography site, he'd just done someone a very big favour.

"Donor." Sophie laughed.

"School fees." Tucker winked. "Extra dosh."

Dr Härma entered the consulting room full of vigour, with the svelte figure of a self-important celebrity. Sitting on the edge of the desk, he looked them both over.

"This will come as no surprise. Our tests match those you brought from the UK. You, Mr Mägi, don't have a shot in hell unless Sophie can do IVF, specifically ICSI. Sophie, you have eggs, but the clock is running out. I suggest I super-groom you with oestrogen and see what we get. You can decide for or against ICSI, which is tricky at this point, moving your eggs inside, then outside and back inside. We can see if they take. Or if we get an egg going, you can try your luck at artificial insemination. If this doesn't work, I can begin to prepare an egg donor for you. I have one that fits your physical parameters perfectly, and because I know this young woman – a chemical engineering student at Tallinn Institute of Technology – she is even temperamentally like you, Mrs Mägi."

Dr Härma flicked the switch on a wall-mounted screen. "Here's the link for donors. Photos, profiles – for sperm or eggs."

Sophie and Tucker studied the images as Härma clicked from one to the next until arriving at one unidentified young woman, who did resemble Sophie – a twenty-two-year-old Sophie. Sophie admired her, thinking for a minute about the generosity of giving life.

"Are they paid enough?" she asked.

"Enough," Härma answered.

"Do they know how tough it is?"

"Yes. All our donors, male and female, surrogate mothers, know what they're getting in to."

"Why do they do it?"

"University fees, mostly. Sometimes to help their family."

A young 'Sophie' faced the camera straight on, with all the beauty of the innocent. Barefoot, in a summer length, diaphanous dress, she looked happy, standing beside a haystack. Several sporty images followed. Decidedly good-looking, the donor truly might have been Sophie, or her daughter, and this might have been a modelling portfolio snapped up by any major agency in London, Paris or New York.

"Let's start with oestrogen," Sophie said, businesslike, "then we can visit the idea of donor eggs."

Tucker leaned forward, as startled by Sophie as she was by herself.

"You will travel two paths," the Estonian consultant added. "I alert her to the possibility of serving as a donor, while we monitor where the oestrogen takes you. Lead time is important. The donor needs it, as much as you.

"Our success rate is high here because I can do things other countries can't. We don't selectively abort, but we can if necessary. I allow a woman three implants; after that I draw the line. I think in England you are allowed two, and of course in America all can come to term if the woman can handle it."

"Thank you," Sophie said, as she took the coffee-coloured oestrogen capsules in their neat, silver packaging.

"Five times a day," Dr Härma instructed. "Let's see what we can do. You are lucky. It's as if your miscarriage never happened. Everything now depends on quality, timing and proximity. Stay in Tallinn. No more flights," said the doctor.

Outside, Tucker pulled Sophie close and offered a modest box from his jacket pocket with his other hand.

"It's only small," he said, "but I want you to know I love you and I'm not giving up either."

Inside, lying on a white satin cushion, sat an intricately carved amber five-pointed star on a simple silver chain necklace.

"Still feeling lucky," Tucker said.

Sophie weighed the protocol for her lookalike, for herself. Should she even consider egg donation at all? The image of 'Sophie II', as Sophie called her egg donor, with one leg kicked back, tumbling blonde hair, laughing in the sunshine, leaning on the haystack, stayed with her.

She took Daisy for a walk as she ruminated, ever captivated by the young children, the rising laughter, the odd spontaneous howl of tears from the odd tumble.

Sophie understood the protocol for this young Estonian woman would be the same as if she, any woman, were using her own eggs. Sophie felt protective. This could be her daughter.

Sophie circled the park, came home and made a cup of tea. What could be the harm to this young donor? There had to be regulations, and no doubt the side effects for her had the same probabilities as for anyone else.

Sophie swallowed the tiny, egg-shaped oestrogen tablets, immediately disliking the sight of them in their tan, silver-backed, Soviet-like bubble pack. She really didn't want any more drugs, or to envision the follicle, the egg or the process of artificial insemination. Even she understood her eggs most probably would be too fragile now to harvest, inseminate and return to her uterus. While she marvelled at the technology, the science of fertility, the big business of fertility – the bright red Ferrari parked outside Dr Härma's clinic in its reserved spot – she thought most about the accident of life, the happenstance.

Babies and toddlers, getting ready now to go home for supper, still squealed in the park. As she sat among the roses in the garden, overlooking the playground, Sophie felt like an interloper. Despite eating well, keeping fit with jogging and yoga, the clean air and Tucker's undivided attention, she had hit a wall. There were moments when she felt comatose, leaden. Was it the oestrogen? She felt out of kilter, off balance; her dreams startled her, increasingly more frightening. In her nightmares, black, wiry hairs sprouted from her breasts… but then, Dr Härma did warn her about side effects.

242

The nausea, vomiting, bloating and headaches were second nature by now, but the tortured dreams arrested her enthusiasm. Even her own body resisted when she picked up the innocent packet of oestrogen – five times a day. Telling herself she was overthinking things, she knocked back the pills like clockwork.

"Millions of people do it," Tucker offered.

"Women," she answered, "millions of women."

Sophie's nightmares continued, including the black whiskers erupting like thorns, turning into vines, crushing her body. After calling the clinic, Dr Härma suggested she come in, but after an examination and blood tests, he said all was well, going according to plan, that her cycle was progressing perfectly, and that now, well into September, Sophie should start the hormone injections for ten days, starting on the third day of her menstrual cycle.

"Let's do the spa today?" Tucker suggested on Saturday morning, after taking the empty breakfast dishes back to the kitchen from their terrace. "Do you know it's got the largest water slide in Eastern Europe?"

"Good idea. I need a break from my work, and I could use a good steam." She packed a bathing suit, swimming goggles and shampoo.

While Tucker got lost in the men's dressing room, Sophie made her way through her own dressing room. Happy and confident, feeling at home in the world, with the most evil nightmares subsiding, Sophie felt pluckier, except for the visceral battle with each dosage of oestrogen. In the showers, before entering the pool, Sophie stood spellbound. An ethereal beauty showered her baby, carefully breaking the water that cascaded down with her hand, as he squealed with delight.

"He's beautiful," Sophie said, telling the woman something she already knew.

"*Jah*," she said, without a second thought and without looking up, as Sophie turned and hurried outside to find Tucker.

"Up here!" he bellowed from the top of the water slide. "Come on up."

Sophie's body still battled every scheduled dosage of oestrogen. Inexplicably she almost couldn't open the pack, pierce another plastic bubble and down the coffee-coloured pill. How many friends had extolled the benefits of oestrogen? It turned back the clock, they said. Tucker liked what he saw; she liked what she saw. It held off the menopause, apparently, and helped others to sleep.

At three days into her menstruation, like clockwork, the visiting nurse from Dr Härma's office came for the next ten days running, injecting the hormones. Even though the process was simple and over within seconds, Sophie felt guilty that she could not inject herself.

"I couldn't do it either," Tucker reassured her.

"You're pretty tough, Sista."

"And why is that?"

"You married me."

"That was the easy bit."

Sophie hoped, like her egg reserve, she wasn't running completely on empty. She would often seek a moment of peace and prayer in one of the many churches now open since Independence. Her favourite remained the Church of the Holy Spirit, *Püha Vaimu kirik*. There she sat, meditating, dreaming and confirming to herself that she would be happy, whatever the outcome, but mostly she prayed for composure.

As her microscopic egg within the follicle grew, Sophie sketched further plans for the company, took notes, studied fabrics, noticed what women wore, especially the older ones – the ones not emboldened by fat new paycheques but living on a pension that might have been useful during the Soviet era but now left most needing to sell flowers, spiced jams, embroidery and knitwear on street corners, under ancient arches and against the city walls.

One day, during her research, Sophie found herself intrigued by a delicately knitted scarf. As she turned the fabric this way and that, mesmerised, it dawned on her. This was the same fine material worn by the woman who had helped her the day she miscarried. For whatever reason, she felt a sudden and urgent need to find the woman who had most probably saved her life.

Sophie left the stalls on Müürivahe Street and ran the gauntlet of flower sellers at the ancient Viru Gates, bursting with the same red roses she'd seen at every arrival she'd made in Tallinn. As soon as she hurried through the double doors leading to the emergency room at the hospital, she realised that this might be an impossible task, a needle in a haystack. She and Tucker had asked previously who the kind Samaritan had been, and the hospital staff had shrugged. They didn't know.

Lost for words, with her meagre Estonian and the receptionist's pop English vocabulary, Sophie realised that they weren't getting anywhere. Finally, she asked for the slender medic who had seen her in the emergency room on the day she miscarried.

"Yes," the receptionist nodded, "I know this."

Within minutes the doctor arrived.

"Technically, we are not meant to do this," she admonished, "but let me see. How are you feeling?"

"Good, actually."

"How's Dr Härma treating you?" she asked, as she scanned the receptionist's computer, and then turned to a tall metal filing cabinet. Registering Sophie's surprise that she knew about her treatment under Dr Härma, the doctor added, "Tallinn is small world. And you stand out like a sore finger."

"Thumb," Sophie corrected her.

"*Okei*," the doctor said, "her name is Arina Tõeleid." She paused. "There is a note."

The young doctor rattled off something in Russian to the receptionist, who jumped up and hurried off to a back office.

"One minute."

By the time Sophie had written the woman's name down, the receptionist returned with a thin package, wrapped in brown paper, tied with string. The doctor handed it over.

"Apparently Mrs Tõeleid left this for you."

"Thank you."

"Mrs Mägi, everyone knows Arina."

Sophie stopped, looked up, waiting for more information.

"She's a world-class violinist – was known at one time the world over. She's quite special to say the least."

With that information in hand, as well as the soft Haapsalu white shawl that Arina had left at the hospital thrown around her shoulders, Sophie practically ran to the Estonia Concert Hall, where the man on the information desk looked her up and down and then, with that Estonian telepathic grin, handed her a smartly written address.

"No telephone," he said.

"*Aitäh*," Sophie said, as if she had just been given a four-leaf clover.

While she wasn't sure then, she knew that one day soon, when she couldn't wait any longer, she would go and find Arina Tõeleid, thank her, but for now, she didn't want to make a scene, embarrass anyone who had only acted as she might have, as a good Samaritan; someone who might want their privacy, not to have it invaded by a total stranger, and a foreigner at that.

"Perfect," Dr Härma said at the ten-day mark. "Ideal."

At home Sophie impersonated the rock-star fertility doctor, saying, "Picture perfect, another Ferrari in the drive, please."

That evening they walked through Kadriorg together. Sophie closed her fingers over the smooth, lucky star she now wore constantly, as if it carried some special power.

"Tuck, doesn't it seem so simple, so right?"

"Straightforward."

"A perfect follicle."

"You might even have two. But the chances are low, Soph. We have to remember that. Even our fertility cowboy said so. Let's not count the chickens before they hatch?"

While Sophie agreed, she did in fact count: on one little towhead, who had made her first appearance back in the small studio overlooking the port of Fontvieille, Monaco.

"By the way, Mrs Mägi, if you can come back down to earth," he paused, unlocking the front door, "I have something to say. I couldn't wait until tomorrow! Happy birthday!"

Back in the kitchen with the music turned low, Tucker placed a bottle of Russian champagne on the table along with a carefully iced cake with the number forty-three written in red.

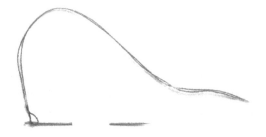

THIRTY-FOUR

Sophie's one follicle and a half grew incrementally by the minute. Härma said he didn't need one as large as the last one that Bertram Conrad had oohed and aahed over, but it did need to grow by one to two millimetres a day for ten days. However, at day eleven, one follicle had all but disappeared, and the remaining one was not sufficient. As Dr Härma conducted the ultrasound, he suggested that with an increased dosage of hormones the growth might be escalated.

"The tricky bit," he explained, "would be the transfer out of the uterus. That may not work. Too fragile."

Asking Sophie to return at the end of the week, he told her, "Just carry on as usual."

Taking longer, slower walks in Kadriorg Park, and out along the sea wall, the Pirita Promenade, to the yacht club, where the yachts seemed to grow in size day by day, Sophie couldn't help but count her one little chick.

She stopped for coffee in an empty restaurant overlooking the harbour and the yacht club parking lot. It seemed every car in the lot was a Mercedes or a BMW. New yachts, still with sticker prices, formed a line as far as the eye could see. Even Tucker had thought of buying one.

Looking away from the lot and out over the Gulf of Finland, then back at the medieval Tallinn skyline and off to the Viimsi Peninsula, Sophie wondered about Estonia's geographical advantage. She counted the international flags gracing the marina. She knew it presented a very different picture from just a few years ago when the locked harbour would have been presided over by a single Soviet star and the marina would have been empty.

Sophie doodled on the restaurant's napkin, drawing a clean image of two Estonian poppies in full bloom, bordered by six miniature daisies, five cornflowers and three sprigs of lavender.

"Do you embroider?" the waitress asked.

"No," Sophie said, "just sketching."

"Very good."

Sophie put the pencil down and reached for her purse. For what reason she didn't know, but today was the day she would find Arina Tõeleid, and just maybe this young waitress might help.

"Do you think you could help me with an address?"

"Why not?"

Sophie handed the waitress the slip of paper with Arina's address.

The waitress stepped back for a minute with that sudden straight face that Sophie recognised as fear left over from Soviet days.

"Please. I just want to thank her."

Again, after a bit of Estonian mind reading, the waitress nodded. "Okay. It's not far from here. You can easily walk. How do you know Arina?"

"She helped me once, after an accident."

"That's Arina," the young woman said before drawing a map. "Just follow along the beach, through the forest to the tip of Viimsi Peninsula."

"Thank you."

The waitress capped her pen, slipping it back into her pocket. "Have you ever heard her violin? I mean, have you ever heard her play it?"

"No. I'm sorry I haven't."

"Pure magic. Who knows? Maybe you will."

Sophie left the restaurant and headed down along the sandy lane, as directed by the waitress. At once engulfed in pine, she walked almost a mile through the wood and along the coast, following the hastily sketched but accurate map.

The house, set back from the main path, might have escaped her attention if it had not been for a small calico kitten grooming itself in short, darting movements in an odd slant of sunlight that found its way through the tall pines, landing on the cat and an old Soviet postbox. Having stopped for a moment, distracted by the animal, Sophie had looked up and back, and there stood the house exactly as the young waitress had described it.

The cottage, practically lost in the wood, had a red door, now faded to pink, matching shutters and planks that matched the ancient firs on either side. From the front steps, a view ran straight out to the sea. Geraniums cascaded down the front steps and onto the lawn.

Approaching the house slowly, at first Sophie thought an odd wind was stirring into a warm melodic sort of sound but then realised someone inside was playing a violin. Sophie sat, listening on the stoop, as the kitten pushed against her leg. She guessed it might be Bach. The chords unbalanced her for a minute but then almost immediately a sense of joy came over her, and the music stopped.

Sophie knocked. Arina answered the door and, recognising her visitor, smiled in welcome.

"Hello, how good to see you again."

"I'm so sorry to interrupt you," Sophie said.

"Never," Arina answered. "Come in, or would you like to sit out here?" She looked up and out at the pines, as if they were friends who might join them.

Sophie stood, unsure.

"Come in," Arina said. "I think I have coffee, or perhaps you would prefer tea?"

"Tea, please. I don't want to trouble you. I just came to say—"

"Thank you," Arina finished Sophie's sentence for her, "and you are most welcome."

For a second, Sophie found herself on the cobblestones on the walk up to Toompea to the Kumu Art Museum.

"Sit here," her hostess offered, as Sophie made her way to a comfortable chair that faced out to the sea in Arina's sitting room.

In no time at all, Arina returned with a lacquered tray, a tall glass press, two porcelain cups and a small silver pedestal with rose-dusted chocolates.

"Thank you, really."

"You are welcome. Truly."

Sophie noticed the violin, set in its case, loosely covered by a soft blue cloth.

"Sometimes," Arina started, lifting her cup, "things hurt."

"Yes," Sophie answered, feeling a million miles away from Kadriorg, Tucker, his business deals and *Project Bébé*. "How can you speak English so well?"

Arina laughed. "Most classical musicians, long before this part of the world was called the Soviet Bloc, were multilingual." Arina turned thoughtful. "I am sorry you lost your baby."

Sophie nodded.

"Pain," Arina continued, "is just another colour that adds vibrancy to your life. It shows you the way, if you will, another string on your bow. I have had to make life-changing decisions, to make tough decisions – like whether or not to leave my family, my homeland, Estonia."

"But how do you know? When to decide, how to decide."

"I don't know. Sometimes, you don't get to decide. Life decides for you. It's different for everyone. For example, those Estonians who missed the Swedish boat, it was just bad luck, bad timing, one of those things like the death of a loved one – beyond your control. Some read the early warning signs and others did not. Many just did not want to believe it, that the rest of the world would let Stalin and Churchill, mind you, carve up the world. We thought the West would come, thought it was just a matter of time before the West would help us, but no one thought it would take fifty years."

Again the two women sat in silence, wondering about the ways of the world, how things could turn on a dime, or how things could change course for reasons unknown. Sophie put her hands in her lap, where she hoped the follicle grew.

"I am sure you've heard this a million times, but your music is…"

"I have heard it many times, and thank you."

"Why didn't you leave? You could have played anywhere – been successful beyond…"

"I could, I did, and I was."

"Sorry. Just hearing you now was so…"

She poured Sophie more tea and offered another chocolate. "I will tell you the story, if you're interested."

"I am interested. Very."

"When there were first rumours that the Russians were advancing, people fled, but not everyone. Before Independence there were opportunities to go, to defect to the West. Today we have a brain drain, as you know. Some are afraid that the Bear might turn again, and we are…"

"The little country that rides the shoulder of the Bear?"

"Precarious." Arina nodded knowingly. "But the truth is, where else could you be an Estonian except in Estonia?"

A sudden shower of rain hit the roof of the house and blocked the grey sea. Sophie felt lulled in a way that she might have been if she had been on her own, sitting on one of those ice-age boulders, now wedged between two ancient pines, daydreaming.

Arina started her story as if it had just been yesterday, as if even a lifetime would not take it away.

"I thought about defecting in the sixties – went to the brink several times. But the ever-watchful KGB, including members of my own family, terrified me. I imagined my fingers broken, my violin taken. Can you imagine? During the odd solo or orchestral performance in Berlin or Stockholm I saw myself quietly slipping away, into any local embassy and asking for asylum, but I never did. I would neatly pack up my dream and my Bergonzi violin that now, instead of belonging to my father, actually belonged to the state. 'Next time,' I would tell myself, 'next time.' I, the Soviet, the world-class violinist would go obediently with my violin back onto the plane with my KGB minders."

Sophie listened, while catching the tiniest sliver of a silver arc out past the pines and against the stark white sky and the blue-grey sea.

"Without warning I was taken off the world-touring list. Clearly, I was now suspect. Would I defect? Maybe it was the length of time I took to pack my violin, or to leave the orchestral venues. Maybe it was a minder's notes, or maybe it was a friend or a relative who had informed. I could never be sure. A boat, hidden amongst the glacial rocks, had been prepared for me to make the crossing from here to Helsinki. Right here." She pointed out the window to beyond the pines and the stretch of sand.

Sophie refilled their cups and took another piece of chocolate.

"I am not sure when I first made the decision about defecting. There had been so many moments, like the one in Berlin, when it hung on a knife's edge. I could have just walked out the door, into the night, the traffic, but I couldn't contemplate being gone forever, even fifty years of exile. I didn't want to think about the KGB agents who may show up at my door, wherever I might be, in the West, to retrieve me, possibly kill me – quickly or slowly, and as always, without a trace. Who cared about a young violin player from Tallinn? Maybe I became suspect after the concert in Sydney, where I froze, almost fainted, when I couldn't pass through the stage door, when the voice in my head shouted 'run' and my accompanist did – straight out into the street and into the American embassy."

"You had a chance," Sophie breathed.

"I had a chance, but there was a last chance. Hidden between the glacial rocks and the windblown firs at the water's edge, a boat pitched from side to side, blown by the night wind. One lone sailor would captain the boat to Helsinki. I was to bring nothing but the Bergonzi – that was the trade. *Free passage for the violin.* I remember it clearly as if it were just yesterday, almost as if I were meant to leave right now.

"The sound of late summer lovers laughing echoed somewhere off in the distance. The scent of pine, fir and mulch filled the air, along with the salty smell of the sea and sand that ran the length of the pristine beach. *Peat and bog.* That aroma, the perfume of Estonia. Waving his lamp, the seaman signalled to me, 'Time to go.' But rooted to the spot, standing there like a fool, the violin case in hand, I couldn't move. We had so little time. I knew the odds, the danger. The radar operators were paid only enough for those few hours. After that, we'd be easily detected, used for target practice or worse.

"Gripping the violin case by the handle, nailed to the spot, I studied the True Lover's Knot at my feet and the other ferns in the gulley two feet away. The smell of the trees made me dizzy. I still could not move, and I watched as the mariner's lamp made a slow arc, and I listened to the low, sharp blow of his whistle.

"'*Kirrusta.*' Hurry up, he said. Every second I delayed I knew was a second less to escape and a second greater that I'd be detected, we'd be detected, caught and punished. I knew the risk I took, the risk the others took, what my family had paid, but I couldn't move. Two alternating woodpeckers hammered away, and a flood of summer flowers poured forth in my memory, especially the lily of the valley at early morning, wet with dew. I saw the carpet of white wild roses spread out before me in the moonlight, and I started to cry.

"'No.' I would not go. Already the stark red berries of my wild roses were showing, preparing for winter. The sailor called out once more, and then left. After all, he had his life, his family's safety to think about as well.

"The small boat receded into the distance, and I knew my beloved Bergonzi would finally and permanently be taken away by the state, but Sophie, I did make that exchange willingly for a simple spread of fragile summer flowers, ones that blow away in the night but leave a bright, inedible fruit that can pass through the coldest winter unharmed. Sometimes a decision is made for you and sometimes you must just make that decision – let it rip right through you. It's either a yes or a no – and no one can do it for you. That is courage."

Sophie heard the distant refrains of Arina's violin, as she walked back up the beach to the causeway and then along the sea esplanade. She watched a Tallink ferry sailing to Helsinki disappear over the horizon.

She thought of Khulan and Arina in the same instant. A thin scent of sandalwood caught her attention, perhaps the seaweed. She recalled the note Khulan had neatly tucked beside the delicately carved fan. *It all gets done...*

"I let fucking go." Sophie railed at the bronze Russalka monument, the angel with its upraised Orthodox cross, facing the sea where the *Mermaid* and all its men went down. Fresh bouquets honouring the dead at the base of Russalka blew away in the hard wind, and crossing the multi-lane highway against the light, Sophie held on to that little thought.

She relinquished hope of whether or not her follicle would grow, if life would or could be multiplied in a Petri dish. She cared, but she unhooked. She just wanted five minutes with Robin to say that she was past holding on, making something happen: *Project Bébé.* Maybe Robin had been right all along, or at least she had found a happy medium between trying and not trying at all.

"No. I'm not doing it anymore. If this doesn't work, I am not going the donor route. I don't want to be an incubator, carry a baby that's not mine – what's the point? Hire a surrogate? Tucker's sperm will have to be 'forced'. ICSI, whether donor eggs or not. That's assuming his sperm is even up to the job. What happens later? Is it more his baby than mine? Do we use donor sperm, as well as a donor egg? Why not just adopt – it's the same thing – but of course there are no babies available?"

Robin listened to Sophie, chiming in with the odd 'yes', 'no' and 'oh'. A lot of what Sophie said made sense and a lot of it was the rambling of a tired woman, drugged with fertility pills, teetering on the verge of perhaps one of life's deepest disappointments.

"Don't give up yet," Robin said. "You've come this far."

"Did you – mother of all reason – just tell me not to give up?"

"Look," Robin said, "focus. What do you have on today, just today?"

"Nothing. An ultrasound on Saturday to see if the follicle is large enough to do anything."

"Okay, so today, just do nothing. Saturday, text me afterwards?"

"Robin, I don't want to do this anymore."

"I know. Just keep it simple, Sophie. One foot in front of the next. You know, keep it in the day. Stop thinking about the Big Picture, you know, Forever. Keep it small. Don't let go, Soph. You are close."

"Okay, maybe."

Sophie wanted to speak about Arina, but she didn't. She felt it was too complicated, and she was sure that any mention of a violin, the wind, the sudden rain, chocolates and coffee, a tiny sliver of a silver arc and the odd slap of the Baltic surf against the reeds would make her sound peculiar.

"Where's Tucker?" Robin asked.

"Today?" Sophie had to think. "Ukraine. Happily, his business is expanding. He's gone for a day or two. He's got a new young partner. Nice kid, young wife. British, always on the go. They run the business in Krakow."

"Exciting life."

"Exciting," Sophie answered genuinely. "Tucker has been fantastic. He really wants this baby. He does care, despite all his posturing. I couldn't do any of this without him."

"Sophie," Robin said, "I've had a thought but have hesitated to say anything – I'm not sure why."

"Go on."

"Call my cousin. Remember, I sent you her number a while back, but you never rang her? She adopted two kids and maybe she might have something to say. I don't know. She's a doctor, could have gone the IVF route but didn't. I never asked her why, but it could be an interesting chat."

Promising to text Robin after her ultrasound, as well as to call her cousin Miriam, Sophie strolled into Old Town. The cobblestones provided an instant transport to another place and time. In the square, she turned to look up at the town hall, where in the form of a green dragon a waterspout looked down.

A fairy tale.

She didn't need to close her eyes to be living any number of the fables Anne had read to her as a child, or she had read on her own. She had stepped straight into any number of Rackham-illustrated stories from her treasured, leather-bound book of fairy tales.

Damsel in distress.

At the Golden Egg, Sophie ordered her favourite Witch's Casserole, and feeling better after speaking with Robin, it dawned on her: Robin had a secret. Something was entirely different. What was it? Sophie grew suspicious as she made her way home after lunch, taking the long walk from Old Town to Kadriorg. Leaving Vabadusa Square – Freedom Square – she circled the Opera House and Symphony Hall, past the massive shopping centre towards

Kadriorg, past the Tsar's Summer Palace and the President's home. Opening the slightly splintered gate to her own home, she decided to sit on the stoop for a few minutes enjoying the October weather. She sat until a chill wind sent her inside, and with a cup of peppermint tea, Sophie called Miriam.

"It's your lucky day. It's Columbus Day. The kids are home, outside playing. Where are you calling from?"

"Tallinn. Estonia."

"Ah yes, Robin told me all about you. Trying to get pregnant, and you are looking for the lucky mojo, putting herbs in your bed and crystals in your bath."

"What?"

"Just kidding. How's Eastern Europe?"

"Amazing actually. Lots of energy, lots of hope. A real buzz," Sophie answered. "Obviously I'm calling you because Robin said you adopted two kids."

"Yes, from Ukraine."

"But why? You have one of the top paediatric practices in California, with certainly access to the very best reproduction specialists."

"It's simple, Sophie, or it was for me – not for everyone, it's not the same, one size does not fit all. I'm a doctor, a medical doctor, a paediatrician, and bluntly, the bulk of my practice is made up of IVF babies with holes in their hearts. End of story. I chose to adopt. I researched adoption and found if I adopted before the age of two, I could have the same relationship with my kid as if I were the birth mother. I know the short- and long-term implications of holes in hearts and I didn't want to risk it. There are all kinds of arguments, but in the end you have to – I had to – just go with my heart, guts, whatever. Make a decision. So I adopted, and I am really happy. One girl, one boy. My daughter looks like me and my son, who originally did, now suddenly has gone ginger. What a surprise, but that's what they are, Sophie – my Beloved Surprise Packages – and

I am deeply content, even in the chaos. Oh, and did I say no drugs for me? No incubator for me?"

"No IVF – despite all the breakthroughs, the miracles, the successes?"

"Definitely not. I love science – don't get me wrong – but I love Mother Nature even more."

"Mommy," a young child rang out, and Miriam signed off, inviting Sophie to call at any time. "I'm happy to talk about my experience. Adoption is the best-kept secret. What's not to like? You need them, they need you. A baby, perfectly formed, all fingers and toes, just handed to you. Easiest delivery in the world. Within minutes they're yours. Not for one second do I think of my son or daughter as adopted. They are just mine! Sometimes I have to remind myself. Really, I don't think of it at all. Best-kept secret in the world! Survival of the fittest? Maybe. But heart of my heart? Definitely."

Feeling almost unbearably light after her phone call with Robin's cousin, Sophie kept her appointment with Dr Härma. Three of 'Härma's babies', identical triplets, played in the reception area with the receptionist in their three-seated pram.

Thumbing through a well-worn baby magazine, Sophie recalled an old refrain from a song she sang as a child, picking daisies, sitting in Anne's lap. They'd pulled petals one at a time from the daisies uprooted from the front lawn. 'He loves me, he loves me not.'

Dr Härma examined Sophie, as they both watched the monitor by the exam table.

"No," he said, "it's not going to work. The follicle is not growing, or not enough. Even if larger, it will be too fragile to move. I am afraid you are out of luck. So what about egg donation? I need to tell my donor. She is waiting. I need at least thirty days to prep her and you."

"What? Wait." Sophie sat up. "Are you saying that the egg will not grow any further?"

"Maybe yes or maybe no, but it is not going to work for IVF or ICSI."

"Can we at least try? See what happens."

"With your husband's sperm?"

"Yes."

"No."

A strained silence ensued.

"Well, should we start the donor protocol?"

The elongated, clinic bulbs buzzed and softly popped. Traffic outside carried on at a steady rate.

"The donor," Dr Härma said, "I need to prep the donor."

"No," Sophie heard herself say. "No." She said it once again, more clearly this time.

"Think about it. Call me later," Dr Härma said, while spraying his hands with the bottle of antibacterial gel on his desk.

"No."

Walking to the street, Sophie flagged a taxi, and at home she double-locked the doors. The house seemed colder than normal, and terribly still. Sophie turned off her phone and felt subdued. She saw her young donor silhouetted against the haystack at harvest time, one leg kicked up and back.

Slipping off her shoes, Sophie climbed into bed and listened. No swallows twittered outside the skylight, where there had been a nest all summer, only a lone goose honking off in the distance. A light wind tossed the tops of the Arctic pines, while children still shrieked in the park across the street.

Curling up deeper, Sophie studied the white eaves soaring over her head and the chalk-white clouds racing past the skylights. Rounding up tighter into her pillow, she found herself slipping away, ice cold, freezing.

Her back teeth ached, as she clenched her jaw, tucking herself deeply into her bed, herself, her fine Scandinavian home. White roses still clung to the bushes, green apples to the trees and geraniums to their bright window boxes. Wrapping the ache of childlessness around her like a blanket, she opened up to the real grief she had long denied.

No father.

All her life she had carried it with her. Never told a soul. Anne was everything, but this big gaping thing had gone with her everywhere.

No father.

Entwined together – no father, and now no child – Sophie closed her eyes, surrendered and let everything slip away. She saw Arina on the shore, a small boat and a sailor waving a lantern, while telling her to hurry. There would never be a link now in that forever replicating chain. She saw the ferns, the True Lover's Knot, at her own feet, riveted to the spot.

It will rip right through you.

'Infertility,' Bertram Conrad had said, 'is not a romantic comedy.' Sophie admitted that 'It' would never happen. She would never have a baby of her own or equally a father who might unexpectedly come home. In a bolted house, in a locked room, in Estonia, Sophie cried. It was over. No one to rail at, not even life in general. She just saw Arina decades ago. Wavering. She heard an audible 'no', then saw the wide arc of the bright lantern go out.

No to donor eggs, no to a surrogate.

Sophie intentionally, perfectly and completely chose to miss the boat.

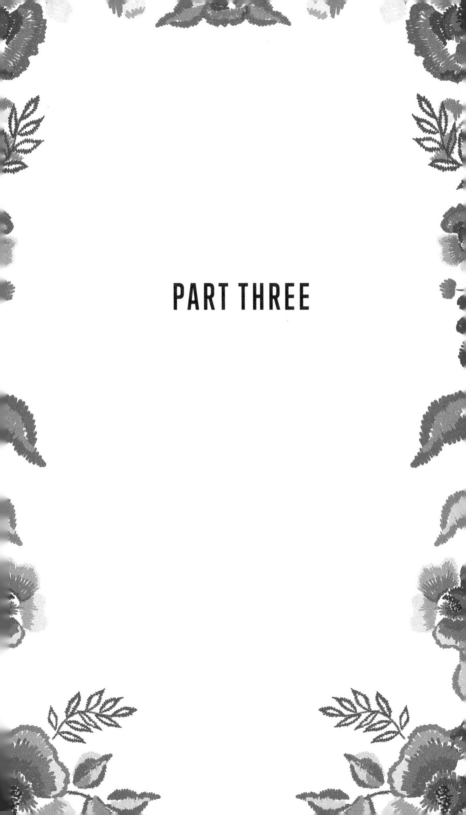

PART THREE

THIRTY-FIVE

"Tucker, listen. I know you are trying to help, but I don't want donor eggs. I don't care how many eggs a twenty-five-year-old has in reserve. I'm not going there. I'm okay with no kids. I don't want a surrogate either."

"Härma said the donor probably has more than seventy thousand eggs left. She can afford to share a few?" Tucker offered.

"No. I'm not interested."

"Okay. That's where I started anyway. Just you and me, kid."

"Good."

"But, Sophie, what about adoption? We'd started going down that route, remember?"

"I know. I need a few days to think it all through, though. I'm already obligated to take the twelve-year-old out for lunch from the children's home – today, in fact. I think they really want me to try on the idea of an older child. I feel committed. They've been remarkable. Amazing women. But I'm not ready to take on a twelve-year-old."

"What are you planning to do with her?" Tucker asked.

"I thought we could at least go for lunch, a manicure, shopping for CDs, whatever prepubescent girls are into."

Sophie sliced and toasted the seeded black bread, poured some coffee, not really hungry but intrigued for a moment by the idea of adopting an older child.

Even so soon after her no-follicle resolution, she felt a certain ease, maybe even a happy free fall after stopping the oestrogen. Sophie smiled, recalling her perfect slam-dunk from across the room as she pitched the remaining silver-backed, coffee-coloured capsules into the wire mesh trashcan.

"Who knows, Sophie, the idea might grow on you. I don't have anything against twelve-year-olds," Tucker said.

"Robin liked the idea," she told him. "Said 'try it on for size'. One of the staff from the children's home is coming along as well."

Lingering over a kiss with his hand touching the small of her back, Sophie promised to fill Tucker in on the what-if-we-were-parents-of-a-twelve-year-old date. Listening to his UAZ as it rumbled out the drive, waking up whoever might have been asleep in the neighbourhood, Sophie tossed the dishes into the dishwasher and went straight to her desk, outside the empty nursery.

"Definitely not for a twelve-year-old," she said out loud, as she looked through the open door. From her roughhewn desk, Sophie studied the room intended for a baby – the towering sunflowers and the swallows. She felt no immediate need to dismantle it, and was impressed with her own happiness, the letting go, and the easy decision-making.

She busied herself, feeling almost impatient for her lunch date, even if only to get it over with and to fulfil an obligation she felt to Krissu and the other staff at the home. At her desk, with the door now closed to the nursery, she sorted through the images of embroidery that Laura Laar had given her. She felt over the sometimes rough and sometimes smooth fabric of the samples she had picked up along the Old Town wall. In particular, she found a blue cornflower pattern striking, then the boldly coloured flowers of Muhu Island, standing out against a black background.

Sophie sketched, envisioning a red linen jacket, embroidered from the shoulder to the waist, then a snug, full-length red sheath embroidered from the waist to below the hips in the intricate Muhu floral designs.

She pulled out her laptop and reviewed her business plan. After fiddling with various sales strategies and financial projections, Sophie sat back. Considering all aspects of the industry, she felt that a niche market would be the only way for her to compete, especially against the likes of India, renowned for its embroidery work.

So engrossed in her work, Sophie almost lost track of time but managed to change quickly, hop into her car and drive to the children's home punctually for the lunch date. There she met the staff member, who excitedly ushered two girls into the car.

"They don't like to go alone. You don't mind?" she asked.

"Not at all," Sophie said, "the more the merrier."

"You know, they've never had a professional manicure," she said. "My name is Rahne. They are Anya and Eeva. Anya is very interested to meet you."

Both girls smiled, as Sophie turned to say hello, and then carried on twittering in Estonian, while at the same time practising the odd English phrase on each other first, and then with Rahne's permission on Sophie.

"It's a good day," Anya said. "Do you like the Backstreet Boys?"

"It is a very good day, and I do like the Backstreet Boys," Sophie answered, feeling immediately guilty. She had no intention of adopting – anyone. As the two girls chatted and Rahne watched the road, Sophie mentally recounted the positives of having no children. 1) No playgroups, no competitive moms, 2) no confusion about priorities, 3) lots of me time, 4) freedom, 5) cinema and sleep at the weekend, 6) use the F word whenever, 7) time, time and more time, 8) sleep, sleep and more sleep, 9) money and 10) time for other people's kids. 'Endless,' she almost said out loud, after she parked. Then after a swipe of lip-gloss and retying her freshly shampooed ponytail, she announced, "Let's go."

At the recently opened New Nail Bar in Old Town, there was much hilarity as the girls negotiated colour options. Each sitting down with her own manicurist, they rattled off in quick succession what they wanted: tiger stripes, zebra stripes. Rahne then chose a neon green, while Sophie picked out the brightest cherry red she could find.

American Pizza around the corner from the New Nail Bar just managed to squeeze them all in and seat them by the window, taking orders on the fly, apologising all the while for the unexpected popularity of their new place.

"If the girls are not back by exactly two o'clock, the police will be called," Rahne announced, as if making a threat or warning. Sophie looked up, momentarily startled, then stopped slicing the pizza altogether.

"It shouldn't be a problem, but maybe, in order to save time, you should run up the street to the music shop. See if they actually have any Backstreet Boys CDs."

"No," Rahne challenged Sophie, now looking at her with suspicion, and checking the girls, as if she had lost them. "Mrs Mägi, I stay with the girls. Where they go, I go. I'm not leaving."

"Okay," Sophie answered, "I understand," which she didn't.

"I'm sorry. You don't. Pretend parents have tried to kidnap Estonian children before. They were on the aeroplane and gone before anything could be done."

"Never mind, let's quickly finish our pizza and you take the girls to the shop. I will pay the bill."

Looking relieved, the interpreter nodded.

Sophie fell silent. On the plane before anything could be done? Young girls. The sex trade? Sophie felt ill and angry in the same instant. Leaving the trendy pizza restaurant, they all walked up the street, across the cobblestones.

Sophie trailed behind the two girls whose heads bobbed together, conferring. They bumped each other at the shoulder and at the hip, and like sisters, they walked arm in arm. The interpreter dropped back to fall into step with Sophie.

Suddenly, Sophie couldn't contain herself any longer. "Do I look like a trafficker to you?"

"No," Rahne answered, "but Krissu holds me responsible. We take our job very seriously and this is all so new. In Estonia we all know each other, but now there are so many foreigners coming in and there is no way of knowing..."

"What their real intentions are?"

"That's right. Please forgive me. I am just trying to do my job. I don't want to lose any children."

"You won't."

"Thank you. May I tell you about Anya and Eeva?"

"Yes, please do."

"Eeva has parents, who can't afford to feed or clothe her, but they come every week, always with the hope of taking her home. Anya has no parents and has lived at the home permanently, since she was four years old. No one has claimed her."

The sense of reverie, bright nails and pizza died away as Sophie took on the seriousness of the girls' situation. However, almost as quickly, looking down at her bright red nails, she regained her sense of buoyancy, of freedom. These were not her children; she had made her choice, but watching them carefully, especially Anya, Sophie realised Krissu and Rahne wanted to find the girl a mother.

Anya worked hard to keep in step with her friend Eeva. Pretending to banter with Rahne, Sophie scrutinised the twelve-year-old. Tourists recently off a cruise ship bumped them as they passed by, and for a few minutes Sophie lost the girls in a crowd of American retirees.

Eeva wore a wool dress with a dark jacket and matching tights. Her long legs strode out confidently. Prancing with excitement, she fluttered her nails in the air. Both girls giggled. A bit shorter, Anya wore jeans, trendily torn and ever so slightly frayed at the cuffs. Captivated by their closeness, Sophie zeroed in on the way they walked. Eeva strode close to Anya in a bit of a lockstep, and then it dawned on Sophie: Anya limped, having one leg shorter than the other. In unison, their movements well-rehearsed, the girls fought to disguise the hitch in her step.

The shop did carry the Backstreet Boys, and the girls blurted out, "Two for the price of one," in their best English.

"One each," Sophie agreed, and paid the clerk.

Arriving back at the home at exactly two o'clock, the girls stepped out of the car, fluttered their striped nails and brandished their new matching CDs.

"*Nägemist*," Sophie heard herself say.

"Goodbye and thank you," Anya said, while Eeva nodded. Rahne smiled in appreciation.

Anya looked back, making eye contact with Sophie, who waved before getting into her car. Eeva pulled her friend into the home as if she would never let her go, while Rahne locked the door twice behind them.

Only too happy to get home, take a shower and have a cup of tea, Sophie continued to think about Anya. It wasn't the limp, the clubfoot, which bothered Sophie. It was the sadness of auditioning a young girl who had obviously been passed over too many times to believe it was possible but still did. It was clear she had, in a sense, a sister, a friend in Eeva, and even if Sophie did entertain the idea of adopting a twelve-year-old, she would never harm that close bond Anya and Eeva shared. That would last a lifetime.

Sophie continued to see the image of the two girls walking in their practised routine, almost seamless, up the cobblestones. Her heart ached with both joy and sadness for them. Would Anya ever understand that it was Eeva's pretence that Anya had no problem with walking that ultimately, and intentionally, highlighted her friend's disability?

"Friends for life," Sophie said before taking a sip of tea, thinking of Robin, and the children's home. The home was so clean, so well organised, and no different from any warm and safe place. The children, well loved and looked after, were a family. Eeva and Anya were sisters.

She remembered the nursery, the youngest babies, from the day Krissu had shown her and Tucker around. She especially recalled the ones without parents; they stole her heart. It seemed unconscionable that they waited, sometimes years, while full investigations had to be played out for any living relative in or out of Estonia to be found.

Wanting to scoop them all up, Sophie recalled having to will her arms down. She still envisioned a baby bouquet wrapped up tightly in her arms. The row of five baby buggies in the garden, backlit by a brilliant shaft of October sunlight, stirred her beyond any monthly cycle website, clinic, support group, proffered cocktail of fertility drugs, technology, replacement of a nuclei or someone else's sperm. Here were five, hooded baby carriages with five live infants, babies who had somehow jumped into the river of life and swam. Why did that memory, that sight, remain so emblazoned?

Home unexpectedly early, Tucker shouted out, "Does this mean we can now have sex for sex's sake?"

"Yes." Sophie chuckled.

"How was the trip to the New Nail Bar?"

"Good," Sophie said, meeting him in the kitchen, "all good."

"So we are not adopting a twelve-year-old?" He kissed her playfully.

"Not today," she answered, wrapping her arms around his neck.

"I'm too young to be a father of a twelve-year-old."

"Definitely," Sophie agreed, kissing him lightly.

"Too much of a reach?"

"Maybe." She laughed, as they both took in the sight of each other and the beauty of their little wooden dacha.

"I think we're lucky," Tucker said.

"I agree."

Luigi Boccherini's String Quintet in E Major played in the kitchen and resounded throughout the house. Streetlights came on around and through Kadriorg Park, as a light wind stirred winter awake and a very light snow began to fall.

"Log on the fire?" Tucker said.

"Yes," Sophie answered, feeling capable of almost anything, even renovating a manor house.

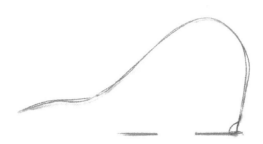

THIRTY-SIX

Packing a small bag, Sophie hummed and chuckled, throwing in a pair of racy knickers. With no *Project Bébé*, and with the embroidery business on a low boil, she felt surprisingly free, happy and herself again.

"Travelling wife," Sophie told her mother, who said no matter what she must see Krakow.

"Of course," Sophie agreed, "how could I forget *The Trumpeter of Krakow*?"

"One of your very old favourites."

"Apparently the tune is played every day at noon. I also want to stand outside the old synagogue, where they say Spielberg decided to make *Schindler's List.*"

'Sexy and fun,' Tucker had said, when he convinced Sophie to come along. Krakow, he had said, would be her field trip alone because he was busy, and Warsaw was not anything to write home about, except, of course, for the reconstructed Old Town.

The previous evening, standing in the wintry Baltic air, regarding the full moon, white against a black sky, Sophie had wondered how October had flown by. Was it really already a

Harvest Moon? With her breath now hanging, visible, in the evening air, winter encroaching, she remembered that promise she had made to herself – no baby, one way or another, by Christmas, she'd divorce Tucker.

Let him go to have a family.

Taking a backward glance at Town Hall Square with its pastel Hanseatic townhouses, her favourite square in the world, Sophie closed her eyes. Feeling once again peaceful, happy and herself, she said aloud, "Never. Not in a million years would I ever let Tucker go. With or without kids, we are a family."

Sophie looked out of the carriage window, as the Polish train rumbled through orchards ripe with apples, farmland rich with wheat. Disembarking in Krakow, Sophie skipped onto the platform. Feeling unrestricted, not weighed down, she tried to remember the last time she'd truly felt spontaneous. It had been in Cassis, the spring-fed harbour, sunbathing on a tilting raft.

Everything once again seemed tangible and alive. Urgency fell away, and sex with Tucker was like falling off a log. Easy. She didn't weigh the odds, consider babies, wonder whether or not Tucker had stayed in the sauna too long. With no charts to keep, oestrogen to take, schedules to make or having to report in to anyone – not Härma or Conrad or even the fertility support group – Sophie smiled. In fact, she laughed out loud.

Walking out of the station, Sophie wanted to fling herself into the buzz. Just like Tallinn, Krakow teemed with it. As she crossed the vast avenues in this once-royal capital, Sophie exuded her own freedom, her own independence. In the shadow of St Mary's Basilica, she unwrapped a sandwich, listening first to the bells and then to the majestic trumpet that broke off in midstream, signifying the player who had been stuck by a Tartar arrow, sounding the alarm.

With striking blue skies, the day brimmed with beauty. Over a coffee and a chocolate brownie, Sophie counted her blessings.

Tossing her brownie wrapper in a street bin, she strolled towards the Krakow ghetto, the Remah Synagogue, where her guide arrived bang on time.

"Welcome to Krakow, the most beautiful city in the world! My name is Jakub. I study physics at the university, and I do this in my spare time. Foreigners don't know our great history, the glory of Krakow."

"So, tell me all about it," Sophie said. "I want to hear everything."

"That's good." He tossed his long hair over his narrow shoulders that sprouted like wings and directed Sophie forward in the same instant. "So this is it! Right here! The exact spot where the famous director Steven Spielberg directed scenes from *Schindler's List*."

From the middle of the quiet lane, Jakub told Sophie all about the story of Oskar Schindler and the Polish Jews he managed to save, as well as those he did not. "This synagogue is special," he said. "Remah was known for its Jewish mystic – Rabbi Moses Isserles. You go in. I'll wait."

Sitting in the dark, empty temple, Sophie prayed, thinking of the congregation that had perished. The enormity of history sat with her, along with hope. The doors of the synagogue, after all, were now open. Lost in meditation and the recall of history for some time, Sophie finally remembered Jakub waiting for her and hurried outside, apologising profusely.

The day turned cooler, but the buzz of Krakow still filled the air. Jakub asked Sophie all the requisite tour questions: Work? Children? Family? Where do you live? Why are you in Poland? Sophie answered all of them, and they chatted easily until she found herself looking over a wall at the Old Cemetery.

One grave seemed covered in snow, but upon closer inspection, Sophie realised it was not snow at all, but small pieces of folded paper, rough origami egrets, doubled up and pleated in various ways, tucked into crannies and set under rocks. The slips of paper, mostly white, looked ready for flight.

"What is it?" Sophie asked.

"The grave of a medieval mystic."

"And the paper?"

"Prayers."

"Hand me a pen."

Sophie fumbled in her bag, finally retrieving the slim envelope that originally held her train ticket, and Jakub lent her his pen.

'BABY', she wrote, not knowing what else to say, and flicked her own little paper egret over the railing, straight onto the tomb, where it wavered for a moment between the mossy lid and the weedy ground.

"Nice." Jakub punched the air as if it were a goal in a penalty shoot-out. He bounced, spun around and made Sophie smile, as if Krakow was not just a royal city but his royal city, even now. He might as well have carried a lute and a sign reading, "I tell tall tales." Waltzing her into Wawel Cathedral, Jakub locked arms with Sophie and commanded her to look.

Falling into step with the other tourists, whose murmurs filled the vaulted air, Sophie knelt in prayer. Candle flames flickered on the high altar and a hint of incense remained from an earlier mass. Liturgical incantation spilled over from a side chapel nearby.

"They are all buried here." Jakub spoke over Sophie's shoulder. "Saint Stanislaus, Saint-Queen Hedwig and too many kings to recount. Make a wish. You can wish on Hedwig's tomb, too, you know. Your wish will come true."

"First a Jewish mystic, and now a Catholic saint?" Sophie laughed.

"What else did you come for?" He chuckled.

"The magic," she agreed.

Sophie stood close to Saint-Queen Hedwig's tomb. It reminded her of Cathédrale Notre-Dame-Immaculée in Monaco, where once, escaping the heat of her MBA and the actual summer sun, she had listened in an almost deadly silence to the sound of her own footsteps, coming upon the unexpected burial slab of Princess Grace of Monaco. She thought then as she thought now. No matter how rich or overflowing a life, eventually it would melt like anyone else's into a stone slab, neatly incised with name and date. She had sworn then as she swore now to use 'it', her life, well.

Jakub amused Sophie with further stories of Hedwig, her holiness, her canonisation, and the tale of a footprint, left in plaster long since hardened, the resuscitation of a drowned child and a Pope who stood at her sarcophagus.

"Did you make a wish?" he asked her.

"I did."

"Okay," Jakub continued to dance around his client, "this is the last thing to see." He unzipped his jacket as they stepped out of the cathedral and into the late-afternoon sun. "Then you better get to the train, if you want to be back in Warsaw by eight."

"Yes," Sophie said.

"This," he said triumphantly "is the Wawel chakra. A power spot. The Dalai Lama, everyone, says so, even the dowsers. Some say it's the old dragon that used to live under the hill. It's like a human chakra, a cleansing spot for the earth."

A group of Japanese tourists stood in a straight line with eyes closed, leaning against the outside wall of the cathedral. Sophie joined in, pressed her back to the wall, feeling its coolness, giggling along with her fellow tourists, while Jakub gave her two thumbs up, while also flashing his watch.

"You've got to go," he shouted, rushing her to the train station, getting her there with no time to spare.

"So now you love me, you love Poland?" He kissed her on either cheek.

"I do," she said, lightly kissing him back, "and Poland, too."

THIRTY-SEVEN

Rolling on once again in a train from what seemed like another century with its rattle and scratchy wool seats, the tragic history of trains in Poland was not lost on Sophie, just as the darkness and stillness of the Remah Temple had not been lost on her either. Yet the thought of Jakub's exuberance lifted her, along with the recollection of the sunny day, blue skies, and Krakow, vibrating with new life, hope and, of course, Independence.

Smiling again, Sophie admitted that not having a baby, like not having a father, didn't spell the end of everything, disaster, as she had once thought. It was just a bit of life's powerlessness, or, as Khulan once wrote, 'a letting go'. Out of that, all kinds of things could happen. As the train clacked away over the ageing rails, she felt liberated in a sense; maybe even like the Polish, she felt independent.

The landscape, dominated by apple orchards, slipped past. Trees ripe with fruit, standing in groves or singularly beside the odd, trackside house caught and held her attention. Her joy seemed to grow as the train travelled on towards Warsaw. With her head resting on the back of her hard seat, Sophie felt pleased to be on a working holiday with Tucker. She'd seen sights she wanted to see, and now, headed back into Warsaw, she'd have dinner with the man she loved. Who could be happier?

In that instant, her phone vibrated, but over the din of the train, she couldn't be sure. She almost didn't want to answer. She let it vibrate, until the passenger next to her tapped her arm, as if she had been sleeping, to let her know she had a call.

"Tucker," Sophie answered. "Yes. Soon." She looked at her watch. "I'm about twenty minutes out."

"Good," he said.

"Why?"

"Krissu called."

"Krissu?"

"Yes. She has your baby."

"My baby?"

"Yes."

"Okay," Sophie said, unsure of what else to say. "See you soon." She snapped the phone closed.

The past seemed to be reaching forward, pulling her back. She'd momentarily forgotten about Krissu, the children's home and adoption. Hadn't all this been put to rest? Hadn't they closed the book on an adoption? Hadn't Krissu heard the news? All of this was over and done with. Like a false alarm, someone shouting 'fire', it had never, ever been true. Sophie wouldn't run. How many ovulations had come and gone in the past two years? How many almost pregnancies, babies? It sounded like a heresy, blasphemy, but as Sophie disembarked from the train she laughed out loud.

A baby?

That night in Warsaw, Sophie and Tucker strolled through the recreated Old Town. He regaled her with the meticulous rebuilding of the site, decimated by the German Army in 1944. They laughed over gefilte fish soup and Polish bread. Who would have guessed Polish bread could ever taste so good? Walking along the Vistula

River hand in hand, the couple might be like any other couple in the world, happy and in love. The baby, mentioned only in passing, seemed like the last thing on their minds.

Tucker played down the call from Krissu. He sensed Sophie had turned a corner of some kind. Unsure what she wanted, he repeatedly said, "I'm easy."

Sophie took her husband's face in her hands. "Tucker, listen to me, I've lived everywhere, but right here, right now, with you, since we got married, and now that is all I care about."

"Me, too," he said, pulling her close. "Right here, right now."

Sophie leaned in, resting her head and one hand against his heart.

With breakfast on the fly and a routine flight from Warsaw to Helsinki, both Sophie and Tucker grew quiet.

"Tucker, I'm okay," she said suddenly, putting her newspaper down, "to meet the baby, but no knee-jerk reactions – promise?"

"Sure," he said, surprised by this apparent change of heart.

"I actually think the chances are zero."

"Why?"

"Gut feel."

"Okay. I'm easy."

"Remember, no matter what, we sleep on it."

"*Okei.*"

"Seriously."

"Yes." He kissed his wife. "I get it."

On the short flight from Helsinki to Tallinn, a small blonde child threw a yellow Teletubby over the seat, hitting Tucker. He handed it to Sophie, who handed it back to the child. The mother smiled, put the toy away, until the child howled relentlessly. Then over the seat came the yellow Teletubby again.

"Do you really want this?" Sophie mouthed to Tucker, as she handed the toy back to the child.

"Got me," Tucker said as he caught the Teletubby with one hand.

Sophie and Tucker ate breakfast slowly, pacing themselves as they prepared for their trip to the children's home to meet Krissu and the baby she assumed was Sophie's. Controlling her inner conflict, Sophie dressed comfortably in jeans, a tulip-splashed T-shirt and a cashmere hoodie. She rehearsed the words she intended to share with Krissu, who had been so kind and so welcoming. 'Thank you, but no thank you.' She pulled her hair back and tied it with a simple ribbon. 'I choose to miss the boat.' She threw on a warm jacket and sprayed, almost as an afterthought, Ralph Lauren's Romance on her inner wrist. 'I'm happy as I am.'

"Apparently," Tucker said as the UAZ shuttered and bounced over the road in a way that seemed improbable with the freshly laid, smooth asphalt, "this baby meets all the qualifications – close to birth as possible, no living parents, an actual orphan and healthy."

"No knee-jerk reactions."

"No knee-jerk reactions."

Both Sophie and Tucker took a deep breath as they turned into the parking lot at the children's home. Snow melted on the tarmac, pooling beneath rainspouts in oily squiggles. Sophie took Tucker's hand, as they entered the building and made their way down the now-familiar corridor. In Krissu's office they waited for what seemed like an eternity, while Sophie recalled the row of tartan prams in the morning sunlight.

Tucker crossed and uncrossed his legs, fiddled with his socks and played with his phone. Finally Krissu rushed in, apologising. An emergency. A young girl brought in with a broken back. Abuse. She had to make a quick decision for the child's welfare.

"She will live, but she may not be able to walk."

"I'm sorry," Sophie said, taking Tucker's hand in the same instant.

Looking over her bifocals at Tucker and more specifically at Sophie, she studied them as she opened the plain file on her desk.

"This child," she said clearly, "the one I have in mind for you, appears to have no living relatives. However, I have an obligation by law to ensure that before putting her up for adoption that is actually the case. Not always easy. You are lucky that this situation is fairly straightforward. Sometimes it can take three years to investigate, and by then, the child has missed the opportunity. Everyone, as you can imagine, wants a newborn. Or at least a child under the age of two."

Krissu inserted a finger in the file, holding the place, before proceeding.

"Mrs Mägi, based on my long and mostly successful experience," she smiled, "this infant girl is right for you, and equally important, you are right for her. If you and Mr Mägi feel the same, she will first become your foster child, then I will work the levers, push this through the system, and hopefully, as quickly as possible, ensure a fast and fair adoption."

Sophie and Tucker listened without interrupting.

"However," Krissu said, "in this case, there is no extreme hurry because, as I said, there appears to be no living relative. We have done our best, and we feel it is in the best interest of this baby to be adopted now, rather than wait. Every minute is precious – for you and for her."

Sophie nodded.

"I am sure nothing new will surface, no matter if the search takes us to the Caspian Sea and back."

"I understand," Sophie said.

"Good. Now. I will take you to the playroom, and leave you on your own." She spoke directly to Sophie, and out of courtesy, nodded to Tucker.

"The baby's name is Arina."

Down a long hall that smelled of astringents and lemon, came the strums of an acoustic guitar and a young girl singing. Then, came a violin, practised carefully, perfectly, with lone single sounds lifting Sophie as she walked with Krissu. Behind the two women, Tucker kept pace, and at the playroom door Krissu touched them both gently.

"I'll be back shortly."

Sophie closed her eyes, put everything behind her and pressed open the natural wood door with its narrow, vertical, viewing window. In the room, a colourful play area directed her eye first to a now-silent television monitor, and then shelf upon shelf of children's books. Strewn on the carpet, as well as the bright linoleum floor, lay toys in various states of disarray.

Sophie looked up and to the right, and there sitting upright in a wooden playpen, built high off the ground, sat an alert little girl, clear-eyed and expectant. A string of blue beads crisscrossed the crib at an angle, and the child, dressed in a soft flannel onesie with a striped bib, looked up. In an instant, she was in Sophie's arms. Sophie knew that face, those eyes, the small, chubby arms, and barely perceptible to anyone else, but clear to Sophie, a click sounded bright and light right over her heart.

Mine.

She might never know the feel of a newborn delivered right into her arms, but it couldn't feel any different than this. Her entire journey had been about this moment, this point in time. All the work, all the effort, all the hope and, maybe most importantly, all the letting go had arrived at this.

Truly speechless, Sophie held Arina, cradling the back of her head as if she had been born to it, done this all her life. Tucker wrapped his arms around the two of them, and in the doorway, Krissu grinned; another right decision.

Sitting down beside Tucker on the miniature, child-sized chairs, Sophie opened and closed her mouth, but nothing came out. For the next twenty minutes, she cooed and cuddled the baby, with Tucker looking on. Finally, unable to put the baby down, Sophie allowed Krissu to softly pry her from her arms.

"Come back tomorrow," Krissu said. "You can visit in my office. Maybe even feed her."

Both Sophie and Tucker knew that it would not be as easy as saying 'yes, we love this baby; we want her'. Krissu still made the final decision, as she did in every case.

Back in the UAZ, Tucker stared straight ahead for a few minutes before starting the ignition. Still wordless, Sophie felt the Russian jeep back out of the parking lot in an uncharacteristically smooth manoeuvre and onto the highway.

Sophie took a breath, again attempting to speak.

"Don't," Tucker said, "I saw everything. She's yours."

Pulling into the local grocery store, where both Sophie and Tucker remained on autopilot, trying to understand what had just happened, they intended to pick up milk, coffee, tomatoes, laundry detergent, make dinner and to sleep on it, but instead Sophie mindlessly picked up bananas, while Tucker robotically ruminated over steak, pasta and marinara sauce.

"Eggs?" Sophie asked.

"Yes," he answered to what might have been anything.

Sophie felt her vision shift. Things seemed brighter, as if the store lighting had been increased. Realising she'd forgotten tomatoes, she hurried back down the aisle and found herself in the aisle dedicated to baby things. Row upon row of pacifiers, small spoons and multicoloured sippy cups dangled in long lines. Disposable diapers, terry cloth bibs and a menagerie of soft toys fanned out in all directions. Without thinking, she plucked a glow-in-the-dark pacifier with a floating astronaut encircling its rim.

Over her head, Tucker tugged a yellow Tellytubby from the wall.

"How about this?" He laughed.

"How about that." She smiled, also touching the soft yellow toy.

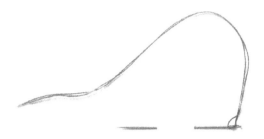

THIRTY-EIGHT

Sophie's phone vibrated insistently, and just as unrelentingly, Sophie ignored it. There couldn't be anything more important than preparing to meet baby Arina a second time, on her own, in Krissu's office. She might even feed her. Sophie felt a sense of urgency, a need to get it right. Krissu held the keys. Checking and rechecking that the yellow Teletubby and the glow-in-the-dark pacifier remained in her bag, she folded and refolded the flannel pyjamas she and Tucker had chosen together.

Not out of the woods yet, Sophie understood completely that Krissu still needed to make a final decision based on all the available information. Any last vestige of a relative needed to be ruled out. She had made that clear. Baby Arina still needed medical exams, mandated by law, despite medical records already on file at the children's home. There would be a battery of tests.

With Tucker having left at the crack of dawn, Sophie sat at the kitchen table, listening once again to Boccherini, while drinking jasmine green tea, unable to eat. Over the music, the clock's minute hand juddered forward, as Sophie held her breath. Who could she tell that, without exception, baby Arina looked identical to the little one that had first appeared to her in Monaco on *Le Rocher*? And the coincidence of the name Arina? Sophie had never even bothered to share that with Tucker.

Suddenly the phone buzzed again, and Sophie once again, seeing an unknown number filling the screen, without a second thought clicked it off. She steadied herself. Arina was hers. There was no going back. Life pulled her forward, and while she promised to pace herself through the formalities, she had a sense that this was a 'go'.

Sophie considered the sonograms, the talks with Bertram Conrad, Dr Härma, the International Women's Club Fertility Group. This was her fertility, and out of nowhere the thought of baby Arina's birth mother came to mind. Gratitude welled up, and Sophie felt the warmth of someone else's love as she cradled her cup of tea.

"*Aitäh*," she said to the mother she would never meet.

The doorbell rang and Sophie suddenly remembered that Krissu was sending an interpreter for her to help with all the formalities. She had told Sophie that Leila was an Australian-born Estonian who had three adopted daughters of her own, so would know just what Sophie was going through.

"Hi, I'm Leila," the interpreter said loudly when Sophie opened the door.

"Good morning," Sophie answered, "doesn't it seem eternally fresh?"

"Whoa, you're in good form."

"I am in good form, Leila. I *do* feel it. She's mine. I know it."

"That is the way it is meant to be. Doesn't always happen, but it happened with all three of mine."

Leila drove them in her car, passing a light green tram, then darting in and out of the midmorning traffic.

"I feel pregnant," Sophie confided.

"That's not unusual. I felt it the moment I saw each of my daughters' faces. They were so tiny, so soft, so mine. I was forty-three with the first one. No mean feat, but I'm ethnically Estonian, even if I was born and raised in Sydney, so I got in under the wire. Krissu must like you, and of course Tucker is an *insider* with his Estonian passport."

Tucker telephoned.

"Yes," Sophie said, "I'm on my way there now, with Leila, the interpreter."

"Now?"

"Yes."

"Good." He paused. "Call me afterwards. Did you remember the Teletubby?"

"Yes. I did."

The two women hopped out of the car and hurried through the parking lot and past the garden, where now only four plaid baby carriages stood in a row. Leila gave Sophie a light pat on the arm.

"You can do this."

"I can," Sophie said.

Sophie's world instantly contracted to the dimensions of that small, upturned face, the warm infant she now held in her arms. As the sounds of the traffic outside disappeared, along with the piercing laughter of children somewhere else, far off in the building. A shrill bell signalled lunch before also dying away. Sophie studied the delicate features of the little girl, who held her in a spell.

With permission from Krissu to feed Arina, Sophie reached into her Stockmann's bag and pulled out a jar of banana baby food with a small spoon. Intrigued and at home in Sophie's arms, Arina cooed, and Sophie fussed back, forgetting Krissu still judging from her seat behind the thick metal desk. Despite herself, Sophie began to sing 'Frère Jacques', while Arina held tightly to the luminescent pacifier with the free-floating astronaut. Finally, without thinking, Sophie pulled the yellow Teletubby out from her bag.

After an hour, with another bell ringing, Sophie reluctantly lifted Arina from the baby blanket, now fanned out over the Persian carpet, where they sat, and handed her back to Leila, who passed her back to the young woman who ran the nursery. Controlling a rising sense of panic, Sophie packed the Teletubby and baby food back into her bag, as the office door swooshed closed.

Catching every nuance, Krissu spoke to Leila in Estonian, before turning to Sophie.

"Thank you for coming today."

"'Thank you for coming today?' What is that? Is that all she can say? A life is being changed here. Three lives are being changed here," Sophie barked at Leila, who started the car.

"That's good. Estonians are very reserved."

"Good?"

"Yes. She's got a lot to consider, like are you the right one? You are not Estonian."

"Well, Tucker is."

Leila paused. "Krissu said that everything is in order, all the documentation. There are a few medical exams, and this is not to worry you, Sophie, but an additional line of enquiry has been opened up. They might have found a grandfather."

Sophie felt her stomach drop at Leila's unwanted words.

"Be brave. Carry on with the tests. The enquiry will come to nothing, I'm sure, but by law she has to pursue it. Max less than a month. You are free to go and see Arina every day. Go at feeding times and stay until naptime. That's what I did. I couldn't get enough."

At home, Sophie collapsed, still smelling of baby and bananas. Closing her eyes, she found it difficult to breathe, or even call Tucker, who she knew would not take easily to the fact that another line of enquiry had been opened up. Sophie knew the truth first hand: eggs can fail to grow, sperm can swim backwards, a baby girl could disappear, and a relative could be found between Tallinn and the Caspian Sea.

The yellow Teletubby sat on the kitchen table, as Sophie made herself a cup of tea, moving from feeling empty, then full, hopeful and then not, yes and then no. She swore at herself for promising not to do this anymore, and yet here she was again – with an 'almost' and the never-ending tug of war.

Just as she was about to shout with frustration, a knock sounded at the front door. She went to answer the door and found Leila standing on the doorstep.

"I'm sorry, I had to come back. I really do understand all of this, personally, from the trenches, so to speak, and it is critical you keep your hand in the game. I mean work, Sophie, any kind. When Christina, my first daughter, landed in my lap, it seemed such a miracle that everything else went blank. My world shrank down to just her. When Krissu started calling me, asking for help with Americans, Australians, Kiwis and South African adoptions, it was a relief. When I got back in the game, I got my sanity back too."

"I get it," Sophie said. "But please do come back in. Can I get you a cup of tea, or a glass of wine?"

Leila lit up with a wide Australian grin. "Hold the tea, bring on the wine. It's well past noon, isn't it?"

Tomorrow came soon enough, and with Krissu's blessing, Leila and Sophie changed, bathed and dressed Arina, who now sat in a car seat ready for the trip to a local paediatrician for medical tests. All the while Sophie held back, praying, trying to erase a potential grandfather, risen up out of nowhere who might take this child away.

"Remember from now on to bring your own clothes for Arina. These kids arrive with nothing and they leave with nothing. Naked as a jay bird." Leila laughed.

As Sophie sat in the back seat beside Arina, tucking in the baby's too-large, hand-me-down snowsuit while letting one tiny hand curl around hers, she smiled at Leila in the rearview mirror. "I am so in love."

"You are."

"True love," Sophie said. "She feels so mine. I mean, I would lay down my life for her. Stand between her and harm's way. I feel like her mom, my mom."

"Yes," Leila agreed, "that's the job."

"Would it be too bizarre to say she actually looks like mine?"

"No. Absolutely not."

In the doctor's office, Sophie read through charts showing heights, weights and birth ages. The doctor smiled broadly and announced, "She's in perfect health. Vaccinations up to date, with another jab coming due right now. Your job is to distract her, briefly."

With all the finesse of a seasoned mother, Sophie held Arina's cleanly scented body next to hers, and chatted away, pointing to the clear blue sky out the window, where an aeroplane drew a soft white line. Sophie spoke the word 'airplane' in a whisper, while Arina tucked into Sophie's neck and chirruped softly in return.

"Amazing," the doctor said, "no words needed." He paused. "I just need to draw a bit of blood now to check for HIV and Hep C."

Sophie looked up.

"It's the law," he replied as he pricked Arina's finger. "I'm afraid you won't be taking her home until we have the results."

"How long is that?"

"Two weeks? If either is a positive, you'll need to rethink things. Do your homework, know what you might be taking on, but the odds are…" He paused. "Don't worry, the results will be negative."

Slipping Arina back into her snowsuit, Sophie noted the weather, a chilly six degrees Celsius, even if a bright, late October day. Sophie held Arina close, and for a moment wanted to run, willed any possibility of HIV or Hep C away. Climbing into the car beside Leila, who had been waiting, Sophie shared what the doctor had said, along with the fact that she would now have to wait an additional, unbearable two weeks.

Leila, who had been dismissed by the paediatrician because he spoke perfect English, looked at Sophie and said without hesitation as she started the car, "It's a scare tactic. Not in any one of my three adoptions was there ever a positive result. It's just the law and a bit of power. I know nothing, but Sophie, I think Arina is yours. Stay with that. You are not going to figure it out. Let go. Lesson number one? Let go. I would assume you've learned that by now."

Sophie kissed Arina on the back of her head. "Yes. I know that one."

"Well, get ready, because you will learn it again and again. That, my friend, is motherhood."

"Okay, but what if?"

"Cross that bridge when you get there. For now, get on with other things like… I know you don't want to take Princess Arina straight back, so we are going to Kadriorg for a bit of Black Forest cake and cocoa."

"But what will Arina eat?"

"*Kohupiimakreem* with a size-appropriate spoon."

"With berries?"

"With berries."

"You've thought of everything."

"That's my job," Leila smiled, "and soon to be yours."

Krissu called earlier than expected, to let Sophie know that Arina's tests read all clear.

"You can take your foster daughter home now," Krissu said, emphasising the word foster, as well as highlighting that the court date now secured for late November could not be shifted, and that the one line of enquiry remained open; a relative in Odessa might be found.

"Thank you," Sophie had said, only too happy to be bringing Arina home to Kadriorg, to a nursery ready and an open heart.

That Sunday, the second Sunday in November, following what Sophie called the 'all-clear Friday', Tucker and Sophie rose before dawn, unable to sleep, knowing they would collect Arina straight after her morning meal.

"It's Father's Day," Sophie said, taking a cup of cinnamon coffee from her husband in their kitchen, where the morning light had just begun to filter in.

"Today?" he questioned.

"Today," she said, blowing ripples across the steaming coffee. "Yes. In Estonia. It's Father's Day."

Finally, upstairs, Sophie threw on a sweater, jeans and boots, while Tucker seemed to have trouble dressing.

"Enjoy it," Sophie teased.

"I am," he said, "I really am, but I just feel slightly panicked."

"You?"

"Me."

Sophie packed a small case with Arina's new onesie, a better fitting snowsuit, a ribbed wool cap and mittens, while Tucker went out to warm up the UAZ, now fitted with a fully certified car seat that he had checked twice.

"Nice car seat," Sophie admired, as she jumped in the front.

"You know," he said, "this is not like going to get a puppy."

"I know," she said, touching the side of his face, "it's not."

Knowing the home well enough now, Sophie punched in the code, and they made their way up to the nursery, where Arina sat wide-eyed and waiting. Sweeping her up and onto a changing table in the next room, Sophie undressed and redressed Arina in her new clothes, with all the finesse of a mother several times over. Gone were the home clothes and on were the spanking fresh new ones, while Tucker, looking on, clutched the yellow Teletubby, and Arina studied her glow-in-the-dark astronaut pacifier.

Finally, with photos and smiles all round, it was time to go. The significance of the moment, the unexpected miracle, was not lost on anyone – the staff, Sophie, Tucker and maybe even Arina herself.

The endless grinning hurt, and with one last photo of Sophie resplendent with Arina in her arms by the UAZ, Tucker finally relaxed and smiled.

"You look like you just won the lottery."

"I did," she said, kissing the top of her baby's head.

At home, Sophie unzipped Arina's pink snowsuit, and Tucker lifted her up and out.

"Nice spacesuit," he said.

After testing the warm milk on the inside of her wrist, Sophie took Arina into her arms, all the while surveying the room, making sure Arina was safe, secure, as she might have been at the home, where she had spent almost the entirety of her young life.

Already planning Arina's midmorning snack, Sophie considered the blueberry *kohupiimakreem*, the proven favourite so far, on the shelves of her stainless-steel refrigerator.

"She's beautiful," Tucker practically whispered from around the corner, where he hung up the coats.

Sophie nodded.

"She looks a bit like you." He now kissed his wife and daughter each lightly on the side of the head.

"I can't put her down," Sophie responded, "but the schedule says 'milk, cuddle, nap.'"

"Play by the rules?"

Sophie agreed, as they both stood spellbound by the infant girl that they both expected and did not. And so the day continued, sticking to the schedule, believing and not believing the joy they now found in their lives, in their Kadriorg home, until bedtime rolled around. Sophie and Tucker found themselves taking turns, reading from Sophie's ancient, leather-bound book of fairy tales with the spidery drawings as Arina looked curiously on.

In the high-backed, white rocking chair in the corner of their bedroom Sophie sang 'Hush Little Baby' along with a number of other tracks from *Peaceful Nighttime* until Arina quietly drifted off to sleep. Once again like Tucker, Sophie found herself both excited and terrified. She had a baby in the house, *the* baby, *her* baby, and a commitment for life. As Arina slumbered in Sophie's arms, as if she had done this every day of her short life, Sophie let a few tears fall. It had all been worth the wait, the struggle – this tiny bundle, this surprising little girl, this poetry of life.

With Tucker downstairs at his desk sorting the next day's work, Sophie continued to cradle her daughter, only standing when the music finally died. She slipped her child into the cot beside the bed, where she had been told to place Arina for the first few nights, so that their faces would be the first thing she saw in the morning and the last thing at night. Only later would they take her to the nursery, once she slept through and the bond was tight enough.

"Imprinting," Sophie said as Tucker sauntered into the bedroom, "so we can get on with being a family."

"Job done," he whispered, kissing his wife. "Remember I have a flight in the morning. I'm getting up very early."

"We will all be getting up early," Sophie said, making room for Tucker beside her.

"That's right," he said, before kissing Sophie again and falling into a deep sleep.

She, on the other hand, ran through the home schedule over and over again in her head. Unable to sleep, lying on her side by the crib, she listened to Arina breathe, to the slight gurgling sounds her daughter made. The baby's eyes fluttered and her breathing slowed. For a moment Sophie concerned herself with crib death. What had she read about that? Might Arina stop breathing? Then other fears grew: the blanket? The pacifier in the crib? The railings? Too much milk?

Nonetheless the softest sound possible distracted the new mother; a tapping repeated itself, lightly drumming on the skylight. Snow. As the feathery snowfall began, Arina's breathing relaxed even more, matching Tucker's even breath until Sophie, too, finally drifted off to sleep, full of gratitude, full of peace.

THIRTY-NINE

"Robin," Sophie said with relief, "I thought we'd never catch up. It's been so busy and a text just won't do. I don't know. It's not over until it is over. We have a court date later this month. The home staff say I have nothing to fear but that there is one line of enquiry still open. Odessa, I think."

"Sophie," Robin breathed, "congratulations. I got your email. The photo of Arina looks amazing, like you, like Tucker even. You've done it. I'm speechless. So happy. Wow, wow, wow."

"It's fostering for now, nothing more. I have to keep that in mind. If someone in Odessa... If they saw her. Robin, she is so mine, so beautiful, and even now, if—"

"Stop, Sophie. Enjoy the moment. Let go. Was it easy?"

"Easy? Did you just say 'easy'? Robin, you know more than anyone how long I've been at this. Two years feels like twenty."

"Sorry, I mean the actual adoption."

"No, not easy. My parameters were narrow in one sense: a true orphan, a child whose parents were actually deceased. A child that really needed me, as much as I wanted her. As close to newborn as possible."

"I've been thinking a little about adoption."

"You?"

"Yes. After the miscarriage, I thought a lot. I did want that baby. So did Eli. We're over it now, but it did make us think. We want a child to raise, even if Eli has adult children. We hardly see them – once a year, maybe. They are busy having children of their own. Sophie, it was the first time I saw Eli cry."

"I'm so sorry."

"Look, congratulations, and count us in. We are coming to the christening – just tell us when and forget the 'if' bit."

"Thank you, Robin."

Sophie clicked the Nokia closed, put it on the kitchen table and went to check on Arina. In the high-backed rocker once again, Sophie watched her foster child sleep. Last night's snow had piled up against the house, and Sophie loved the feeling of warmth, of safety.

"Eternal," Anne had said. "That feeling, of mothering, is eternal."

She thought of her father momentarily, and admitted the loss. Her whole life Anne had said how happy, how 'over the moon', her father had been when she was pregnant with Sophie and how much Sophie had been wanted. But now in the warmth of her own home in Tallinn, with a blanket of freshly fallen snow muting the sound of even the snowploughs, Sophie understood what she might have meant and what she might have almost missed.

Practically afraid to move, Sophie could hardly express her joy. Sleeping, even napping, seemed out of the question, despite Leila having warned her to rest when Arina slept because she would need her strength. Finally with a slight stretch and a gentle roll, Sophie's daughter awoke. Up and out of the rocker in an instant, Sophie then paused, observing Arina as she collected the glow-in-the-dark pacifier from between the rails, where it had lodged, and looped it over one finger.

"Wake up, my love," she said, kneeling down beside the crib, stroking the baby's cheek until she was fully awake. Finally, Sophie lifted her daughter up, feeling the small warmth against her chest. She kissed the tiny cheek pressed close to hers, and surprisingly Arina kissed Sophie back.

"Mmm," the baby cooed.

"Mmm," Sophie clucked right back. "That's right, Arina. That's me. Mommy."

Bundling her up, Sophie strolled Arina out from the garden and into the park, stopping here and there to catch the winter sunshine or to give the infant swings a go, holding Arina carefully in her lap.

Sophie, again, reminded herself to 'let go', and with her baby, even if just for today, swung in a gentle arc, with children laughing all around. This was not *Project Bébé*. This was Arina, Sophie and Tucker, her family, formed out of love, luck and longing. Who would have guessed? Sophie beamed, having grown comfortable now, resting her chin lightly on her baby's head.

Strolling further into Kadriorg, around the pink President's Palace, by Peter the Great's hunting lodge and finally back around to the café in the Tsar's Summer Palace, Sophie unzipped Arina's snowsuit and then her own jacket. Her latte arrived with an evenly dusted cocoa heart. The slender waitress, without even asking, as if she were a cousin or an older sister, just the way in Tallinn, emptied Arina's warm milk into the bottle standing beside the pacifier.

"*Ilus*," she said, rubbing the back of her hand softly against the baby's cheek.

"She's exceptional," a rosy-cheeked Swedish woman said as she stirred her coffee and broke a cardamom pastry in two.

"Thank you," Sophie said.

"How old?"

"Seven months."

"She looks just like you."

"Thank you."

This flow of attention continued as she left the café and made her way back through the playground, by the Swan Pond and home, from Estonian women, Russian women and a robust Finn.

"Identical." They nodded and studied. "Lucky you."

On the stoop, in front of her own home, Sophie talked with Arina, who murmured and grinned as the Baltic sun set.

"You," she told her daughter, "look like you."

Inside, they stopped in front of the hall mirror.

"What do you think?"

Sophie turned to the right and to the left, admiring their profiles.

"Mother and daughter?"

Arina explored her own reflection, and clapped.

Sophie laughed aloud, "Krissu, you did get it right."

Tucker arrived home early, having made the trip to and from Riga in record time, impatient to see Arina, to toss and turn her, to play 'Wipe Out' on kitchen pots and pans, to dance, the three of them together, to 'A Hard Day's Night'.

"Prize fighter," he called his daughter, as Sophie picked up the phone buzzing on the kitchen table.

Line of enquiry closed. Call me!

Turning the music down, Sophie sent Tucker to rock Arina, as Leila spilled over with the good news.

"Job done. I am so happy for you. The relative in Odessa was too distant, no interest in Arina and probably too poor. The case is closed. She is yours now and forever more! The court date is Thursday, November 23rd. Nothing can stop you now."

"Thank you, Leila. Thank you."

"She is safely home, my friend, and so are you."

Later, with Tucker deep in thought in his study, thumbing through paperwork, Sophie continued to rock Arina long after 'Hush Little Baby' died away. The baby's head lay over Sophie's shoulder, heart over heart.

Sophie's father came to mind again. She imagined for the

millionth time the eternally effervescent man, who existed only in black and white portraits and oversized oils; and in Anne's quiet, undying love. As Arina's steady heart beat over Sophie's, a seemingly missing piece slipped into place.

Sophie said goodbye to the sliver of emptiness she carried all her life, the painful shard buried in busyness, projects and management, the emptiness that had driven her finally, *thank God*, to this place, to the love for her new daughter. Sophie felt the love and loss of the father she had never known, and she let it go.

As she placed Arina in the crib and tucked what appeared to be her favourite stuffed toy, a soft, big-eyed, flat pillow-like Estonian caribou, within easy reach, the phone screen lit up.

"Sorry," Sophie whispered, moving down the hall and into her office, realising there had been multiple calls now, "my phone was on silent, Leila. Baby sleeping."

"I just wanted to gently remind you, remember, keep your hand in the game."

"Yes." Sophie laughed quietly. "Hand in the game."

As she listened to Leila talk, Sophie ran an open palm over the neat embroidery, the stitching, at the hem of the handmade christening gown from Muhu that lay across her desk with a myriad number of yet-to-be-opened colour swatches.

"Good," Leila said emphatically, "is your mother over the moon?"

"Yes. She's coming for the christening."

"Me too?"

"You too, Leila, with your whole brood. December 25th, at noon."

"Christmas Day?"

"Yes."

"Total miracle."

"I'd say."

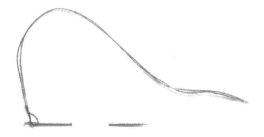

FORTY

Layer after layer of pristine Baltic snow fell all night, and in the morning, the muted sound drifted away, giving way to a deep quiet that only those living in the Far North could appreciate.

"You prayed for a white Christmas, a blizzard, six feet deep," Tucker boomed from the shower.

"I did," Sophie laughed, "and Tallinn delivered."

Poking his head out, dripping wet, Tucker reminded his wife, as if she didn't know, "It's Christmas, Sophie, and we have a daughter, who is being christened today."

"Really?" She pushed him playfully back into the shower.

"Troika to the manor, *Frau Mägi*?"

"*Jah*, why not?" She laughed.

In the kitchen, Sophie put water on for tea and slipped opened the blinds. Looking out from her gingerbread house, decorated in the same colours as a Carl Larsson painting and landscaped the same, Sophie imagined the wild rose bush, now completely buried in snow, and the crab apple just barely poking out from above. The expanse of white carried on as far as the eye could see, as an intermittent snowplough droned now louder in the distance.

Sophie recalled for an instant the odd cold morning when she'd sat in her mother's embrace with her voice purring, telling the tale of the Snow Queen. Arctic geese had flown off and away from the pages of a leather-bound book of tales. Why had she fallen in love with Lapland? How did she arrive in Estonia? Wind stirred the snow from the limbs of the firs across the street.

The Snow Queen's sleigh had pulled up and away, and Sophie once again recalled her favourite deep blue fabric embroidered with red from years gone by. How could a dark, below freezing morning, on a Christmas Day in Tallinn, be called the brightest day in the history of the world? Padding upstairs in her warm slippers, Sophie paused at Arina's crib, where the baby had only begun to stir from her midmorning nap. The scent of Tucker's aftershave spilled down the hall and into the room as Sophie tiptoed to the high-backed rocker once again.

Everything she loved most was in that house, that home, in Kadriorg. The journey of the last two years lay round her like the morning's snow. Her gratitude for Tucker, her marriage, all the people who had helped along the way, including all the dead ends, spilled out. Mostly she was thankful for Arina, her daughter, their daughter, hoped for, longed for and loved. Sophie knew Arina would be fully awake soon, and that they would prepare for the christening, but she just wanted to take a few minutes to say thank you to God, to the mystery and to 'letting go'.

Arina was hers and Christmas Day had arrived. At noon, in the Church of the Holy Spirit, *Püha Vaimu kirik*, her baby would be baptised. Sophie picked up Arina and settled into the rocker, wrapping her baby a little more warmly in the cashmere throw. Instantly, the baby snuggled into her chest, and a second stirring in the tops of the Arctic firs sent a cascade of snow tumbling down outside.

Sophie sat humbled for a minute. Who would have guessed the journey would arrive at this?

"Up you go," Sophie sang out, as Arina opened her blue eyes.

Back in the kitchen, Sophie flicked on the UV lamp, swivelled Arina around on her hip, deftly warming a bottle, pressing juice and testing the rice porridge almost all at once. Upstairs, Tucker belted out 'O Sole Mio', competing with Boccherini's string minuet playing on the stereo downstairs. This was the din of a family on the move, the din of a family finally preparing for a long-awaited Christmas christening in Tallinn, the capital city of the newly independent Republic of Estonia.

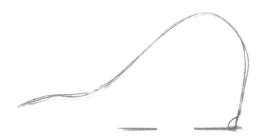

ACKNOWLEDGEMENTS

Thank you, once again, dear Reader, before anyone else, for reading Mine. After you, there are so many people to thank, and as usual, I apologise in advance for those I may have forgotten.

Thank you Paul Oberschneider.

Thank you Christian Hauser Oberschneider.

Thank you Harry Coventry.

Thank you David Roche.

Thank you Wanda Whiteley.

Thank you Lynn Curtis.

Thank you Tamsin Shelton.

Thank you Ali March.

Thank you to all the brilliant staff at The Book Guild.

Thank you Lizanne Christopher.

Thank you Noreen Sawar.

Thank you to the Hauser Family, especially to Marianne Hauser Macaulay.

Thank you Linda McFadden.

Thank you Libby Rohovit.

Thank you Summertown Villa Writers Group, especially Lucien Quincy Senna.

Thank you Wimpole Street Writers Group, especially Jill Robinson.

Thank you Tortugas Writers Group, especially Sara Johnson-Weyer.

Thank you Maimu Nõmmik, Liivi Laos, Kaja Kirsch and the entire Ober-Haus Family.

Thank you to all the personnel worldwide who work to help women and men find their way through the labyrinth of fertility options, standing with them whether procedures succeed or fail. ⟨

And most importantly, the deepest thank you to all the women and men who work tirelessly in caring for, loving, nurturing and protecting, the hearts and souls of those children yet in search of a mother and a father.